Some women
are made for scandal....

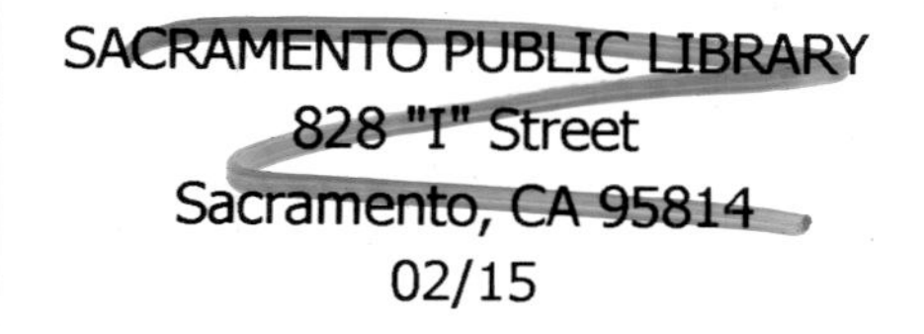

"Simply delightful. . . . From beginning to end, I was totally captivated." —Night Owl Reviews

"As always, Hunter hits the mark, drawing readers into her three-dimensional characters' minds and hearts, and delighting [readers] from the delicious start to the satisfying conclusion." —*RT Book Reviews*

"I had a blast with this one. . . . I am definitely going back for more." —Delighted Reader

"Filled with witty banter, passion, secrets, danger, deceit, treason, betrayal, and love. Did I mention passion? A must read!" —My Book Addiction Reviews

"Humorous . . . hot . . . fun reading."
—Romance Reviews Today

The Mistress Memoirs

"Hunter knows how to combine sensual romance with a mystery, and passion with tenderness." —*Romantic Times*

"Another wonderful winner." —Fresh Fiction

"Exquisite . . . filled with action, mystery, sensuality, love for extended family, rotten children to love, and a bevy of eccentric characters . . . a rare treat for historical readers."
—Romance Junkies

continued . . .

Praise for the Bridal Pleasures Series

The Duchess Diaries

"There is so much to love about this book. The witty dialogue and the fantastically paced writing, the characters who sparkle and come to life on every page . . . a romance tale at its finest." —Smexy Books

"The reader will have a hard time putting it down."
—Fresh Fiction

"Another completely captivating combination of wonderfully madcap plotting, wickedly humorous writing, and wildly hot passion." —*Booklist*

"Fast-paced, sexy, and hilarious. . . . Run, don't walk, to get a copy." —*Romantic Times*

A *Bride Unveiled*

"Sizzling sexual chemistry and rapier wit . . . a thoroughly romantic literary treat." —*Booklist*

"Hunter draws the reader in with a compelling plot and engaging characters in this smoothly written tale of love lost and found." —*Publishers Weekly*

A *Duke's Temptation*

"A sinfully sexy hero with a secret, a book-obsessed heroine in search of her own happy-ever-after ending, a delightfully clever plot that takes great fun in spoofing the literary world, and writing that sparkles with wicked wit and exquisite sensuality add up to an exceptionally entertaining read." —*Booklist* (starred review)

“With humor and charm, sensuality and wickedness, Hunter delights.” —*Romantic Times*

“This is the first in what looks to be a very promising, and extremely seductive, new quartet. Few can resist a novel by Jillian Hunter!” —Huntress Book Reviews

More Praise for the Novels of Jillian Hunter

“One of the funniest, most delightful romances I’ve had the pleasure to read.” —Teresa Medeiros

“An absolutely delightful tale that’s impossible to put down.” —*Booklist*

“A sweet, romantic tale . . . full of humor, romance, and passion. Historical romance that is sure to please.”
—The Romance Readers Connection

“A lovely read.” —Romance Reader at Heart

“Enchanting . . . a fabulous historical.”
—*Midwest Book Review*

“[It] bespells, beguiles, and bewitches. If romance, magic, great plots, and wonderful characters add spice to your reading life, don’t allow this one to escape.”
—Crescent Blues

“Romantic and sexy. . . . Read it—you’ll love it!”
—The Romance Reader

ALSO BY JILLIAN HUNTER

The Bridal Pleasures Series
A Duke's Temptation
A Bride Unveiled
The Duchess Diaries

The Boscastle Affairs Series
The Mistress Memoirs
The Countess Confessions

A SIGNET SELECT BOOK

SIGNET SELECT
Published by the Penguin Group
Penguin Group (USA) LLC, 375 Hudson Street,
New York, New York 10014

USA | Canada | UK | Ireland | Australia | New Zealand | India | South Africa | China
penguin.com
A Penguin Random House Company

First published by Signet Select, an imprint of New American Library,
a division of Penguin Group (USA) LLC

First Printing, February 2015

ISBN 978-0-451-47013-3

Printed in the United States of America
10 9 8 7 6 5 4 3 2 1

PUBLISHER'S NOTE
This is a work of fiction. Names, characters, places, and incidents either are the product of the author's imagination or are used fictitiously, and any resemblance to actual persons, living or dead, business establishments, events, or locales is entirely coincidental.

To Gunilla with love

Acknowledgments

As always, a huge thank-you to my agent, Mel Berger, for his support and insight.

Also, a special thank-you to my editor, Kerry Donovan, for staying on board with the book until her own production schedule took precedence.

I am grateful to Isabel Farhi and Claire Zion for filling in during my editor's absence and to the art department for creating yet another wonderful cover.

Prologue

London
1808

James had pursued his alluring prey midway to the ladies' retiring room. A black silk mask concealed half his face, but the more experienced guests at the masquerade ball knew his identity. A duke's heir rarely went unnoticed at a party, especially when he paid attention to a particular lady. To his amusement, the object of his infatuation seemed to be the exception.

The lady acted unconcerned by his pursuit, perhaps even oblivious to his interest. She hadn't once glanced over her shoulder or faltered in her steps to show she cared that she'd captured his fickle attention. She swept down the corridor like a *princesse royale*, oblivious to whoever fell or trailed in her wake.

He admired her demeanor. Was it possible she was blithely unaware of his existence? He had to remedy that situation before he had half the guests at his heels. But he was starting to wonder whether he wasn't hunting her as much as she was leading him somewhere.

She certainly wasn't dressed to entice a man. Her skirts belled out over a metal-framed Elizabethan farthingale that bumped a pair of footmen on either side from her hurried path. It was quite the costume. If James hadn't become so instantly enamored of her angelic face, he might not have gone on the chase with so many tiresome debutantes warning her, between giggles, that a scoundrel had her in his sights.

"Hurry up, my lady!"

"He's going to catch you."

"Do you want us to escort you?"

"She isn't from London," one of them whispered to another, looking at James through a bejeweled mask. "He'll take advantage of her innocence."

The silly geese dispersed as soon as he approached her—his personal attendants had made an art of protecting his privacy. They crowded the hall until he caught her by the hand and led her to a corner beyond the betraying lights of the wall sconces.

He neglected to ask her name, or to speak at all, while memorizing her face. And he ignored her initial resistance as he pulled her into his arms and kissed the lovely mouth that had lit an unbankable fire in his blood. Her body refused to mold to his, but neither did she push him away. The feather in her tall hat poked him in the eye. As soon as he had noticed her in the ballroom, he had wanted to take her home and remove her square-necked Elizabethan lady's costume. But now he realized she was too young to dishonor, as badly as he desired her, and beyond that, he'd enlisted in the infantry. She would belong to someone else when he returned home.

Stolen kisses on this night would have to suffice.

"Sir, I don't even know who you are," she whispered when he gave her a moment to breathe.

"If I told you, would you allow me greater liberties?"

She laughed at his bold question, evidently delighted at the prospect of a season of romance and gentlemen to vanquish ahead of her. "I should warn you—my father has a hot temper."

"I have a hot temperament." Which she did nothing to cool. How could he offer her anything except trouble when he was about to leave for war? He brushed his hand down her back, over her stiff skirt and petticoats, then around and up to her bodice, seeking the true shape of her body. She was well built, and he laughed at the delicate hand that arrested his quest.

"That's quite enough."

"Not for me."

"Who do you think you are?"

"Isn't it better sometimes not to know?"

"I couldn't say. I've never attended a masquerade."

He stared down into her sweetly indignant face and proceeded to ravish her tempting mouth until the rumble of background voices forced him to release her. He had acted rashly, and it was his responsibility to protect her reputation. After all, she was presumably at the ball to find a husband.

He brought his hand to her warm cheek, murmuring, "My body servants will stand as a barricade for you to slip away. I'm sorry if I offended you, but I simply couldn't resist. And I'm not sorry that I kissed you. Tell me the truth—are you? Do you regret my actions this evening?"

He knew even before she replied that she wasn't. He'd felt the shivers she had tried to control when they kissed. Still, he didn't expect a lady to willingly admit that she had shared his inexplicable surge of desire.

She surprised him with her answer. "I'll tell you the truth," she said under her breath. "This was my first kiss. From what I've heard, as far as first kisses go, yours was fairly decent. But if you try anything like this ever again, I will call you out. I won't let you kiss me a second time. My father is looking for a husband for me tonight. I'm his eldest daughter, and that's all you need to know."

"My goodness."

"You're everything a lady should avoid."

"I might be."

"Well, it's never too late to repent."

"At my age? I have absolutely no intention. Save the sermon for the next rake you meet."

"I'll tell you something else," she whispered. "It's a good thing I can't see your face, because in the event that someone has seen us together, I can't identify *you* to my father."

He laughed. "Or to your future husband, who, it is becoming apparent, must kiss decently and be on his guard against scoundrels like me. You do have a delicious mouth. Are you certain I can't entice you to meet me in a more private spot at midnight?"

"This is my debut," she said, with a catch in her voice. "Would you ruin it for me? Would you ruin me for the rest of my life for your passing pleasure?"

He crushed her to him, closed his eyes for an agonizing moment, and released her with a regret he'd never known he could feel. "I suppose it's too much to ask you to remain pure another few years?"

She laughed again. "If you had your way, I wouldn't remain innocent for the rest of the night."

"Let's make a bargain."

She shook her head, the feather in her hat tickling his nose again. "I don't think so."

"Hear me out first."

"Hurry, then. I've left my sister alone in the ballroom."

"If you don't have five proposals by noon tomorrow, I shall offer for your hand."

Her eyes widened. "Now I know you're mad."

And at that moment he let her slip away, unable to disagree, convincing himself it was for the best. What did he want with a woman who made him lose his head?

Ivy had felt quite beautiful during the short interlude with the masked stranger, bedazzled by his attentions. In fact, she so wanted to believe the scoundrel had meant what he said that she made one excuse after another not to dance with anyone else for the remainder of the night. If they spotted each other across the room and he broke through the crowd of dancers to reach her, well, she wasn't sure what was supposed to happen next in a romance.

She expected there was a good chance that she'd catch him flirting with another lady, in which case she would simply stand with all the poise she could muster, smiling until her face ached, and count the hours until she could escape.

At least she wasn't alone in the crowded ballroom. She had an ally at her side; of her three sisters only Rosemary had been old enough to accompany her to the ball. Rosemary had met a young gentleman, too, one who shared her passion for literature but was too shy to ask her to dance, and he had disappeared when his aunt complained that she had felt a need for air.

Ivy hadn't yet dared to confess to Rosemary what had happened, but of course one day she would. She wanted to savor the secret for the evening and not appear gullible in Rosemary's eyes. Her sister could be counted on to lecture Ivy for behavior beneath the Earl of Arthur's eldest daughter, and then, even worse, she would demand that Ivy describe every detail of the rake's kisses so that she could include it in one of her future novels.

Ivy doubted she could describe the alchemical transformation she had undergone in the stranger's arms. The magic of it still shimmered through her veins. She intended to keep it private for as long as possible.

Five proposals.

What a bounder.

"Ivy?" Rosemary nudged her. "Who are you looking for?"

"Who—oh. Papa, I suppose."

"He's upstairs gambling." Rosemary unsuccessfully attempted to fit her skirts into a Chippendale chair. "Bother. Are you enjoying yourself?"

Ivy nodded. "Yes. I think so. And you?"

"It's amazing how much one can learn about life from watching what goes on in a ballroom. I'd love to take a stroll down the corridors. Are you game?"

"Not in these skirts. I'd rather remain here and observe the crowd."

Just before the midnight supper the evening's festivities turned ugly. Another debutante, one who had attended the same boarding school as Ivy, had been caught in a bedroom with a married baronet. Ivy comforted her in the retiring room while the other girls talked of nothing but her disgusting behavior. Later Ivy persuaded herself she should feel fortunate that she had not been witnessed in an indiscretion herself. After the guests had settled down from the excitement, her father's footman appeared during the supper and the two sisters were whisked home to the town house.

By the next morning their father, Thomas Fenwick, the Earl of Arthur, had been accused of cheating at cards and killed in a duel. In the rush of sorrow that followed, the scoundrel's kiss faded into a sweet memory that Ivy buried beneath her grief for so long that at times she even wondered whether it had happened at all.

Chapter 1

England
1813

The Duke of Ellsworth met his match on a Tuesday afternoon while plotting ways to pleasure the woman he had left only hours before in London. He anticipated months of uninterrupted bliss in a bedchamber where rather than producing an heir with a suitable wife he would concentrate on seducing a new mistress. He had gone to war, survived an injury that should have killed him, and returned to a dukedom that any man in England would envy. His tenants needed reassurance that he would carry on tradition. He was supposed to provide them with security through the hard times predicted for his country in the years ahead.

He planned to give a feast and toast his farmers with the potent apple cider that their orchards produced. Duty fulfilled, James then intended to submerge himself in months of uninterrupted sexual impropriety to purge his mind of the war he had fought and would still be fighting if a well-placed bullet hadn't stopped him.

In less than a week he would be a satisfied man, one whose body was soothed by a woman's attentions, not battered by every bump in the country road he'd insisted his coachman take. Why had he demanded this detour? he wondered as the carriage approached a small stone bridge.

He turned his head, remembering the reason with a jolt of surprise. To his right stood what centuries ago had been a majestic Tudor house. His father had admired the manor since James was a boy, and James had inherited the late duke's appreciation of traditional English architecture.

Was it abandoned?

Could he purchase it for his mistress? She wouldn't care for it, he decided. The house needed extensive repairs and would be too isolated for a lady accustomed to the bustle and excitement of London. Elora loved her parties. She thrived on the gossip of infidelities and jewel thefts and bankruptcies that brewed in the beau monde. She had attended more balls and routs than any woman he had ever known. She sought constant entertainment. He needed sex. Still, the steeply pitched roof and dormer windows intrigued him. Perhaps it would suit one of his aunts.

He noticed a hawk perched on the branch of one of the ancient oaks that ringed the manor. A bird of prey, the hawk kept its sight on an object in the garden below. What it was James couldn't see. But he saw something else.

Was that a woman standing at the bottom of the garden? He banged hard on the carriage roof and opened the door before a footman could attend the task. He set his boots to the dirt road as the wheels stopped rolling.

The hawk remained motionless. He could not help but wonder again what innocent creature it had in its sights. He walked down a sloping path buried in leaves and passed a once-grand gatehouse.

"Your Grace?" said his coachman, a musket under his arm. "Shall I accompany you? I've heard stories about this house."

"Tell me one."

The coachman squinted up at the roof. "Dangerous women abide within. Women who bend men to their will."

James grinned. "What is it they make their victims do?"

"Wicked things, from what I gather."

"They sound like women I might like. Now I am compelled to continue."

"And as for me?"

"Let me sacrifice myself first."

He wandered into what remained of the original Tudor garden, a riotous shambles that threatened to consume the house. James predicted that in another year only the chimneys would rise above the thicket of thistle and rose, weed and bramble. From what he could see, it was only a matter of time before the roof collapsed into heaven only knew what lay beneath.

He'd never seen a caretaker or an occupant in the few times he'd driven by. But then who could find a human being in this overgrown mess? Hard to believe that the grounds had once been designed in geometric knots and patterns as precise as a chessboard.

He felt a sudden whimsy to ask his land agent about purchasing the place. Despite his coachman's warning, the only rumor James could recall about the manor was that four spinsters lived within. Perhaps they would be amenable to an offer.

He blinked. The beguiling figure in white was half-hidden beneath an unsightly trailing arbor of honey-suckle vines. She stood completely still as if caught in a misdeed. Or was it a statue of a Greek goddess? He would have noticed such an anomaly on the Tudor estate before.

He cleared his throat, pushing an intrusive thorn out of his face. "Good afternoon," he called out in a gruff but pleasant voice. "Allow me to introduce myself."

The goddess came to life. Before he managed another word, she bent, scooped up a wriggling ball of fur, and fled up the path. James couldn't decide whether she was a maidservant or a gentlewoman. She moved too spryly for a spinster. How irritating that she ran at his polite inquiry.

Ladies usually chased after James, especially when they discovered he was an eligible duke with nothing better to do than indulge their whims.

"Please," he said, quickening his step. "All I wish is a few words with you." Which might not be entirely true, but he couldn't be certain of his own motives until he convinced the woman to give him a chance to introduce himself.

There was something about her that reminded him of the past, of sweet days lost and unappreciated. But that was fancy, the influence of the manor's charm. She didn't appear to feel this absurd connection.

She muttered something under her breath and gripped her skirt with her free hand. He decided she was desperate, indeed, if she'd display her stockinged ankles to make an escape. He noticed that she had nicely shaped calves.

Perhaps she ran away from men all the time. He could have pounced on her in two masterful strides. Or so he was convinced until he walked into an obelisk concealed behind a wall of hollyhocks.

The impact should have knocked him to his senses. The woman clearly knew the garden's snares as well as how to elude persistent gentlemen.

Her white sleeves and skirt fluttered out, a taunt and a symbol of innocence at the same time. He felt like Hades pursuing Persephone.

He wouldn't be surprised if everything in the garden began to wither, and he found himself sitting with her in the underworld, trying to justify his position.

"Miss! I'd like to speak to you about the manor house."

He reached out for her, not certain which part of her person he would grasp. She looked fetching from behind. But then she dodged another obstacle that he hadn't anticipated. She seemed to fly through the heavily overgrown garden.

He stumbled over a sack of weeds and stones. Perhaps it was the dead body of the last visitor. He regained his balance but lost the advantage.

"Stop!" he said in his ducal voice, to no effect. Either she disrespected the peerage or she was too upset to acknowledge his rank.

Dangerous women abide within.

Women who bend men to their will.

"Wishful thinking," James muttered.

A heavy beat of wings in the air drew his gaze to the sky. The hawk flew over the house. Its sudden ascent disturbed a family of jackdaws that appeared to reside in one of the manor's numerous chimneys.

The woman jumped a small urn filled with geraniums and disappeared into the house. A bramble bush snagged his trousers and slowed his pace.

"I have a sword, you half-wit!" a female voice from inside the manor shouted.

Then the door slammed, the sound reverberating in the garden. A swarm of angry bees circled his head.

He stood, breathing hard. He half expected the rose-bushes to grow claws and hold him captive. "Another time, then," he said; he was no longer merely interested but enthralled. "I'll send a message ahead. Make proper arrangements."

He heard the crunch of boots from behind the over-growth. He followed a weed-choked footpath to the side of the house.

"Pardon me," he said to a tall gate smothered in strands of verdant ivy. "Is anybody home?"

He tunneled his hand through the vines and made a peephole. The ivy concealed a back garden of such well-maintained Tudor symmetry he believed he'd discov-ered a secret paradise.

The illusion soon perished. A rheumy eye met his. A voice that could belong to either a beast or human being snarled, "Begone! All and sundry creditors and other trespassers will be roasted on a spit!"

He drew himself upright. It took more than a reclu-sive lady and an ill-tempered gardener to force a duke to retreat. "I wish to speak to your master or mistress about ownership of this property. And I shall have none of your surly impertinence."

The gnome hurled a handful of dirt over the gate in answer to his demand. James glanced up, realizing he had an audience. The lady in white stared down at him from a lozenge-shaped oriel window of what he guessed to be a hall in the upper story. Her face blurred behind the leaded glass. He noticed other indistinct figures standing around her like guardian angels.

"Your Grace?" his coachman called from the gatehouse, a footman at his side. "Have you been assaulted?"

James gave a laugh and brushed the dirt from the shoulders of his greatcoat. "Hardly. Let's return to the carriage. And be careful where you step."

"I did try to warn Your Grace about those women."

"Yes, you did. Danger comes in various forms, doesn't it?"

The coachman looked back in curiosity at the house. "Some of those forms are quite attractive, if you'll forgive me for saying, Your Grace."

"How can I not forgive you when we share the same thought?"

He ambled back through the garden. The bees had disappeared. Rose-tinted shadows enhanced the enduring beauty of the house. Its outward simplicity deceived the unknowing. The Tudor manor represented the essence of England, of what James had fought for, what his younger brother and so many other valiant soldiers were fighting for now.

In the false twilight it didn't seem to matter that the windows lacked a few panes, or that time had peeled strips from the ornate wood framework.

He had coveted this house for years. He wanted to learn its secrets. He wanted to know about the woman who lived inside. He thought he should explain that he hadn't meant to frighten her, that he wasn't a man who went about accosting young ladies on their property.

His arm throbbed, a welcome diversion from finding

reason for his behavior. Soon enough Elora would arrive to make him forget all about Tudor houses and reclusive women. He desperately longed to give himself over to a season of pleasure before he settled down and found a wife.

Chapter 2

The soft but protective arms of Ivy Fenwick's two younger sisters dragged her across the threshold. The door slammed in the stone archway on the face that Ivy had not even seen. His persistence told her all she needed to know about his character. He had shouted to the world what he wanted. Every man who braved the garden had one objective in mind: taking possession of Fenwick Manor.

"Who was that?" her youngest sister, Lilac, whispered. Lilac's light hair shone in the darkness of the hall. Heavy drapes covered the belowstairs windows. It was too early in the day to waste a candle. The housekeeper kept them on a strict allowance.

The sisters hadn't always scurried into the house like mice at the approach of male callers. Once the clip-clop of horses paraded across the bridge by hopeful gentlemen had added a measure of excitement to their afternoon tea. With their father the Earl of Arthur's approval, a young gallant might stroll through the enchanting gardens with one of his lordship's daughters. All four Fenwick girls had been well dowered and never lacked for company, even though Rosemary tended to sneak off with a book half the time and Lilac had walked with a limp ever since her accident.

But Lilac was fair and intrepid and laughed when her gait slowed her pace. She had fallen in love with a neighborhood boy when she was fifteen. He had never come back from the war; three years ago his parents had died. She insisted that she would be with Terence one day and that she didn't need a courtship until then.

"Who was that?" Lilac asked now, her voice low with dread. Even Lilac recognized danger when it stood at the door.

"I didn't stop to ask his name," Ivy said, disengaging herself from her sisters' custody. "It's obvious he came to put a lien on the property."

"But you said we paid the last of our debts." Rue Fenwick hadn't taken her dark blue eyes from the door. She had coal black hair and fair skin, and was bitter to Lilac's sweet.

"I thought we had," Ivy said. She bent to put down the puppy squirming against her neck. "Go, you morsel of trouble. You don't know how close you came to being snatched up by that hawk. Quigley has to fix that hole under the gate."

Rosemary, the second eldest of the Fenwick sisters, trudged down the stairs. "What is all this commotion?" she asked with a resentful frown.

Ivy assumed Rosemary had been at her desk. Ink stains of various shades smudged her sleeves. Her hair hung in a messy plait over her shoulder. But then the sisters never received callers these days. Why should they dress for company that never appeared?

"I assume it was another land agent hoping we'd sell the house at a pittance to pay off one of Papa's debts that has just come to notice. I don't think he was a bailiff."

Rosemary leaned against the heavily carved balustrade. "He arrived in an expensive carriage for a debt collector."

"How do you know?"

"I saw it parked on the bridge from the hall upstairs."

Ivy ran toward the staircase, Lilac at her heels. Rue stayed below to guard the door, although what her delicately boned sister thought she could do to ward off a man of such a determined nature, Ivy didn't want to speculate.

At the top of the stairs, she and Lilac followed Rosemary through a dark bedchamber into a narrow hall. The watchful stares of ancestors, Welsh and English, followed their progress to a window where the drapes tumbled to the floor in fragile condition. No one dared touch them. The last maid to do so had mummified herself in moldering silk.

Ivy glimpsed a large black carriage disappearing down the road from the bridge.

"That was not a creditor," Rosemary said. "But he might have been something worse. What did he look like?"

Ivy sighed. "For the last time, I didn't dare stop to find out. He missed capturing me by mere inches. Details might be important to a writer, but a woman running for her life doesn't care whether the man chasing her has blue eyes or brown."

Lilac rubbed a smudge of dust from the windowpane.

"He had gray eyes, I believe, and a noble face, although it looked not overly pleased when Rue and I slammed the door on it."

"The jackdaws took off from the chimney as if the house were on fire." Rosemary was studying Ivy now in concern. She usually needed a good hour after writing to return to the world. "And I haven't heard Quigley threaten anyone to stay away from the gate in years. How did you outrun the man, Ivy?"

Ivy guided the others away from the window. "I didn't. The garden slowed his chase. I knew the pitfalls and thorny places. He came up against every one."

"You shouldn't have gone outside in view of the road." Rosemary pulled a foxglove blossom from Ivy's hair. "I'm almost finished with the story. Can we hold out for three more months?"

Ivy stared through a chink in one of the windows to the back gardens of Fenwick Manor. The front of the house might deceive the unwanted visitor into believing that chaos ruled. But behind the back walls, the land was immaculately maintained by her sisters and Quigley, the gardener, and displayed geometric beds, fruit orchards, and knot parterres that remained true to their original Tudor design.

As did the manor house, for all it was crumbling into decay. Time held its breath within the walls. Few structural changes had been made since the first Earl of Arthur had built the house over three centuries before.

Rue's voice startled her from her musings. Her sister had climbed the stairs so quietly that Ivy hadn't heard her approach. "Didn't you say that most of our bills have been paid?"

"I thought they had. Even so, the roof can't hold up

through another barrage of storms. And I won't make our only footman clean the flue again and get stuck in the chimney. We have to do something besides hide."

"But what?" Rue asked. Her hair was blacker than Ivy's, her nature more secretive than her eldest sister's intense sensibility.

"We'll decide after supper," Ivy said.

"After Rosemary reads her latest chapter," Lilac added, bending to pick up the foxglove bloom from the bare floor. "These are poisonous, as you know. I wonder we shan't have a sick puppy on our hands tonight."

"Or an unwanted visitor," Ivy thought aloud. She felt vulnerable after that man's pursuit, caught outside with only herself and Quigley to blame. "To be truthful I don't care that society believes living in seclusion has turned us into spinsters, or that it has forgotten we even exist. It rarely crosses my mind what others think of us."

"It seems hard to believe that we were once popular and had our dance cards filled at a masquerade ball in London," Rosemary said, not truly wistful, either.

"I've never been to a ball," Lilac offered. "I've forgotten how to dance. Besides, I was never good at it."

"You play the virginal beautifully," Ivy said, smiling at her. "That's worth more than being able to dance."

"Except that we sold the virginal last year," Rue reminded her. "I do miss listening to Lilac's music before going to bed. One can play an instrument by oneself. You don't need a partner to accompany you."

Lilac frowned. "But you need someone to appreciate what you play."

"And that's why you have sisters," Ivy said, hoping a little cheer would counteract their ominous mood.

For the first time in years a persistent stranger had

stolen a glimpse into their secret world. Her sisters might not have admitted it aloud, but Ivy knew they must have been feeling as shaken up by the intrusion as she did. Then and there Ivy took a silent oath to do whatever was necessary to keep possession of Fenwick Manor.

Chapter 3

It was no secret to the staff of Ellsworth Park that the duke had returned home to indulge in a liaison. He had written a fortnight earlier to alert his estate manager of his impending arrival. The letter was a mere formality. His servants kept abreast of the master's affairs as reported in the gossip papers. His housekeeper followed the details of his intimate life with embarrassing pride.

It was almost twilight when his heavy carriage rolled to a stop in the drive. The estate looked as elegant as ever. Yet without his family it stirred in him a sense of loneliness and loss.

Still, he wouldn't be alone for long. He might not have appreciated the park's seclusion in the year since he had inherited it and lost his father. But in another week he would spend his days entertaining Elora and allowing her to return the favor at night. He only hoped there were delights in store once she arrived, rather than disappointments.

He had known her for years. But in the last few months she'd begun ambushing him at parties for unplanned trysts that he soon realized were part of a plot to tantalize him. These private affairs left him largely unfulfilled and, as Elora surely intended, prepared to outbid any competitor for the privilege of making her his mistress.

She was beautiful, amoral, and practiced in the carnal arts. He wasn't sure whether their longtime friendship would benefit them in the bedroom. Yet they had nothing to lose by trying.

He stirred. The scar tissue around his upper right arm ached from the bullet he had taken at Albuera. His fruitless pursuit after that lithe woman today had aggravated his mood. At least he could laugh at himself now, remembering the other lady's shocked voice at the door. *I have a sword, you half-wit.*

Half-wit?

A sword? What manner of spinsters resembled young deities and resorted to swordplay to ward off unwelcome gentlemen? James might deserve their suspicion for his display of aggression—he really had no excuse. Still, he had to wonder if an apology, a small gift, would be returned by an invitation inside the manor.

"His Grace is home!" the porter at the gates shouted to the servants assembling. James frowned, staring out the window of his carriage.

Where *were* the servants? Had they misunderstood his letter? Were they hiding from him in fear that he had brought Elora home with him? Had something happened?

The estate looked peaceful. His footman opened the door, his face also puzzled. James stepped down. A lark's melody drifted from the shadows.

He strode toward the house.

He had not been home since his father had died six months earlier. Their reunion had not been pleasant. He hadn't even known his father was ill.

At the time James had been drinking too much, infuriated that a single wound had ended his military career. His father had shown him no mercy. But then, James would have refused any suggestion of sympathy. What man wanted to be thought weak?

Their final conversation still stung when he thought back on it. "You are my heir. You will inherit Ellsworth Park and the tenants who depend on you. I know you hoped to rise in the army, but that is for your brother now. Are we agreed?"

"Do you honestly expect me to pretend I have the least desire to lord it over acres of apple orchards?"

"I don't give a damn about your desires. Keep them to yourself. Hundreds of men and women depend on our orchards. The cider we produce is famous the world over. You had more pride in your birthright when you were a child than you do now. What happened?"

"The apples can wait. Battling in foreign fields can't."

James looked around again. Where was everyone? Had he forgotten a festival day? His tenants *did* work hard and brewed a heady cider that brought a good income to innumerable families. Apples mattered. They had mattered in Tudor times.

He thought of that alluring woman from the garden again, when he should be thinking of Elora and her reputation for bedsport. Soon enough he would accept his responsibilities and respect his father's wishes.

"I shall make you stop moping, James," she'd teased,

using her body to promise a forgetfulness he realized would be fleeting at best. He could only chase pleasure for a time.

"An Englishman does not mope. He dodges life's slings and arrows to battle on."

"Well, you could smile once a week. Your face is always so forbidding. It gives me the shivers."

But he *had* smiled this afternoon, and all because he'd pursued a woman who found him even more forbidding than did Elora.

"Your Grace! Your Grace!"

The illusion of peace dissolved. Although only two servants appeared to greet the duke, the greyhounds had been released from their kennels and bounded across the lawn in howling welcome. Mr. Carstairs, his estate steward, detached himself from one of the crouching stone lions that flanked the drive. The urgency of his pace suggested that, unlike the hounds, he would not be satisfied with a romp in the park and a juicy bone.

"Your Grace. Thank goodness you have arrived." Carstairs bowed between gasps of breath. "I did not attempt to contact you about the trouble while you were traveling. I thought you would prefer to be told in person."

A shriek drifted from one of the upstairs windows in the wing reserved for visitors. James lifted his head in alarm, aware of the questioning expression that must have shown on his face.

"It might be better if you come inside and have a taste of brandy while I explain, Your Grace."

"That is not a child, is it, Carstairs? A paramour from my wilder days is not bringing a paternity suit because I have become a duke? I have never been a man-whore. My indiscretions were few and sincere."

"It is not your child. Children. Well, they are, in one sense, but—"

James stepped around the smaller man. "I'll take that drink in my study. And I hope your explanation will not be of a nature that interferes with my plans."

No. That burden apparently fell to Mrs. Halliday, his housekeeper, who startled the wits out of him when she ran up the side of the house wailing, "Thank heavens Your Grace is home." Her red-rimmed eyes meant she had been weeping. But then the woman sobbed over scorched muffins and the obituaries of people she had never met.

He stilled. "There has been a death in the family?"

"Nothing is as bad as all that," Carstairs said, giving the woman a look.

But clearly upsetting news loomed on the horizon. James considered jumping back inside his carriage and taking a ride to the village pub.

But no one had died.

The news could not be anything to run from. He would face it like a man.

Chapter 4

On most evenings, after a supper made from whatever the hidden gardens of Fenwick Manor had produced, Rosemary beckoned her sisters to her bedchamber to read from her latest work. Ivy had come to adore the tradition, but since this had once been her mother's secret retreat and Mama had allowed her girls to play with her jewels and perfume, Ivy felt both her absence and her presence keenly whenever she entered this room.

"Anne Boleyn slept in this very bed for two nights when she was young," Rosemary used to inform everyone who would listen when she was younger. "Imagine how the course of history would have changed had she lived."

Ivy took pride in *their* history and their house. But this was the true heart of the house, where secrets were shared, children and stories conceived over the years.

Rosemary had claimed this chamber as her own the year she turned twelve and her mother had moved into a larger room. She found out from the servants the identity of its most notorious guest. On the first night that Rosemary had slept there, her sisters had gathered solemnly in the doorway and predicted that she wouldn't survive to see the sunrise.

Not only had she survived, she soon lured the other girls to abandon their rooms to stay with her. Night after night they'd fall asleep in her bed, lulled by her early attempts at storytelling. It took their mother an entire summer before she caught her three other daughters sneaking down the hall one September dawn.

"So it is Anne Boleyn I have to thank for those circles under your eyes and nodding heads at supper."

"No, it's Rosemary," Lilac said innocently.

"It's Henry VIII," Rue said with a yawn, and her mother, who might have punished them at any other time, seemed to take that under consideration and forgave the girls their conspiracy.

Where had those pleasurable years gone?

"I feel safer in here than anywhere," Lilac admitted as they huddled together on the bed. Rosemary sat at her desk, writing with her quill, a smile of contentment on her face.

Whether the incident earlier in the day and the realization that they might lose their home provoked Lilac's confession, her fear seemed reflected by Rue, who added, "So do I."

"It has history," murmured Rosemary, who for all practical purposes might as well be on another continent. "Don't you remember who we are descended from?"

"Yes," Ivy said, smothering a laugh. "You wouldn't let us forget if we wanted to." She cleared her throat. "The first notable personage in the family rose to prominence as a faithful bodyguard to Harri Tudur, who rewarded his English retainer with an earldom in Wales."

"This gift," Lilac continued, "included a castle on a seaside cliff that was pounded every winter by violent gales."

"Then one December morn," Ivy said, flapping her arms, "the birds took wing. The dovecote disappeared in the rock-strewn waves below."

It was Rue's turn. "The earl declared the castle uninhabitable. To mollify his loyal guard, Harri Tudur bestowed on him a charming manor house in Kent."

"In exchange for which," Lilac said, "the earl turned a blind eye when Harri took the earl's wife to bed and a set of twins, one boy, one girl, was born of this clandestine affair."

Rue finished with a grin. "The first Earl of Arthur might not have liked this bargain, but as it happened, his two natural children died in battle, and he and his wife were richly compensated for their discretion and devotion to the Tudur line. The end."

Rosemary closed her book, put down her pen, and rose to stretch her arms. Her long braid swung between her shoulder blades like a pendulum.

Ivy sat up straighter on the bed, looking at Rosemary. "You aren't about to launch into one of your *'Horresco referens'*—'I shudder in relating stories'—are you?"

"One about my three disrespectful sisters and what became of them?"

"What are we to do, Ivy?" Lilac dropped from the bed to play with the three puppies whining at her on the floor.

Ivy sighed. Unless a gentleman with a heart or purse

of gold could overlook Lilac's awkward gait and dreamy nature, Lilac, for all her fair looks, was liable to end up on the shelf for the rest of her life.

Perhaps it was Rue, with her sultry eyes and ink black hair, who would suffer the most heartbreak. Rue was a young lady of extremes. Hadn't she threatened to take a sword to that intruder in the garden? Sometimes Ivy couldn't decide which characteristic was Rue's fatal flaw—her heritage, her deep passion, or her beauty.

"We can't hide in this house forever," Ivy said. "Someone will take it from us as the debts mount. We need a source of income other than Rosemary's writing."

Rue rolled across the bed. "Why don't we sell off the rest of the paintings?"

"Because Foxx rehung them to cover the water damage that the Flemish tapestries we sold were hiding," Ivy said. "And now the paintings are damaged."

"I'm starving," Rue said. It hadn't escaped Ivy's notice that she had gone slim and whiter than melting snow lately. But then everyone in the house had been forced to take in their clothes with the exception of Lilac, who thrived on apricot syllabubs in cream given them by a local farmer whose wife remembered their mother's past kind deeds.

Ivy stood up. "I feel a little faint-headed with hunger and desperation myself. We've spent the last of our money settling Father's debts and legal disputes. We've sold off heirloom by precious heirloom. Mother's pearls are the only valuable possession left to us."

"No," Lilac said. "It's a rule. Nothing goes that carries her warmth. She wore them against her skin."

"The pearls will only see us to the end of autumn, if

then," Ivy said. "I'll have to go to London, and after that, there is only one sacrifice left to make. I'll find a position."

Rosemary pulled her braid loose and shook her head. "You can't. It's too humiliating."

"It's not as humiliating as going hungry," Lilac said. "If we can't feed ourselves, we won't be able to support the staff. We'll be beggars."

"Are you willing to let out the house to strangers?" Ivy asked, a lawyer negotiating at an empty table.

Rue wrinkled her nose. "No one would want to stay here. I wouldn't mind acting as a maidservant, but I'd lose my temper at the first guest who complained about the service. I would give it a try to save the manor, though."

"What sort of position do you have in mind?" Rosemary asked in a pinched voice.

"A governess. In a house nearby, if possible. I don't want to be far from home."

"No," Rosemary said as if Ivy had announced she would become a professional chimney sweep or vampire. "I'd as soon sacrifice my head. Can you imagine working in a house of someone we once knew? What if one of our old friends hires you? They'll laugh at you behind your back. An earl's daughter."

Rue sent Ivy an encouraging smile. "There must be other ways to earn money, Ivy. But I'll be at your back and your front. No one will ever marry us. Do what you need to do. We will follow your lead."

Rue had a point, of course. The four of them might once have soared in society, eligible daughters of a nobleman with pristine names and plump dowers. But several witnesses swore that Lord Arthur had been cheating at cards during the masquerade ball. The last thing he told Ivy was that he'd been desperate to win back enough money to pay back the "few" debts he'd kept secret from the girls.

In fact, Ivy had heard the servants whispering that he'd been cheating for months, and not one gentleman stood up for him before or after the duel. His family was tainted by association.

His daughters loved him, of course, despite the damage he'd done to the family name. After his funeral Ivy and Rosemary reviewed his account books and had charted his decline from the time of Mama's death. They soon learned he'd wagered away their dowries as well as his other estates and mortgages in Sussex.

The only hint the sisters had prior to his death of any financial troubles was the sudden disappearance of the rare book collection from the library. A third of it had been saved due to Rosemary's penchant for "borrowing" books and hiding them in her room.

The earl died without a will or male heir, leaving his daughters an old manor house and a sea of debts. The four sisters, who had been invited to more social affairs in a month than one could cram into a year, received curt notices of cancellation. After all, no one expected them to attend a party while in mourning.

Unpaid bills replaced cards from admirers. It was something of a blessing, Ivy came to realize, when they could no longer afford newspapers and read the libelous stories published about their family. One reporter claimed that each of the four daughters had been born of a different sire.

In the year following the earl's death, the family's infamy grew until it subsided into a fairy tale. The sisters, who struggled to exist on their own, were glad to be forgotten by society. In all the rumors written about them the only truth was that their father's scandal had ruined their reputations overnight.

But at least they still had one another.

Chapter 5

James Merrit, Duke of Ellsworth, bachelor and returned soldier, who had promised himself months of shallow pleasures before succumbing to society's expectations, found himself in an intolerable situation. His younger brother had gone off to war, which was good. But his brother's wife had gone off to Sweden with another man, which wasn't good, and James had a bewildered niece and nephew occupying the bedchamber that Elora had chosen for her suite when she stayed at Ellsworth.

A gnarled hand touched his arm. It brought him back to the present. "Your Grace, are you well?" Carstairs asked with a troubled look at the brandy bottle clutched between James's hands.

James raised his head from the desk. "There's only one solution."

"You would like me to pen a letter advising Miss Denman that this is not a proper time for a visit?"

"No, Carstairs. I would like you to pen an advert for a governess to protect my niece and nephew from the appalling behavior of their mother. And myself."

"But the process of interviewing suitable applicants for a noble household is not one to be taken lightly, Your Grace."

"That is why I depend on you, Carstairs, to research all character references." Although with Elora's arrival imminent, James might hire the devil's handmaiden to assure his personal affairs weren't interrupted. "Have the children gone to bed?"

"Yes, Your Grace. Unwillingly, I might add. They are eager to see you."

"Under other circumstances, I'd be delighted to see them, too." James pushed aside the bottle on his desk. "Carstairs, do you remember the Tudor house by the stone bridge that runs through an oak wood?"

Carstairs straightened his bony shoulders. "Indeed, I do. Such a tragedy, Your Grace. To tumble from splendor to shame virtually overnight. It shocked those of us who knew of the family."

James sat back in his chair. "Are you sure you and the staff don't write for the scandal sheets?"

"Your Grace, really."

"I've caught you reading them. Tell me what you know about the place."

"It's called Fenwick Manor. The earl who owned it left it to his four daughters, in addition to an inheritance of debt and disgrace. He died in a fool's challenge."

"Over a woman?"

"He cheated at cards. How the sisters have survived one dares not speculate."

"Four of them?"

"Unless one of the sisters has perished."

James didn't feel this was an appropriate time to admit that at least one of the young ladies seemed fleet of foot and another two capable of mustering a strong defense against a duke who thought himself persuasive and quick on the offense. “Do you suppose they’d consider selling the manor?”

Carstairs threw him a poorly veiled look of contempt before he returned to his usual respectful mien. “That would be a sacrilege, Your Grace.”

“Why?” James asked, thoroughly amused. “Was the manor built on the ruins of a sacred abbey?”

Carstairs lowered his voice.

James leaned forward.

“The ladies who reside within Fenwick Manor are of royal descent.”

“Well, no wonder they slammed the door in my impertinent face.”

“I beg your pardon.”

“Find out more tomorrow, Carstairs. Tonight I wish you to write that advertisement and have it posted in the morning.”

> Wanted, immediately, a respectable young woman as governess, for two young children in a nobleman’s household. She must be honest, well educated, and unencumbered. Wages no object. Interview, Friday next, Ellsworth Park.

> WANTED, EMPLOYMENT as GOVERNESS, in a respectable house. Knowledgeable in French, literature, history, and finishing. Available immediately. Inquire at Fenwick Manor.

It was James, and not Carstairs, who realized that his notice had been printed in the newspaper directly above that of the goddess he had pursued in her private garden. A mere coincidence. It meant nothing. His was a need motivated by selfish desire, while she sought the job out of desperation.

For a moment he imagined himself in her place. It must be humiliating for the descendant of Harri Tudur to apply for service.

His moment of empathy passed. He needed a governess. She needed the position. Hostilities would have to end the instant she came before him.

He would not take advantage of her in any manner. Not as means to buy her house or as a man could do with a woman in a vulnerable situation. He hadn't even seen her face. A Tudur governess, indeed. She could look like a gargoyle for all he cared, although her posterior view had shown promise. No matter, he would treat her with the respect she deserved.

And he would count the hours until Friday came, because she had stirred more than his curiosity.

Chapter 6

It wasn't even daybreak when Ivy closed the door of Fenwick Manor behind her. For some peculiar reason Rue, pushing on the other side, could not get the latch to hold. Listening to her sister's struggles, Ivy suspected she and Lilac might have damaged the frame the other day when they slammed it on that arrogant man.

So, what was the sensible thing to do? She could count on Rue to do the opposite. Rue threw herself upon the door again. This time the tarnished metal door knocker broke loose from the bolts that secured it and dropped to the steps.

Ivy stared down in trepidation at the dragon lying between her feet. The dragon was her family's adopted heraldic beast, and his fall seemed to portend something dire. Did it mean that Ivy should not go on this interview?

Rue's muffled voice startled her. "Was that our dragon?"

"I'm afraid so. He's broken."

"What?"

"No. His bolts have snapped. It could be a bad sign."

"Nonsense. He wants to protect you."

Ivy laughed. "Do you think so?"

"I know he does," Rosemary said in a louder voice. "Take him with you. And do go now or don't go at all. There are women who would die to work for a duke."

"Yes. I love you all. Stay safe until I return."

She bent and, with some difficulty, slid her reticule up her arm and stuffed the dragon into her fur muff. She might not look fashionable. But she felt presentable in a blue-sprigged muslin dress, a warm overmantle, and Rue's gray shoes. Ivy had ruined hers while helping their only footman clean the chimney. When he had gotten stuck, Ivy had climbed up in the soot to rescue him, shouting for help that never came. Eventually he had wriggled out and fallen into the hearth.

Every day brought another deprivation, another embarrassment. But at least Ivy was taking a step to alleviate their misery. She wasn't leaving Fenwick Manor forever, she assured herself during the carriage ride in the dark.

However, the moment the gates of Ellsworth Park came into view, she wondered what had possessed her to apply at an elegant estate obviously built for entertaining, when she had been hidden away for years. She doubted the duke would consider hiring her.

"Be careful, my lady," said the coachman, who often served as footman and the family butler, as he handed her down from the lopsided carriage.

"It's almost light," she said, her eyes widening in chagrin. "Look how many other ladies are here to apply! I'm too late. Rue was right. These women would do anything to work in the duke's household."

"Forgive me for speaking my mind," the coachman

said. "But they aren't you, Lady Ivy. Not one of 'em could hold a candle to you in a crisis."

"How kind you are," she murmured. "I wish I shared your confidence in me."

Before she could assess the competition that lined the driveway, a slight silver-haired man in a plum jacket and gray trousers appeared from the top of the line and marched toward her.

"Good. You are the first, I believe. Your name, please?"

"Fenwick." She hesitated. She couldn't bring herself to use her title. It was too degrading to admit she was of nobility. "Miss Ivy Fenwick."

"Pardon me, sir," a woman in a bonnet said, squeezing Ivy off the path. "I believe I was first."

"I believe you are wrong, madam. This lady had an appointment, you see. Please wait in line. The reception room will open in a few minutes. Hold your patience until then, if you will."

Ivy's heart thumped. Her reticule bumped the other woman on the wrist, earning another cross look.

Appointment? There had to be a misunderstanding. Should she correct it? Or was it possible the duke's manager had already investigated the applicants' backgrounds before their arrival?

She had been chosen first. Why?

She walked down a winding hall, rising sunbeams dancing across the marble tiles. The study into which the steward escorted her was neither light nor dark. And it didn't seem to matter what she had worn to the interview.

The Duke of Ellsworth undressed her in a single look from the desk where he sat, his long booted legs propped between piles of letters and books. Ivy fought back a wave of panic, remembering the reason she was here.

"Please, sit down," he said in a pleasant voice, indicating the chair his steward had brought to the desk for her comfort.

But the steward had disappeared.

And the duke's voice awakened a chain of conflicting memories in her mind.

"Oh, no," she said after an eternal silence. "You're the man who chased me through the garden."

He grinned. "Yes. It's me. I don't believe we were ever properly introduced." He drew his legs off the desk.

She lowered herself into the chair before her nerves could betray her. This was the time for Tudur courage. She would not lose her decorum over a man whose stark masculinity made her mouth dry. So, he had ensnared her, after all. She had walked into his trap. And she had no plans to escape—her sisters' future was resting on her shoulders.

James stood, more as a defensive instinct than to be polite. He recognized the woman the instant she entered the room. Even though he'd had but a fleeting glimpse of her, her memory had robbed him of sleep and provided fodder for countless daydreams until he had convinced himself to let her go.

He recognized her not merely as the woman whose privacy he had violated just this week, but as the young debutante he had kissed at a masquerade ball before he went to war. She had been clutching a velvet mask in her hand. And he had searched for her the next morning at the breakfast party, wondering how many proposals she'd received and whether she would recognize him without his mask.

He never learned her name. He had never forgotten

her face. He stared at her intently as she rose unexpectedly from her chair.

"Sit down, please, Miss—"

"—Fenwick. And I prefer to stand."

Lady Ivy was her correct title. God help her, he knew about the royal mischief in her ancestry. But she showed no sign of recognizing him, which disappointed his male pride. How self-collected she was. A man wanted to know he'd made an impression.

"I'm expecting a female guest to arrive next week," he said bluntly.

"And I am to be her governess?" she asked with a composure beneath which he detected the slightest hint of reproach.

"No," he said wryly. "While she and I were making our arrangement, there was an emergency in my family."

"An arrangement." The mouth he had kissed lifted at one corner. "I understand."

He made a face. "Good. I don't understand it myself. My niece and nephew have been sent here until their situation at home can be remedied. It's a most inopportune time for me."

"I'm sorry, Your Grace, to hear this. I hope it isn't a grave matter."

"It is from my point of view, and for my brother," he added hastily, lest she perceive him to be the selfish demon he was at heart.

She lowered her eyes. "There's no need to explain."

"Sooner or later one of the servants would tell you. I prefer you hear the truth from me. The children will ask. It is better we agree upon the story they are to believe."

She frowned as if questioning the wisdom of this strategy. "But if this story is untrue and they learn the truth?"

"We'll cross that bridge when we come to it, won't we? First things first. Let me finish."

"Pardon me."

He could pardon her a hundred sins for the secret they had shared in the past. "My brother, Viscount Bramhall, is in the thick of battle," he said. "His wife abandoned her children to the care of servants for another man. The servants sent my niece and nephew here and then deserted the household, citing an immoral atmosphere and lack of wages for their actions."

"I can't say I blame them," she said, then bit her lip. It was obvious that she was no more born to serve than was he. "I shouldn't have said that."

"It's nothing I haven't thought." He walked around the desk to motion her into the chair. It was an excuse to move closer to her, to test his self-control, his memory. He recalled that her eyes were an extraordinary shade of green. But he couldn't peer into her face without seeming a little peculiar. What if he had the wrong woman? How could he find out without seeming like a complete scoundrel?

There was no need to frighten the lady half to death. But he'd rather she knew what she was getting into now than run off in a panic later because she remembered when they had first met and how.

"I need you to know who I am," he said, reaching for her hand.

She gave him a smile that drew the air from his body. "I do remember, Your Grace. But I'm willing to forgive and forget if you are."

Chapter 7

The last thing she had expected was to be greeted by such a breathtaking man. It was his voice she recognized. The pitch sent ripples of forbidden delight straight to the toes of her ill-fitting shoes. It carried a command that she might have ignored in her garden, but in his domain, and in his captivating presence, there was no question of ignoring him.

He was a peer of the realm, a duke, even if he looked rather young and offhanded about his role, with his long coat unbuttoned and his shirtsleeves rolled up to his wrists.

A grin counterbalanced his brooding stare. "If you aren't comfortable sitting before me, I insist you at least put aside the muff and reticule you're holding like a battle shield. They appear rather awkward." He reached to unhook the reticule from her wrist, lifting his teasing face to hers. "I thought you clanked against the door when you entered. Is there a dagger or gun on your person? Are young governesses so imperiled these days that they must carry weapons to their interviews?"

"I wouldn't know," she said, miffed at his mockery and disconcerting charm.

"This is your first interview?"

His smoky eyes studied her intently; she wouldn't dare lie when she needed this job. The newspaper notice promised good pay.

"Yes." She lowered her reticule to the empty chair. The dragon and its accoutrements slid from her fur muff to the bare wooden floor. An embarrassing clunk echoed in the room. A governess, like the children in her care, should not draw the master's attention. Yet the duke stared down in bemusement at the brass ring, dragon, and plate.

Quickly, she bent, aghast at her clumsiness. He looked down at the floor in astonishment. So much for the door knocker bringing her luck. The duke studied it a moment longer before looking up again. "That's an unusual token to bring to an interview. Does it hold a personal meaning for you?"

She winced. "It's our door knocker. The bolts severed when I closed the door this morning to come here. You saw the condition of the manor house."

They went down on their knees at the same moment. Ivy swallowed; his hard chin brushed her head. She supposed it was too much to hope he would act as if it were completely normal for a potential governess to carry a heraldic door knocker to her first interview. Perhaps he'd excuse her as an eccentric, and not an impoverished lady who'd brought along evidence of her desperation on her person.

"It's a sanctuary hold," he said in surprise, "not a door knocker."

Their fingers met across the ancient brass ring.

Warmth suffused Ivy at the unexpected contact. "Yes," she said, caught off-balance. "It belonged to the medieval monastery on the grounds behind the manor before it was built. Cromwell's troops destroyed the priory during his reign, and my great-great-grandfather salvaged it from the ruins."

"A dragon is the insignia of my regiment in the infantry."

"The dragon is our Welsh talisman."

She started to withdraw her hand; his fingers closed over her knuckles, a strong grip, alive, in contrast to the cold brass.

"In days past a fugitive had only to lift it once to receive sanctuary," he said. "The question is— "

Ivy's heart pounded. "What is it doing in my muff?"

He smiled. His eyes drifted over her inelegantly poised form. "That's a good question, yes. But what I meant to ask is which of us at this moment is in greater need of sanctuary."

The warmth turned to smoldering heat that reached deep inside her.

Sanctuary?

She wasn't sure of that.

Never had she felt so drawn to a man, it was true. Although she didn't know whether she should trust him. She needed this position. If he offered it to her, it should not be because his smile made her clumsy and . . . his attentions made her weak. Somehow it was almost as if she knew him.

His eyes shone as if they were keeping a secret, too. He probably thought her a fool for bringing a sanctuary hold to his house. "I might have been better off applying for a position at an alehouse," she thought aloud.

"Does your dragon breathe fire?" he asked, grinning at her.

A little of her anxiety melted. "I suspect he does when no one is looking."

He raised his other hand to her face. "Do you think he's looking now?"

"Looking at what, Your Grace?" she asked blankly.

"At us," he said, and stretched forward to kiss her with a sweet familiarity she did not understand.

She had been kissed only once before, just like this, and as romantic as she remembered the moment, her entire life had fallen apart afterward. She had attended a party in the hope of meeting a suitor who would make a good husband. Instead, a masked scapegrace had flustered her, as the duke was doing now.

Did she *want* to be employed by a man who was kissing her during her interview? What favors would he demand at a later time? He drew back slightly. Moment by moment she regained her wits. Then he pressed his forefinger to her lower lip, and she lifted her eyes to his. His arrogant smile seemed too familiar. But it couldn't be. . . .

"It is you!" she said in astonishment. "The man at the masquerade in London."

"I was rather hoping you'd remember me," he said ruefully. "I knew right away who you were."

"I was unmasked," she said in self-defense. And he'd swept her off her feet.

She laughed then. It was unwise of her, but really, she couldn't imagine how the duke's kisses could portend anything but problems.

He had risen to his feet, however, and it was impossible to appear self-possessed while she remained on the floor in a worshipful pose. Not, she supposed, that he was unaccustomed to worship. But she wasn't used to sprawling and dropping door knockers about. He didn't seem to care what impression he had made on her. But then he had no need to impress anyone.

"You could have simply introduced yourself to me," she said. "Or never have mentioned our meeting in London at all."

"Think of how awkward it would be for you to remember where we met while you were in the middle of a history lesson."

She glanced away before he could see the disbelief cross her face. He was offering her the position. Were there strings attached? She had to accept whatever crumbs he would throw her way. Still she said nothing. He'd made no secret of the fact that he wanted Fenwick Manor. Was she to be his means of acquisition?

He couldn't have known, years ago, that they would meet again like this.

His voice filled the silence. "We could consider it a kiss to seal our agreement."

"It's hardly how I expected to begin service."

He smiled at her. "It was rather uncivilized."

It was more of a Norman conquest. He had made up his mind. Should she ask for a day to consider his terms, whatever they might be? She thought of the other hopeful applicants gathered like a horde outside these walls and decided she couldn't take that risk.

"Remember the children," he said, extending his hand. She stared at his wrist for a moment before he pulled her off the floor with a strength that brought their bodies together.

"Children?"

"Mary and Walker." He drew her around the desk and placed a pen in her hand. "I know this seems rushed, but they need a stable influence in their lives. Do you mind signing the contract right now? It would take a burden off my shoulders, I'll admit."

"Shouldn't I read it first?"

"It's a standard contract. You will be committed to me for a year. Your wages will be forty pounds, which I think you will agree is more than fair."

It was twice what a top governess would earn, and now that Ivy had begun to emerge from her initial shock, she could hear voices rising from the hall. "We are about to be stormed like the Bastille," he said, shaking his head as if sharing a weighty secret.

She smiled dryly. "How difficult it must be for Your Grace to turn down all the women who desire to work under your roof."

"It won't be difficult for me," he said with a smile to answer hers. "Carstairs will inform them."

"Then thank you for your time. I'm grateful to have been chosen."

Again those gray eyes took an experienced survey of her person. Already her doubts rose up. Had she made a mistake taking the position? A peer of the realm might assume he had certain rights over a governess that she did not wish to relinquish.

Her gaze met his. His eyes betrayed no further mischief. She'd like to think he had been studying her for neatness instead of as a woman he could take to bed. She lowered her gaze to the desk, staring at the contract she had signed. "Should I have read that document more carefully?"

"Why aren't you married?" he asked unexpectedly.

The question would have mortified her had she not noticed the letter sitting on his desk.

Dearest James,

I am more excited to be with you than words can express. How long we have waited to be alone.

The duke's voice put an end to her spying career. "Lady Ivy?"

She looked up in embarrassment. He'd asked her why she had never married, and she had discovered he was expecting a lover to arrive. Or so that letter seemed to suggest. Of course it could be old correspondence. Of course she could mind her own business.

He shook his head. "Have you loved and lost, perhaps?"

Only you, she thought, *on the most tumultuous evening of my life.*

She could invent a story, but she was too taken aback to think on her feet. So this was the unabashed rogue who had offered to marry her if she didn't have five proposals by noon the next day.

He looked gorgeous without his mask. More gorgeous than she'd imagined, and he had figured in her imagination on innumerable occasions since then. Sometimes he'd gone beyond kissing her. In her dreams she had met him at midnight and he'd seduced her until morning so that he had no choice but to marry her. His proposal had interrupted her father's duel. Instead of a funeral, there had been a wedding and honeymoon composed of wicked and wistful moments.

"Lady Ivy?" The duke's deep voice drew her back to the present dilemma. "It was a personal question. You don't have to answer."

Question? What question? Oh, the one about marriage. She really should make up a story. The truth sounded quite unimpressive.

She thought of the eligible gentlemen she had once turned down. Only two, it was true. But surely if she'd married one, she would be in a better place than where she and her sisters currently found themselves.

The duke had investigated her background before he'd agreed to this interview, hadn't he? He couldn't know that Billy Wilson had proposed to her at Fenwick, vowing her father's scandal didn't matter, only to retract his offer a week later.

Then again, the duke wasn't a man to underestimate.

She sighed. "I never found the right gentleman before our family fell from grace. Or perhaps, I was always the wrong woman."

His eyes searched hers until it became a battle to maintain her dignity. She had told the truth. He could order her out the door if he disapproved.

He nodded slowly. "Your father's sins are not yours."

So he *had* heard. "You're one of the few men I've met in society to think so."

"Society is comprised of sheep. I care more about your present behavior. I assume you are not given to flirtation?"

She could've hit him with her sanctuary hold. How presumptuous. Given to flirtation, he asked, and with a straight face. She blushed at the memory of the two of them on the floor. She certainly hadn't initiated that kiss. And in no manner was that to be interpreted as a prelude to a liaison. It was criminal what a handsome man could get away with.

"I assure Your Grace that *I* am not given to kissing or

flirting with random strangers. At masquerade balls or on floors."

He rested his hip back against the desk. "Good. We're no longer strangers, by the way."

"We were never introduced."

"We know each other now." He assumed a somber attitude. "As governess you must hold yourself to be the North Star for the children. The last thing they need is another person drifting off on a whim."

"Yes, Your Grace." She knew how deeply a parent could damage a family.

"Can you start on Tuesday, please?"

"But that's only a few days from now."

"The sooner, the better."

She panicked. She needed a wardrobe, shoes, food for her sisters until she was paid and could give them a little to live on. She'd intended to make a final journey to London to pawn her pearls before committing herself to service.

"Your Grace, please, may I start on Friday next?"

He wavered. She remembered what he'd said. She must not drift off and be caught staring at him every time they crossed paths. It was rather difficult, however, when his eyes traveled over her person, stopping at every button and indentation of her gown as if learning the topography of a map.

"Fine," he said. "My carriage will collect you early on Monday morning at Fenwick Manor."

She curtsied, turned again, and darted through the door the steward held open for her exit. "Welcome to Ellsworth Park, Lady Ivy," he said warmly.

Good heavens. She did feel wanted.

"Thank you, Mr. Carstairs. Thank you ever so much."

She must have regained enough decorum to satisfy the steward, for he granted her an approving nod and politely overlooked the fact that she almost fell through the door he had opened. The duke, she feared, would not be as easy to please.

By the time she reached the end of the entrance vestibule, Ivy understood why Carstairs had warned the duke to remain hidden until the grounds had been cleared of hopeful governesses. Gentlewomen of all ages soon filed from the receiving room, Carstairs dismissing them like cattle. Within moments the wrathful eyes of the rejected noticed Ivy sneaking down the hall.

A cry went up. "Is *she* the one? The *first* one?"

"He never heard about my experiences working in Siam."

"She isn't much to look at."

"Which is a benefit, you ninny."

"Well, I'm ordinary, too!"

Ivy quickened her step. The applicants had multiplied like rabbits since the time she had arrived at the estate.

Her heart sang with guiltless joy. This early bird had caught her worm, although nothing about the duke reminded her of a measly creature she could crush beneath her foot. In truth, she had signed a contract pledging her subservience to him.

Strange that he had already put his signature to the document. What made him so sure of her? What if one of the other applicants proved more qualified than Ivy and pleaded the chance to prove herself the better governess?

He had chosen her.

And if a long-ago kiss and her door knocker—she stopped in sudden realization, turning slowly. She had left her reticule and dragon behind in her rush to escape before he could change his mind.

The dragon would have to wait.

She wasn't about to brave those parasols.

Or face the duke alone again.

Carstairs closed the door on Ivy's rather graceless exit and approached the desk. "I hope you will not make a habit of that," James said.

The steward stared at the floor. "Of what, Your Grace?"

"Of eavesdropping, you rapscallion."

"I was only standing guard in case you required my assistance."

"Against a governess?" James asked, grinning at the thought.

"You haven't seen the mob in the reception room, Your Grace. There must be a hundred of them, and more arriving by the minute. Some of the ladies are poking one another with parasols in such antagonism I fear hostilities are about to break out."

"Well, tell the parasols that the position has been filled and send them on their way."

"Sight unseen?" Carstairs glanced down again at the floor. "Excuse me for asking, but what is that by your desk?"

James looked down at his feet, laughing quietly. "Damn me. She forgot her reticule, and her dragon."

"Oh, dear," Carstairs said. "Shall I run after her with the items?"

James went down on one knee. "Don't bother. I shall return them to her myself."

"But she hasn't left the property yet."

"Are you suggesting I subject myself to a horde of hostile umbrellas?"

Carstairs shuddered. "I will brave them for Your Grace. Stay hidden until the grounds are cleared."

"Take reinforcements. I can't afford to lose you, Carstairs."

Chapter 8

Rosemary ran down the garden path ahead of the others to greet Ivy at the gatehouse. She took a long look at Ivy's flushed face and drew back in disappointment. "It didn't go well, did it? You didn't get the job? Cook heard that a parade of carts left the village carrying applicants for the job to his estate. Never mind, Ivy. They'll be other positions."

"Not in the duke's house," Lilac said, staring at Ivy in chagrin. "I was hoping you'd come home with a basket of food."

"I forgot my muff and reticule," Ivy explained. "His Grace is really going to think I'm absentminded, practically dropping the door knocker on his foot and then leaving it there after all the fuss over it."

Rosemary grinned. "I understand why he didn't hire you."

"But he did," Ivy said, taking a deep breath.

Lilac blinked in disbelief. "Then why do you look so unsettled?"

"Because—oh, what does it matter?"

Rue gasped. "Congratulations."

"You must have made quite an impression," Rosemary said, looking her up and down. "Either that or he has impeccable taste."

"It's a miracle is all I know," Ivy said, eluding further questioning. "And I have to start on Monday, which means one of you has to come with me to London to sell the pearls so I can buy a dress and food to see you through until I'm paid my wages."

"I'll go with you," Rue said, slipping her arm around Ivy's waist. "That way Rosemary can keep on writing and Lilac won't be jostled around in the streets."

Ivy turned to Rue. She looked so wan that Ivy started to say she would be fine with the footman. But Rue, reading her mind, would have none of it.

"Nonsense, Ivy. If you're willing to make a sacrifice, then so am I. This is good news, isn't it?"

She felt a niggle of uncertainty about Rue's offer, but she let it pass. It wasn't a long journey, and they had just enough money for lodgings. "I'll be grateful for your company."

The evening of that same day, Rue was helping Ivy pack their bags for their journey when they heard rain on the roof. Seconds later they hurried into one of the upper halls with oil rags to stuff the broken panes. The branches of the ancient oaks quivered in the rising wind.

"It's not raining heavily yet," Rue said, scanning the moonlit sky through the window. "And there aren't many clouds."

"It has to pass by tomorrow morning," Ivy said, and turned, her eyes widening, at the momentous shudder that rent the lower regions of the house.

"What is it?" Rue whispered, slipping her icy fingers over Ivy's hand.

Lilac materialized at the bottom of the staircase with Quigley in tow, three puppies following at his boots. "There are two men hammering something onto the door," she said. "Shall I have the servants shoot them?"

Ivy went to the stairs, descending in uneven steps. "It must be a lien against the manor. And no, we can't shoot agents of the court, as much as I would cheerfully do so if I could."

"A notice?" Rosemary had emerged from her room, stuffing one arm into her robe. "At this time of night? In the rain? I don't believe even a bailiff would brave this weather."

Ivy marched toward the door, her voice echoing to the dark beams above. "Rue, put down that sword or we shall be arrested for—inciting a riot."

"In our home?"

"Perhaps it is no longer ours," Ivy said, swallowing hard. "To think I spent the morning convinced I was our heroine."

And convincing herself that, despite his questionable behavior, she had found sanctuary in the duke's employment. What would he think of her now? He could not be expected to keep a governess who had spent time in debtors' gaol. Would he show her any kindness?

The hammering at the door had stopped, and the house was plunged into a profound silence. Cook had been awakened to appear from her bed with a candle stub that threw the chaotic scene into relief. "Don't open that door, my lady. They might spirit you off in your nightclothes."

"I sold my soul this very morning to the devil," Ivy muttered, lifting the heavy bolt. "If I'm taken away, perhaps one of you can explain to him why I will not be available for work on— "

She opened the door to the collective gasp of those gathered behind her. Rain splattered her face, temporarily blurring her vision. Even so, she recognized the nobleman in the black hat and greatcoat who stood before her, two menservants bearing hammers at his side.

"Your Grace," she said in disbelief, conscious of his warm gaze and the damp air traveling over her at the same instant. "What do you think you're doing here at this hour?"

His smile was the stuff that sent maidens to the couch, an act Ivy might have considered had she been capable of movement. The effect of darkness on his chiseled face gave her the quivers. In fact, if not for the rain, she might have stood there forever, a prisoner of his dark charm.

But it was cold, and above all else she was practical.

She lifted her arm to stay the gun that Quigley had raised in her defense. In the middle of the stairs hovered Rosemary, clutching, of all despicable weapons, the mate to the dueling pistol that had failed their father on the night of his death.

"Put down those guns," she said over her shoulder. "It's only the duke." She turned back to him in time to glimpse another smile that amplified his general manly appeal. "May I ask Your Grace what you are posting on my door with enough clatter to awake those at eternal rest in the family vault?"

He removed his hat, rain sloshing around the black rim and dribbling to the step. He would stand there and be soaked for all Ivy cared. If he had tricked her into signing a contract today to test her desperation, only to sink his talons into Fenwick, then she might order Rosemary and Quigley to fire a few shots in his direction, after all.

"It's very wet out here," he said, shifting his feet. "My men are getting cold."

There wasn't any point in manners. If he planned to seize her property, then he could find another governess to kiss and mislead.

It was a heartless deed, she thought, that had brought him out on a night like this. She felt Rue trembling at her side although, knowing her sister as she did, Rue was more liable to be shivering from fury than apprehension. "What were you posting on my door?" she demanded.

"Oh, yes. That." He grinned, rain sliding down his broad cheekbones to his jaw. "The sanctuary hold, of course. You forgot it. And this." He withdrew her reticule and muff from the folds of his coat. "I assumed you would want these to travel to London. You said you were leaving tomorrow?"

She opened her mouth in astonishment, staring briefly at her reticule before she stepped outside, braving the rain, and looked at the other side of the door. "We'll leave if the weather improves."

"Ivy," Lilac whispered in embarrassment, "you aren't dressed for company."

To which the duke replied, casting a surreptitious glance at Ivy in her night rail, "It's my fault. I shouldn't have called on you without notice. But I'm a bit superstitious. I fancied that the dragon wanted to be home. He's a protector."

"And are you?" Rosemary asked rather dubiously from the position she had taken behind Quigley.

"I certainly hope I am," the duke said, gallantly removing and shaking off his coat before he placed it around Ivy's shoulders as if to prove his claim.

Ivy's breath caught. The wool enwrapped her in his warmth and a sense of ownership she was defenseless to fight. She felt as if he'd put his mark on her. "Please put your coat back on."

"It's no inconvenience. My jacket and gloves are sufficient. Let me draw it around you a little tighter." His big hands cocooned her in the coat. "That's better. What do you think of our dragon?"

She lifted her hand to the sanctuary ring, tracing her bare fingers over the dragon's unfriendly face. Tears came to her eyes. It was a dramatic gesture. She did not completely trust the duke's motives, knowing how he coveted the manor, and how, in less than a week, he had thrown her life into chaos.

"It's wonderful," Lilac said, poking her bright head around the door. "Very kind of you, Your Grace. We're falling apart at the seams, you know. I'm not sure whether Ivy told you, but you were our last hope. Won't you come in and take shelter from the storm awhile? We don't have much to offer in the way of refreshments, but Cook usually saves a bottle of sherry for Christmas. You will have to excuse the condition of the house. As much as we adore it, we are not blind to its faults. Still, there is no place like Fenwick Manor. If you're lucky, you might even meet a ghost tonight who is grateful for your good deed. Quigley, please take the duke's men to the kitchen. We can at least offer them a bit of warmth by the hearth."

* * *

James didn't look at Ivy. He didn't dare. She removed his coat, handed it back to him as if it were a castoff, and curtsied with a resigned sigh. "Welcome to Fenwick Manor, Your Grace. I'm surprised that you survived the garden at night."

He allowed himself a covert glance at her curvaceous form before one of her sisters brought her a dressing robe. The damp air had moistened her night rail so that it clung to what appeared to be a lovely pair of full breasts and a rounded belly. It wasn't a long enough look to appease his curiosity, but he felt uncomfortably hard and looked forward to a restless night. However, with a chorus of suspicious sisters and servants in the wing, he would simply have to keep his carnal longings for the governess to himself. Fenwick Manor would help distract his fancies.

While his servants melted away to the kitchen fire, he entered the house that had sheltered the four noblewomen in secret if shabby glory.

What a magnificent study in English architecture, both the manor and its mistress. What a sin that Fenwick had suffered from the lack of care it deserved. The quartet of impoverished sisters should receive accolades, not condemnation, for keeping the manor in the family's hands.

The fireplace loomed empty and bleak in the great hall. James guessed it cost too much to light coals, even on rainy nights. He noted the absence of a fire screen and iron firedogs. In days past the family would have gathered before a robust blaze in comfort.

Lavish carvings of roses and dragons covered the walls between linenfold paneling. Ivy followed his stare and said, "There used to be tapestries where you are looking."

"They fell," Lilac said eloquently. "Then we sold them."

"It's incredible." He shook his head.

"Yes, it is," said the tall, dark-haired woman with the gun hidden in her skirts. "And it belongs to us."

He blinked. The four of them couldn't possibly hope to maintain this house much longer on what he would pay Ivy as a governess. Brave spirits wouldn't carry anyone to the bank. It would be a tragedy to watch this manor and its beautiful gardens come to sorrow all for a want of funds. The urge to protect rose inside him, only to clash with his possessive nature. What could he do, knowing any benevolent act might cover a selfish motive?

"I've returned the sanctuary hold to its home," he said, lowering his stare to Ivy's face. How lovely she appeared in the candlelight. Her dark green eyes had turned hazel. He saw her gaze lift guiltily from his mouth and felt a sting of gratification. She would not forget him again. "I should have come earlier in the day. Or sent my servants alone, but I thought I'd at least look familiar. I shall leave now."

The palpable relief in the room amused him. He had made a poor impression. Never had he been so aware of the power he held and so uncertain of how to use it.

"Thank you," Ivy said with a thin smile. "Perhaps you might call at a better time and tour the back gardens."

"In the daylight," Lilac added.

"Perhaps next spring," Rosemary said, making no attempt to hide her distrust or her pistol. "The rose walk shows beautifully in May."

He granted her a cynical smile. "I'll wait for the invitation, then."

He turned to the door.

"Your coat isn't even dry, Your Grace," Ivy said hesitantly behind him.

"That's fine," he said, his servants reappearing at his side. "My carriage is supplied with coal braziers and brandy. As you'll learn when my coachman collects you on Friday. Until then, ladies, I bid you good night—with apologies yet again for the intrusion."

Ivy stared at the family portraits lining the hall while Rosemary stood at the window, watching the duke's coach disappear into the rain. One painting of a Restoration ancestor seemed to smile at Ivy in understanding. Ivy's father had insisted he was a rogue courtier who didn't belong to either side of the family. Her mother contended he had slipped into the gallery because his ghost could not give up flirtation. He stood with a sword at his side, and even though his eyes sparkled with questionable integrity, the sisters had decided to adopt him. His mischievous presence lifted their spirits.

Ivy smiled up at him. The duke uplifted her, too.

"I swear he's winked at me more than once," Rue said, putting her head on Ivy's shoulder.

"I believe that." Ivy smiled. "You're beautiful enough to stir a ghost's passions."

"Speaking of passions," Lilac said. "I do believe he desires you, Ivy. I can still feel it in the air."

Ivy turned to see Lilac propped against the balustrade at the top of the stairs. "The rogue? He's never winked at me in his life. Or death, I mean."

Lilac shook her head. "I mean the duke. He wants

you. It was ever so obvious. For a moment when you opened the door, I thought he had come to abduct you. It would have been terribly romantic except for the rain. What a pity he couldn't have met you when you were on the market as a wife and not governess. You might have mentioned how handsome he was. He's truly a magnificent man."

Ivy laughed in embarrassment. "What are you talking about?"

"The duke. If he ever calls again, I hope it's on a clear evening."

Ivy sighed in exasperation. "You don't understand. He wants this house. He didn't chase me through the garden the other day out of romantic fantasy. Couldn't you tell how eager he was to look inside and assess our poverty?"

"I agree with Lilac," Rue said, frowning as Ivy's shoulder was immediately withdrawn as a cushion for her head. "He might wish to acquire Fenwick, but his eyes gave his other desires away. Think about it. If he wanted a proper look at the house, he could have come in the morning. But it was Ivy he wanted to see, and he couldn't wait. You should tell him to find another governess, Ivy."

"Well, I signed a contract," Ivy said bluntly. "And I'll do whatever is necessary to keep the manor."

Rosemary glanced around in amusement. "Will you do *anything*?"

"We'll have to see," Ivy said. "I might."

"You wouldn't," Lilac said, laughing in delight.

"That's how the family started. Let's hope that isn't where it ends."

Chapter 9

Ivy woke up, stiff and cold. The journey to London had drained her. She took a moment to adjust to the dim atmosphere of the unfamiliar chamber. It was supposed to be a respectable hotel, but during the night there had been a party in another room that had gone on into the wee hours. Ivy wasn't certain whether she had dreamt Rue sneaking into the hall to investigate.

She sat up in bed and shook Rue gently awake. "It's not raining. With any luck we'll make it to the pawnbroker's shop and be home before supper. I'll have to buy a new dress in the village and shoes and stores for the pantry. We all need cotton stockings and shifts. If we have enough money left over, we'll buy rose water and gloves."

Rue sat up and combed her fingers through her hair. She was avoiding Ivy's eyes. "What a horrible place this is."

"Why did you leave the room last night?" Ivy asked.

"There was a party down the hall, and I was hoping to catch a servant in passing and have him ask the guests for a little consideration. You were sleeping peacefully. I couldn't sleep at all." She slid from the bed. "Come. We'll do what we have to do."

Ivy glimpsed her sister's face in the mirror. "Do you feel well? Look at those circles under your eyes. I wonder if you took ill in the rain." But then the four sisters had all been on edge lately. "Everything will be better soon."

Rue smiled wanly. "Yes. I believe it will."

Ivy told herself that whatever was wrong with Rue would have to wait until they returned home. She had to keep her wits about her when she dealt with Mr. Newton, the pawnbroker. She'd never had the sense that he cheated her, but business was business, as he said, and he paid her the best price she could expect due to the fact that he'd once gotten into trouble with the authorities for receiving stolen goods.

An hour later she watched him open her mother's old jewel casket on his counter to examine the diamond-and-pearl necklace. Rue stood at the door, her face turned to the street. "Oh, Lady Ivy, this is a magnificent necklace, crafted indeed to be worn by a noblewoman. I cannot pay you what it's worth."

"I'll take whatever you can pay me, then."

"It's come to that?" he said in a worried voice.

"Take the pearls, and the casket. Fenwick is at stake."

He removed his spectacles, laid the pearls on a velvet swath, and turned his attention to the intricately carved casket. "Keep the box," he said after a while. "Only a few were made during Royalist times and carried secret messages for the exiled king."

"It will only make me miss the necklace."

"This is a unique item. There are panels hidden within that held secret messages, but, alas, all appear to be empty."

"Yes. We opened them countless times as children."

"I will pay you, my lady, but I do hope that this is our last encounter. You deserve better."

"I've nothing left to sell, sir."

When the time came, she almost could not bear to part with the necklace—ten pounds was generous for a pawnbroker but little compensation for what her family had lost. Rue stifled a sob, which so upset Ivy that she accepted her payment with a hurried thanks and steered her sister out of the shop. "It's all right, Rue. Everything will be fine once we're back at Fenwick."

Rue pushed through the throng of pedestrians, presumably to reach their parked carriage. "Nothing will ever be right again. We should never have come to London. It's only a place of endings, and dreams that can't ever come true."

Ivy hurried after her in concern. "You're not making any sense. Stop a minute. You're going the wrong way. I wouldn't have sold the pearls if I'd known you felt like this. Rue, *stop*."

But Rue didn't stop.

And in her distress Ivy stepped straight out into the street in front of a speeding phaeton. The driver swerved to avoid hitting her. The lady in a plumed hat beside him covered her face with her hands.

Ivy would have done the same had she not reared back and fallen hard to the cobbles. A crowd drew around her, preventing her from getting to her feet. The driver jumped down to the curb and instructed his companion to move the phaeton from the flow of traffic. As his long brown hair swung against his face, Ivy braced herself for a public scolding.

Instead, he looked her over for obvious injuries and

shook his head in consternation. Ivy wished he would speak his piece and allow her to disappear. She was famished, weak, and worried sick because Rue was acting oddly, and Ivy suspected that her behavior was not due only to the sold pearls.

The gentleman standing before her spoke in a museful voice. "I almost hit you." He grasped her by the wrist and helped her to rise.

"It was my fault, sir," she said, shaking out her skirt.

He glanced past her to the pawnbroker's shop. "I shall write a sonnet to you. What is your name?"

Ivy studied him. She could hardly hear what he was saying for all the chatter that had arisen. "What in the world is he wearing?" she whispered to the kind matron who was brushing off Ivy's cloak. "That long coat and ruffled shirt look like the castoffs of a pirate captain."

"Oh, no. He pays a fortune for his wardrobe on Bond Street," the matron assured her. "It's essential for an artist of his standing to represent the romantic without appearing to try. He gives me palpitations."

"Is he an actor?" Ivy asked.

"I am a poet, my dear," the gentleman answered, apparently amused by this conversation. "You must be from the country not to recognize me."

At last, a constable arrived, and the poet's admirers broke apart. Ivy looked about for an avenue of escape and spotted Rue, waving to her from their carriage. She was laughing helplessly at Ivy's predicament, a welcome state compared to her earlier despondency.

Still, Ivy couldn't help noticing that Rue seemed to be stealing glimpses of people in the street as if she were searching for someone she knew.

But Rue didn't have any friends in London. At least

none that Ivy was aware of. She couldn't be looking for an acquaintance, unless, against all odds, she had met someone during the night. Her sister in a rendezvous with a stranger? Never. Rue chased away callers from Fenwick.

Sir Oliver Linton found it disconcerting that a lady would ignore him in public. The unfortunate woman appeared unaware of his fame. In this case, however, perhaps it was for the best. Upon reflection, he decided that being seen entering a pawnbroker's shop did not enhance his reputation, and so he drove about for a good half hour before he parked, leaving his adoring passenger to manage for herself. Alone, he walked back, his head bowed, to the shop he frequented more and more these days.

The pawnbroker did not glance up at his entrance. "Good afternoon," Oliver said with false cheer. "Any steals today?"

"For me or for you, sir?"

Oliver approached the counter, his gaze lighting on the strand of pearls laid out by the man's gnarled hands. "Are those genuine?"

"Yes," was the curt reply. The pawnbroker rubbed a soft cloth over the necklace and slipped it into a bag. "A sad transaction, though."

"I'm no judge of jewelry, but that necklace appears to be very old. Did it belong, by any chance, to the lady in the gray cloak I noticed outside?"

The pawnbroker looked up steadily. "It was her last valuable possession, or so she believes."

Oliver laid his elbow on the counter. The pawnbroker nudged it off. "Is hers a tragic tale?"

"As you shall never meet, I suppose there's no harm in telling you. She lives far from here in an old manor. As legend goes, in days past, a royal visitor to the house hid a treasure inside. As a thank-you for the family's hospitality."

Oliver mulled this over. "Wouldn't the visitor have gifted the owner in gratitude before leaving?"

"I have told you enough. History has it that the royal visitor escaped the house an hour before his enemies descended upon it."

"Then there wasn't time to explain."

"One assumes."

"Does the young lady know of this?"

The pawnbroker evaded an answer. "I underpaid her."

"How ruthless of you. She seemed to be an innocent lady in dire straits."

"And that is why she is grateful to accept whatever I offer her." He gave a droll laugh. "I show you the same courtesy."

Oliver glanced up at the weapons mounted on the wall above the counter. "Except that I'm not a gullible young lady in dire straits."

"You're always in trouble, sir. That's why I enjoy your visits. By the way, Lady Moffatt's husband was in the other day. He noticed the cuff links you had pawned and remarked that his wife had bought him a similar pair."

Raising his brow, Oliver turned briefly to watch a potential customer peer into the window. For an instant he thought the owner of the necklace might have changed her mind. "So," he said, returning his attention to the pawnbroker. "Did he buy the cuff links back?"

"No. He was looking for a bracelet as a surprise for his mistress. He was also looking for the man whom he suspects cuckolded him."

Oliver shook his head. "London is such a sinful city, isn't it? Where did you say the lady who pawned the necklace lives?"

"I didn't. Leave her be. At least when she comes to me, she returns home with something to show for her trouble."

"Do you believe that the tale of the hidden treasure is true?"

"I'd stake my life on it."

At that moment the doorbell gave a discordant ring. The pawnbroker made a face, indicating Oliver had overstayed his welcome. Then he turned to greet his new customer. Oliver tipped his hat and inched to the end of the counter where an account book lay open. A smudge of fresh ink drew his eye to the last entry.

Receiv'd a double strand of pearls from Lady Ivy. Fenwick Manor. Kent.

Oliver murmured his farewell and hurried out into the street. He should be sitting in his garret working on the ode he had promised to write for Lord Moffatt on the occasion of his fortieth birthday. But Oliver had spent the advance a month ago, and his lordship was neither pretty nor in need of rescue.

Oliver, however, was in need of funds to buy those pearls and return them to their owner. This was the second time today he'd been warned that his affair with Lady Moffatt had been discovered by her husband. It wouldn't hurt to have a place to escape to in the country. Oliver had fought and won two duels in the past year. There was no point in pushing his luck.

He ought to wait until January before fighting the next.

A treasure hunt appealed to his imagination. It was a gamble, of course. But it was preferable to being arrested for killing a nobleman in a duel.

Chapter 10

James was playing cards with his neighbor, Captain Alan Wendover, when Carstairs brought a letter into the library on a silver salver. "This arrived early today for you, Your Grace. I believe you might have overlooked it."

James had forgotten the letter, in fact, in favor of spending the afternoon researching the history of Fenwick and Tudor days in general. He knew right away from the handwriting on the letter that Elora had written him. And so, with his intuition for females, did Wendover.

"Let me guess," Wendover said, putting down his hand of cards on the table. "She's changed her mind and has a sudden hankering for me. Shall I go to London for our rendezvous?"

James broke the seal, snorting in derision. "If you can make it there with two broken ankles." He started to read, then lowered the letter, releasing a sigh.

"Bad news?" Wendover said, instantly contrite.

"My arm, that's all." He loathed admitting how the pain could suck the breath from his body. "Listen to this."

Darling,

I trust you don't mind that I shall arrive several days later than I promised. I forgot that the Earl of Axbridge invited me to his birthday ball. I haven't forgotten your warning that you are not ready for a wife, but as we have not signed our formal commitment, I assume you understand that I still need a husband.

I know what you need, James.

Yours wickedly,
Elora

"Several days?" Wendover said, laughing. "How will you manage? Does the governess arrive before then?"

James felt the tightness in his arm descend to his ribs. "That's none of your affair, you rude bastard."

"Ah." Wendover brushed a lock of hair from his forehead, turning his head to the window.

"'Ah,' yourself," James said testily. "Is it foolish to hope that in several days my brother's wife will experience a change of heart, realize she is a faithless doxy, and return to her children?"

"Do you *trust* a faithless doxy to raise Mary and Walker?"

"Definitely not. They've only come to trust me in the last day or so. However, I have the feeling they're aware of every step I take in this house. It's unsettling to think that my sister-in-law's adulterous lover has influenced their upbringing."

Wendover raised his brandy glass. "Cassandra isn't exactly what one would call demure."

"She used to be," James said, frowning. "She was always sweet and quiet at our family gatherings. I wonder what happened to her. And now I'm in a devil of a bind.

I invited Elora here for fun and games. Not the sort that children play. This is a bachelor's nightmare."

"You should have stayed in London."

"Even then I couldn't have let the children run wild on the estate."

"But you'll have the governess soon."

James took a deep breath to control his temper. "Would you kindly not refer to her as a possession I have acquired?"

"Be on guard, James."

"Against a lady who has been forced into a humiliating situation?"

"Against yourself. You haven't been the same since the day of that interview."

"I haven't been myself since the children arrived."

"As you say."

It was Ivy's last morning at Fenwick Manor. Rue brought her a breakfast in bed of tea and a slice of plum cake. Whatever had troubled Rue in London seemed to be wearing off. Perhaps she had merely been upset about losing the necklace.

"Are the others up?" Ivy asked, unbraiding her hair.

"Not yet. I wanted you to know before I tell Lilac and Rosemary that I've applied for a position."

Ivy set aside her tray. She was too nervous to eat and afraid of being late. "As a governess?"

"As a companion to an older lady. I saw the notice in the newspaper the day yours appeared. It sounds like a peaceful position. She has a town house in London and a home not far from here."

"It sounds safe," Ivy said without thinking. "You're too pretty to work for a gentleman, married or not."

"What about you?" Rue asked, a hint of her old spirit returning. "Lilac pinned the duke for a devil the moment she met him. Even you didn't deny how handsome he is."

"Denying how handsome he is and denying him privileges beyond our agreement are two different matters."

"Perhaps not to him."

"You're not helping my nerves!" Ivy exclaimed, sliding off the bed to dress.

"Ivy, I'm only teasing. What if the duke realizes how well educated and skilled you are?"

Ivy shook her head. "You saw him in person. All it takes is a few minutes in his company to realize the sort of woman he wants need be educated in only one art."

"Needlepoint?" Rue said, grinning.

"How did you guess? That's why he's waiting for his London mistress."

"So he can point his needle at her?"

"You have it backwards. Now stop this nonsense, or I shall blurt out some inappropriate remark about needlepoint the next time I see him."

She went to the washstand, and in the next minute, Lilac and Rosemary crowded into the room to dole out useless advice while she dressed. It seemed that Lilac had only fastened Ivy's last button, giving it a good tug to secure it in case "the duke was tempted," when the dragon's knock resounded through the house.

"It's time," Ivy said. "Don't kiss me. I'll cry and look unstable in front of the children. I'll visit on my days off. I love you all. Be good. Keep me in your prayers. I daresay I shall need them."

As she descended the stairs, she had never felt so sorry for herself in her life. The ancient oaks that embraced the manor would surely bow their branches in sympathy when she embarked on her crusade to keep her home. And even if the trees stood oblivious to her plight, she had worked up enough self-pity to populate an entire forest.

A footman in black and red-braided livery confiscated her small trunk. Another assisted her into the waiting carriage.

And the duke took her hand to draw her down gently into her seat.

"I did not expect that you would collect me personally," she said, which was all she could manage to say. She could not do more than stare at the man and hope that she would grow to take his breathtaking maleness for granted.

"I had business in the village." Humor glinted in his eyes as he appraised her tightly buttoned dress.

"The children are anxious to meet you," he added. "I warned them not to overwhelm you all at once."

Overwhelm was the exact word for how he affected her. What had she gotten into? How could she live with him in his house when sitting with him in his carriage challenged her composure? She had not learned anything on how to deal with scoundrels in the years since they had first met.

He leaned forward, his dark eyes hypnotic. "I should apologize for kissing you on the floor the other day."

"Yes, you should."

"But I'm not going to."

Ivy braced herself against the squabs. "Whyever not?"

"Because I've wondered about you for years. I convinced myself that another man had married you. Now that you're a governess in my house, I'll have to convince myself you are still unattainable."

"I certainly hope to be." She raised her chin and gave him a frank look. "Am I going to be safe in your house?"

"I think so."

That was not exactly the reassurance she had sought. In fact, it wasn't comforting at all. "What do you mean 'you think so'? Either I shall be or not."

"You won't have to worry about losing the manor."

Her eyes widened at this evasive tactic. "What does that mean?"

"Carstairs has taken care of paying the interest to your moneylender and the wages owed to your servants."

She couldn't believe this turn of events. Was the duke merely generous or putting her in his debt? She was too stunned to decide. "Thank you. However, if you expect me to give you certain liberties in return, then I shall have to refuse in advance."

His dark eyes traveled over her in detailed appraisal. "It's too late for that. Consider it a selfish decision on my part. As I explained, the children need order, and our family's reputation will not be enhanced by another scandal. It's bad enough what their mother did. Let me not be accused of employing a governess who lives in fear of her own shadow."

Ivy looked down at her lap. She *was* unwillingly touched by what he'd done. He might have his faults, but he was generous.

In that moment she concluded that he wasn't a bad man, after all.

In the next, she decided that he was an utterly depraved one whose sensual appetite canceled out whatever virtues he professed. Scoundrel. Rake. Rogue. Man with only one primal goal in mind.

He had continued speaking. "I expect my mistress to arrive at Ellsworth Park next week. She is not my mistress in physical fact yet, if you understand what I'm saying. We have not consummated our arrangement, although we've come— "

"I understand," she said hastily. "And I must admit that I'm disappointed. How is this a moral example for your niece and nephew?" And why had he kissed her and hinted at a romance that might have been when all the time he had been planning an association with another woman?

"You *don't* understand. She isn't my mistress. We are close friends."

"Who desire to become closer?"

He smiled reluctantly. "Well . . ."

"In the presence of children?"

"The children's arrival was a complete shock to me," he said, speaking in such an aggrieved voice that Ivy was tempted to smile.

Poor decadent duke. Imagine having life ruin his naughty scheme. But perhaps she wouldn't be smiling when the mistress arrived. Protecting her charges from the duke's behavior was above and beyond the duties Ivy had anticipated.

"Why are you smiling?" he asked suspiciously.

"I wasn't," she lied without conviction, looking up at his face.

"Yes, you were. Your lips curled up at the corners. I even detected a little gleam in your eye. That was a smile, albeit a sly one, if ever I've seen one." He lifted his brow, assessing her until she would have confessed to anything to escape his scrutiny. "Please explain what you found so amusing."

"I'm afraid I can't remember now."

He leaned forward and took her chin between his fingers. Had those attractive lines creased his face beneath the mask he wore long ago in London? "Come, come. We share a past. There's no need for secrecy between us."

"Your Grace, if you wish to unburden your soul of its secrets, perhaps you should speak privately to the vicar. A carriage is hardly the place for a confessional."

"But the vicar isn't as pretty as you."

"For heaven's sake."

"Exactly. He'll make me repent of my past sins so that I'm worthy of heaven."

"What is wrong with that?"

"I just told you. I don't regret the past."

It wasn't what they'd done in the past that worried Ivy, either. It was the present she had to contend with.

She wondered if she was about to feel those firm lips against hers again. Against her better judgment, she let her mind wander. Was his clean-shaven cheek cool or warm to the touch? Had he learned to subdue his amorous desires?

"May I ask you something, Lady Ivy?"

She focused her gaze on his cravat. It was infinitely less befuddling than his face. Safer. "Yes, Your Grace."

"What advice would *you* give me if you were the vicar?"

Her eyes flew to his. "The first thing I would tell you is to let go of my chin. I assume you have not made a habit of kissing the vicar?"

He smiled. "Did I give you the impression I was about to kiss you?"

Ivy was not about to show the scoundrel that he'd unsettled her. "You asked for advice. If I were a duke of your means, I would find a separate, *discreet* lodging for my mistress."

"I might as well admit this, too—I was considering your manor house for such purposes."

She gasped. So much for remaining composed. The very suggestion. How dare he? "How thoughtful of you. I suppose I should consider it an honor that you wish to gift your paramour with the house that represents more history than either of you could ever appreciate?"

He released her chin and slipped his hand inside his coat. Ivy wondered if this last admission had given him a case of indigestion. "My family's ancestry also traces back to the mists of time."

"And it is your mutual love of history that sparked your affair?" she asked innocently.

"If that were true," he said, smiling as he slid his arm back to his side, "then there is a possibility that you and I could continue where our history began."

"We couldn't."

"How can you be so sure?"

"Because I wouldn't."

"You don't even know what I was about to ask. I might have been about to propose we collaborate on a literary work regarding the local architecture."

"Then consult an architect. Or my sister Rosemary. She's better versed on the history of Fenwick Manor than I am."

The carriage slowed. The duke's eyes gleamed. He looked unchastened and full of himself, an attitude that reminded her of her place in their contractual agreement. As if he'd read her thoughts, he said, "We are at

Ellsworth Park. Once you begin your duties and I resume mine, we shall not be tempted by each other."

"The thought never entered my mind."

He grinned.

She bit her lip. The irreverent man lived in a grand house. She would learn the layout down to the last corridor to avoid him as if she were a courier sneaking across enemy lines. He would soon enough have his mistress to tease and kiss and seduce out of her stockings.

She would overcome her attraction to the duke. It didn't matter at all that he had been the first man to kiss her and most likely the last. She would disappear to him in a few days as all governesses tended to do in a household.

She would not be swayed by the sensuality infused in her blood centuries ago. She would not weaken as her ancestors had, even though she was now indebted to the duke. Charmed, perhaps. And in trouble—unless she watched her step.

Chapter 11

Four days passed, and to Ivy's relief the mysterious London mistress failed to arrive. The duke had behaved, although Ivy felt his presence in every corner of the estate. At night she fancied she heard his footsteps outside her room. Once she awoke from a dream with a start, not certain if the door to her dressing closet had opened and closed.

Had the duke entered while she was asleep? One of the children? A servant perhaps? Whoever it was should be punished for invading her privacy. Still, she could hardly complain when her imagination might be the guilty party.

She missed the creaky floorboards and familiar ghosts of Fenwick.

Until she could return home, this would be her sanctuary.

She wasn't sure what to make of the children. Mary was eleven, dark-haired and quick, burdened with the emotional perception of a seventeen-year-old girl who has not only seen too much of life but has understood its coarser elements. Walker, at seven, was noisy and bold, not developed enough to elude either his family or life's foils, although for all intents Mary stood as his primary defender and foe.

Ivy thought them charming, manipulative, and self-indulgent, much like their uncle. She was grateful to have been guardian of her own sisters; learning their peculiarities had prepared her somewhat for her role as governess. If Rosemary and Rue had not chased each other through the gardens at sword point, Ivy might not have understood that an unsupervised girl could be as bloodthirsty as a boy.

Nor did it strike her that a boy weeping into his pillow was a sign of weak character.

The children were late to lessons as usual that morning. She marched impatiently into Walker's bedchamber. "Mary," she said to one of the two forms huddled under the covers, "why are you crying?"

Mary pulled down the sheet to reveal her guileless face. "It's Walker, miss. I'm comforting him. He won't get up."

"Walker, what is the matter?"

He rubbed his nose. "I am not crying."

"Yes, he is," Mary said. "He's afraid our father will be killed at war, and our mother will never come back." She scrambled across the bed, fully dressed. "Papa will kill her lover if she does. He might kill them both."

Walker howled.

Ivy braced herself. "Walker, I insist you wash your face so that your valet can come in and dress you. That is not my responsibility. No matter what happens, your uncle will take care of you and Mary."

Mary pulled the covers to the floor. "Until his lover comes."

"I beg your pardon," Ivy said, battling a sudden compulsion to carry the children off to Fenwick for safekeeping. "That is not how one should refer to His Grace's houseguest." *Houseguest* being a euphemism for several other choice words she refused to utter. She didn't particularly want to witness the duke's depravity herself.

"Do you have a lover?" Mary asked ingenuously.

"Certainly not. I wouldn't be employed as your governess if I did. And now I'll expect you both outside in the garden in half an hour. I'll have Cook pack a small hamper for your breakfast."

Walker sniffed. "Are we studying French?"

Ivy returned to the door. "No, morals. I shall read to you. Perhaps Aesop and a good dose of sunshine will chase away the darkness in your young minds."

James found Ivy under the weeping willow by the lake, reading "The Boy Who Cried a False Alarm" to the children. He stood back, listening to her, and wondered when Aesop had become a writer of torrid fables that put immoral thoughts in a man's mind. Surely that was not the fabulist that James remembered from his early days. The tales James recalled had been told to frighten him and Curtis into behaving. The ruse hadn't worked on him then and it didn't now. He doubted it would do much to change the children's behavior, for that matter, even though Ivy appeared to have their complete attention.

It wasn't the fable's fault, of course. Or Aesop's. It was the appealing voice of the storyteller who read the tale with unselfconscious vigor, acting out a part here and there for her enthralled audience, one of whom spotted James in the background and gave an unholy shriek.

"It's the wolf!" Mary cried. "Run!"

James growled at her. "And I'm going to eat you for ruining the reading, not to mention giving me away."

Mary's eyes widened as if she wasn't sure he was only teasing. The truth was he had been enjoying himself. He didn't often catch Ivy unawares. She was different with the children, her defenses down. Now she had to worry about a wolf.

Or perhaps two. James might be overreaching, but he had reason to suspect that she had another admirer.

"Let's get the wolf!" Walker shouted.

Ivy closed the book, giving James a look. "Stop it, children. These dramatics are not appropriate. You're too old to behave like this."

Walker vaulted over Ivy's lap, snatching a willow branch on his way. Ivy started to rise from the blanket, only to be lifted without protocol to her feet. In the process she bumped against James's hard chest and he refused to budge an inch.

"Walker. Mary," he said to the children, but he was staring into Ivy's eyes as he spoke. "Go inside the house. I must speak to Lady Ivy alone."

"Is she going to be dismissed?" Walker inquired, his willow branch drooping.

Mary sighed. "Elora must have arrived."

"Go inside," the duke said, his stare so forbidding, Ivy knew that her dismissal could be the only explanation.

She hadn't lasted as long as the least valued of Henry VIII's wives. She'd be happy to leave with her head, not to mention her heart and virtue, intact.

“Have I done something wrong, Your Grace?” she asked, running through any actions on her part that might have offended him. Perhaps she had not fallen into his arms as he expected. Perhaps she had been meant to serve as an unwilling lover until a voluntary one appeared. All his talk of fulfilling her contract, and—he looked a little annoyed. What could have happened?

“You have been sent a gift,” he said in an accusing tone, his left hand behind his back.

“A gift? Sent here to me?”

“That is what I said. And I believe you said that you did not have any present admirers to distract you from your duties.”

“Well, I don’t. This gift is most likely from my sisters.”

He lifted his eyebrow. “It was sent from London. Do you have another sister in town that you’ve forgotten to mention?”

“Of course I don’t.”

Ivy forced herself to meet his stare. Her last journey to London had reinforced her sense of loss and defeat. “Are you going to give it to me or not?” she asked, not caring how discourteous she sounded. She hadn’t done anything wrong. He didn’t need to be so abrupt. Why on earth should he resent her receiving a package?

“Here.” He produced a black velvet oblong box wrapped in a scarlet silk ribbon.

Ivy took the box reluctantly. “How do you know it came from London?”

“A footman from Fenwick brought it here this morning. Evidently it was sent to you at the manor and your sisters opened the outer wrapping. Aren’t you going to open it?”

"Do you need to watch?"

"Not if you have something to hide."

"What would I have to hide?" she asked, feeling guilty without knowing why. She and her sisters had never received gifts, only bills, after their father's death. She didn't know anyone well enough in London who would send her a present.

Did this have anything to do with Rue's disappearance that night in the hotel? She had an awful sense that night would come back to haunt them.

"Would you like me to open the box for you?" the duke said, looking for all the world as if he wanted to.

Ivy frowned at him. "I'll open it myself, thank you."

"Then, unless you suspect it contains some embarrassing or unsavory contents, I suggest you do so."

Her mouth pinched, she untied the ribbon and stared at the diamond-and-pearl necklace carefully pinned to the bottom of the box. "This belonged to my mother," she said, biting her lip. "I sold it as a last resort."

He stared at the necklace, his eyes narrowed in speculation. For a moment Ivy thought he understood more about its reappearance in her life than she did. At length he said, "Perhaps there was a mix-up, after all. Could your sisters have sent it to you as a token of family affection?"

Ivy shook her head, afraid to voice her suspicion. She could only assume that Mr. Newton had discovered the pearls to be paste and had sent the necklace back, demanding a return of the money she had already spent.

Still, she couldn't imagine her mother in artificial pearls, unless these were a copy she'd had made of the original necklace to foil potential thieves.

"I think you need to come inside and sit down," the

duke said, taking the box from her hand. "You do not look yourself."

"I'll be fine."

"I said you need to come inside. You are upset. I can see it in your eyes."

And his voice implied he was not giving her a choice in the matter. For five years Ivy had made all the decisions for herself and her sisters. She questioned now whether she could submit to this man for a year, when after only five days she balked at following his orders.

James led her from the garden into the house and ordered her to take refuge in his study. He kept a tight hold on the box. Evidently she'd been too upset to notice the card inside, which he was inordinately curious to read. Her reaction to the pearls had provoked his suspicious nature. His initial thought was that she was unaware she had an admirer, and he would sew his lips together before admitting he was relieved she didn't appear to care for another man.

The red bow disturbed him. Red indicated passion. Someone's heart involved.

Was someone blackmailing her? Could it involve an unpaid debt she had overlooked, or an old insult on her father's part? James would not tolerate such goings-on in his house. Intimidation of the weak aroused his wrath, an emotion that simmered close to the surface of his skin since he had been forced to return home.

He poured a small measure of sherry into a glass and offered it to her. She wrinkled her nose. "I don't want it."

"I insist." And when in obvious reluctance she raised the glass and drank, making a face, he surreptitiously reopened the box and unfolded the paper inside.

My dear Lady Ivy,

Consider these pearls small compensation for the careless act I committed in London. This necklace is only the beginning of the amends I must pay to redress my wrong against you.

I have not been able to put you from my mind.

May I dare to hope the same of you?

Your servant,
Sir Oliver Linton

Her voice startled him into dropping the irritating message. "Did you just read my personal correspondence?" she asked in an incredulous voice.

"Sorry," he said insincerely. "It's a bad habit. I tend to peruse anything that comes across my desk. Here." He pushed the box and its offensive missive toward her and reached for the bottle. "Have another drink. We can't have you reading fables when you look frayed at the edges."

"I can't tend to the children when I'm foxed."

"You can't watch over them when there's a wolf prowling after you, either."

"Are you referring to yourself?"

"Take that drink. One of us needs to calm down."

"Stop plying me with sherry and false sympathy."

"He's plying you with pearls."

"I don't even know him."

"It would seem he wants to know you. His name is Sir Oliver Linton."

"He almost ran me over in the street," she said, her voice growing high enough to hurt his ears. "An accident is not the start of an affair."

"It can be. Most men don't need an excuse, only an

opening." He scowled, watching her slide the letter into her lap as if she weren't boiling herself with curiosity to read it. He shouldn't have made that remark; his father had often said that the devil found a willing helpmate in his eldest son. "Why does his name seem familiar?"

Ivy was reading the message now, blinking and blushing as she did. "I've no idea," she said, not bothering to look up. "Perhaps he's sent you pearls in the past."

He surprised her by walking around the desk and pulling her from the chair, the letter crushed between them. "If he's trying to cause trouble, I'll take care of him."

She blinked again. He noticed that her breath came faster, and he wondered if her response was due to some guilt on her part or, as he preferred to think, her reaction to their closeness. "You can trust me," he said somberly.

"It certainly doesn't appear so from our present position."

He laughed to subdue an uncontrollable urge to prove her right. His throat tightened as he fought his baser instincts. He was used to acting on his urges. But then he hadn't found a woman this appealing in a long time. "I'm not surprised that another man desires you." What surprised him was his resentment of the fact.

"That isn't at all what he said. He wants to make amends."

Amends, his sweet arse. James recognized an overt move on a woman when he saw it. She ought to have recognized it for the cheap trick it was, too. Playing on her sentiment. Returning her mother's necklace. Surely she wasn't so easily swayed by the rogue's gesture. James could smother her in pearls if that was her pleasure. The thought of her in nothing but pearls brought his blood to a boil.

"How did he come into possession of that necklace?" he asked, deciding that there was a gap in her explanation.

Ivy balked, eyeing the door. James decided that if she moved another inch, he would be justified in taking her into his arms until she regained her composure. Or he did his. "I pawned it," she whispered.

"Before or after you signed our contract?"

She moistened her lower lip with her tongue. He realized, in the midst of lusting for her, that she had come to him out of sheer desperation and that he could have been more bloody helpful. "Why didn't you ask me for the money? I would have been happy to give you an advance of your wages to cover whatever you needed."

"I was afraid of what you would demand in return."

"That isn't fair. Have I asked you for anything yet that you did not expect?"

"Yes. You're asking me for something right now."

She had him there. "Anything you give me of yourself has to be given willingly." And would be willingly and most gratefully accepted.

She raised her face. "Your Grace, you say that now, but your actions speak otherwise. Pardon me for saying this, but you are rather acting like a wolf."

He frowned. "Would you like for me to give you an advance on your wages?"

"I shall have to be a better governess to Mary and Walker in order to deserve that, which reminds me. It's time for history."

"History. My favorite subject."

She rose and skirted the chair, curtsying twice while she backed away. "Mine too, Your Grace."

"Recent years, I meant," he said as she slipped into the hall, the jewelry box clutched in her hand.

He felt thwarted, aroused, infatuated. Both determined he would find out about her admirer and puzzled that she mattered enough for him to bother. She had taken care of herself for five years. She needed an income, not his personal interference. And he needed—well, so much more from her than *Aesop's Fables*.

Ivy didn't know how she managed to hide her vexation from the children until her day off. She avoided their uncle, although she could have sworn he kept her under his surveillance, and it was all the fault of that presumptuous poet who had made her appear to be a deceitful woman. One with a secret admirer, no less.

She left the house as planned before breakfast and headed toward the gates where Foxx was to pick her up for the drive to Fenwick. She hurried through the mist, feeling guilty for no actual reason. It *was* possible that Sir Oliver had only meant to send the necklace as an act of penance. The duke's insistence that he witness her opening the box had transformed a simple gift into an artful deed with covert motives.

Ivy had let the duke influence her.

She was afraid that, given enough time, he could influence her in any number of ways. But it had felt rather nice to have the masterful man make a fuss over her and show concern for her well-being, even if she knew what he had in mind. And she wasn't about to agree with him, but Sir Oliver had overdone his apology.

Still, what would a poet want with an impoverished lady? Was his conscience so sensitive that he would seek out her prior activity at the pawnbroker's shop and attempt to redress a wrong with this flamboyant gesture? Ivy simply didn't know. And quite honestly she preferred to remain in her ignorant state.

One scoundrel of a duke was enough to deal with.

One scoundrel who sneaked up behind her in the mist with such stealth that the cry of surprise in her throat died to a gasp before he spoke in her ear. "I hope I didn't startle you again. The children wanted to wave to you from the front steps."

She spun around to stare up into the duke's face. "I am merely traveling to Fenwick, Your Grace, not to France. I don't need a farewell party."

His grin said that her forgiveness was assumed. "I know that. But they don't."

And while she turned to wave at the two children who, looking utterly miserable in their nightclothes, had obviously been dragged from their beds as an excuse for the duke to—to search her carriage? "What *are* you looking for?" she said indignantly.

His dark eyes shone in the breaking light. "Blankets."

"I beg your pardon."

"Blankets. Brrr. It's cold these mornings, and as you know, my coach is designed for comfort. Do be home by six. Mary and Walker tend to work themselves into a frenzy if they're left alone too long. They're too much for me to manage."

"You underestimate yourself, Your Grace."

He smiled. "Return to us safely, Miss Fenwick. We've come to rely on you."

"It has only been a week."

He motioned the footman out of the way to personally help Ivy into her creaky old carriage. She felt the pressure of his hand upon her hip, the hardness of his body against hers.

"Ivy," he whispered against her cheek.

She restrained the urge to turn her face to his. His closeness devastated her, filled her with reckless desire. "What?" she whispered back.

His mouth slid to the corner of hers. His fingers lifted to the underside of her breast, a sinful caress that fizzed her blood like champagne. "Do you have to go?"

"I'll come back."

He drew himself upright. "You'd better."

"Good day, Your Grace," she said.

He glanced back at the house. "One can hope."

Chapter 12

Sir Oliver was as unimpressed by the exterior of Fenwick Manor as he was unprepared for the impact of its interior. With obvious reluctance, Rue Fenwick, recognizing his name, had invited him into the great hall. He managed to overlook her loveliness for several minutes as he cataloged the interior of the house.

In his mind he heard drums and cymbals, the music of revels and whispers of Tudor political rivalries. His imagination caught fire.

How could four young women have spent their lives in this splendid ruin and not have found the hidden treasure? They must have heard of it. And how would he delicately approach the subject without appearing to come across as the fortune hunter he was?

Poetry, of course.

Words of flattery. He made his living writing sonnets to noblewomen who in turn supported him with little baubles, which he sold and professed to have lost.

"Darling Oliver, how can you be so careless with your watches?" his last countess had asked him as she lay naked and squashing him to the bed.

"Perhaps because time flies when I am with you."

"You adorable cad."

Yes, he was a cad, and were he a more talented cad, he wouldn't have to write poetry to wealthy ladies of the beau monde in order to survive. He wasn't much of a gambler. But this endeavor, a treasure hunt, inspired him. He disregarded his stirrings of guilt and allowed Rue to introduce him to her sisters.

Naturally, he would share in whatever hidden fortune he discovered. But what a complex puzzle of a house. It could take months to search every nook and cranny, and how was one to do so without appearing obvious?

"Sir Oliver, please come into the drawing room and take refreshment," said a tall, dark-haired lady whose stare, he swore, pierced his innards.

"Lady . . . ?" he asked, hinting for a first name.

She gave him a vague smile. "Sometimes."

"Oh, yes. Of course."

Arrogant woman. She hadn't even properly brushed her hair for his visit, although neither had he. But then Oliver found the look of tousled artist appealed to most females, and God knew it wasn't as if he lived on Park Lane and had a reliable valet to keep him in style.

She didn't appear to be a typical daughter of the nobility. Neither of the two other sisters, Lilac and Rue, were dressed to receive guests, but with their natural beauty, what did clothes matter?

The unfriendly siren led him into a sunlit room and to a hard chair that sat beside a large golden lyre. It looked like something a giant might own; he wondered when the golden hen would appear so that he could snatch it and run. But on closer inspection the lyre's strings were so worn that Oliver doubted it would play a chord.

"Is Ivy—*Lady* Ivy—at home?" he asked when he realized the women awaited an explanation for his appearance. "I do have the right day this time? I sent a box here last week and received a letter in return that she would be at home on Wednesday."

The statuesque lady whom one of the sisters had referred to as Rosemary gave him a curt nod. "We sent the box to her place of employment, which we shouldn't have done. She hasn't been gone from home all that long. I'm not sure she'll be ready to receive callers the minute she walks in the door." She crossed her arms. "You are the poet Sir Oliver?"

He warmed. "You know my work?"

She sniffed in reply.

He glanced at Rue for support, only to find an impassive expression that indicated she wouldn't take his side over her older sister's. "But I owe her a personal apology, don't you agree?" he said. "I've thought of nothing but her since that day in the street. I can't write a decent verse. I'm rather hopeless. I have to see her."

"This sounds like more than an apology," Lilac said candidly. "Are you hoping to court her?"

He lowered his gaze. Odd. At a soirée in London his looks could melt stone, but these women appeared to be made of the stuff. He'd feel a damned fool if Lady Ivy refused him as a suitor.

Beggars couldn't be choosers, and after the scandal her sire had created, she ought to be grateful that a man of Oliver's renown would consider reintroducing her to society. True, it was half-world society, and his motives might be tainted, but if by his deep thinking he discovered in this house a fortune, then everyone would benefit.

He shuffled his feet, staring past the sisters, who were studying him as if prepared to torture him with one of the weapons on the wall.

Where in this house would he began to search for a treasure?

A half minute later Ivy stood before him, looking not as grateful as he would have hoped. He had rescued a family heirloom. Perhaps she did not remember him? He rose, bowed.

"Sir Oliver," she said in a hoarse voice that sent a prickle down his spine. "How unexpected to see you at Fenwick."

He straightened in surprise. Her condescending manner challenged him. It was a good thing she was fair on the eyes. He might enjoy this match. "Lady Ivy," he said, flicking back his coattails. "I am enchanted to see you again."

She turned and inhaled as if to breathe in—what? The odor of mildew rising from the floor? Did she think he would be dismissed that easily? He stood back in amusement. Her sisters divested her of her cloak, revealing a figure that took no deception to appreciate. A smattering of servants appeared in the passageway to rejoice at her return.

"Lady Ivy," he said, clearing his throat. "If this is not a convenient time to call, I understand."

She glanced back at him as if she had forgotten his presence. In a fortnight's time, he swore, he would have her eating out of his hand.

Ivy had been dying for a private welcome and a chance to divulge all that had happened to her at Ellsworth Park. Now she had to entertain Sir Oliver—and was she supposed to repay him for the necklace? Yet, after an hour of small talk, when she broached the subject, he became incensed.

"That was atonement for the accident, and a chance to deepen our friendship."

"So you *do* want to court her," Lilac said gleefully from her chair in the corner.

"Honestly, Lilac," Ivy said, choking on the bite of biscuit she had taken. "Must you always speak your mind?"

"It's quite all right," Sir Oliver said with a laugh. "I don't have a family of my own. I was an orphan, you see. This is quite pleasant for me."

"It's pleasant for us, too," Lilac said. "Some people think the four of us are dangerous, if you can believe it."

Sir Oliver glanced at Ivy. "Dangerous to the heart, they must mean."

"No, no," Lilac said, shaking her head. "'Dangerous' in an unpleasant way."

He smiled thinly. "I assure you, no one will insult you in my presence with impunity."

"How unpoetic," Rosemary murmured.

Lilac frowned at her. "Were you really an orphan?" she asked Oliver, returning her attention to him.

"Yes. But don't waste your pity on me. How can I regret my life when it has brought me to this present place?"

At that point Rosemary excused herself to work and left the hall without looking at Oliver.

"Work?" he said into the silence that followed her departure. "Is she a seamstress?"

"She's a writer," Lilac said.

Sir Oliver's remark reminded Ivy of her other "family." What if the duke's soon-to-be mistress had arrived during Ivy's absence? She might gratify the duke, but her arrival would also pique the children's curiosity. Ivy ought to be there to act as a moral barrier, so to speak. Of course Ivy didn't care if His Grace diddled a spoon while she was gone. But she had promised to oversee Mary and Walker's upbringing.

She frowned, trying not to picture what the duke might be doing while she drank tea with an attractive rascal who had just scooted his chair closer to hers. She flinched at the unsubtle scrape of wood against stone. Oliver's eyes moved languidly over her face. He started to talk about London. She didn't listen.

Surely the duke would wait until dark to bed that woman.

What a naive assumption.

He had kissed Ivy just after sunrise on his study floor.

"What time is it?" she asked in alarm, noticing the lengthening shadows on the carpet.

Sir Oliver consulted his pocket watch. "It's not gone six yet."

"Six o'clock? I have to return to Ellsworth before it's dark."

"Is the duke that strict?" Rue asked in sympathy.

No. He was that unstructured. "It's the children, you realize," she explained, handing Lilac her cup and rising for the cloak and gloves she'd removed what seemed only minutes ago.

Sir Oliver stood at her side. "What a shame. Do you think it would help if I put in a word? On your behalf—you know, explain to him that you had been in the company of a well-known person?"

"Don't you dare," Ivy said quickly. The last thing the duke would appreciate was knowing that she'd spent the afternoon with Oliver.

"And I was hoping for a tour of the house."

"Come next May, Sir Oliver," Rue said, her shadow falling between him and Ivy. "You can admire the gardens at their finest. You will be inspired."

His strained smile intimated that he hoped for more than a horticultural tour for inspiration. "My traveling carriage will be quicker than that antique which brought you here, Ivy. Honestly, my dear, you'd have been faster gliding on a sleigh without snow."

"That's not the vehicle that almost ran me over?" Ivy could not resist teasing. "Oh, forgive me. I shouldn't have mentioned it again."

His smile transformed his face. For the first time Ivy saw past his superficial veneer to the charisma of the poet who sent the ladies of upper-crust London into raptures. Yet Ivy didn't feel the least tug of attraction toward him. "But of course you should. Tease me all you like. It is the reason I am here."

Ivy rushed through her good-byes to her sisters, even though she felt unsure about abandoning them to a man as ingratiating as Sir Oliver.

"I feel responsible for him," she whispered to Rue as they embraced beside the straggly hollyhocks.

Rue smiled rather wickedly. "Don't worry. Rosemary is keeping her eye on him."

"What about Lilac?" Ivy asked under her breath.

Rue laughed. "She considers him useful for some odd reason."

Ivy considered Oliver to be an annoyance. He'd

wasted the precious hours she'd wanted to spend at Fenwick with his aimless flirtation. Yet on the bumpy ride back to Ellsworth, she managed to forget him entirely.

She promised herself she would make up the time she'd wanted to spend with her sisters on her next visit. Perhaps by then, she thought, as the carriage drew into Ellsworth and she hastened through the house, she would have collected a few more anecdotes about the duke to share with her siblings.

She walked into her bedchamber and peered at the clock on the mantelpiece. Half an hour late. The old carriage horses couldn't travel these country roads as they had done years ago. The journey to London had taken its toll on the faithful bays. She stripped down to her shift. Well, at least the duke hadn't caught her.

She bent over her washstand, splashing water over her face, and stared in the mirror. She froze, not at the cold, but at the reflection of a man sprawled across her tidily made bed. The duke might not have caught her.

But she had caught him, sleeping, in *her* bed.

She lifted the pitcher, counted to ten, and reconsidered. She set the jug down silently and picked up a towel, draping it over her bare shoulders.

She looked at him again in the mirror. He hadn't moved.

She turned, water slipping down her breasts, and walked to his side. She wondered if he was dead drunk or flagrantly courting an invitation. Clearly the woman he awaited had not made her eagerly anticipated arrival, which meant that while Ivy was envisioning the duke engaged in unspeakable sins, he had been *here* . . . snoring softly on Ivy's bed.

What was she to make of this?

Why on earth had she rushed back to the park, terrified of being late?

"Your Grace," she said, nudging his big stockinged foot. "Are you in your cups?"

"Cups." He opened his eyes, perusing her semiclad figure like a man who'd never tasted a drop of liquor in his life. He was alert, keen, a waking beast. "I couldn't find you at the appointed time, so I came in here to check. I must have dozed off. The children exhausted me. Did something happen at Fenwick to keep you?" He glanced at the clock. "You're late. We can't allow that. A governess should be prompt."

Her temper simmered. She hadn't been able to enjoy a decent visit at home with her shoes off and now this—this—intimidating spectacle expected her to behave as if it were acceptable for him to await her return in her bed.

"Your Grace, I might not have moved about in high society as often as you. But we both know that a duke doesn't nap in the governess's bed. I am in the act of undressing."

"Don't let me stop you." He sat up, crossing his legs in the middle of her bed. "I'll cover my eyes."

"You shall leave the room."

"You could use the screen."

"Excellent idea."

He folded his arms behind his head, giving Ivy cause to appreciate the breadth of his shoulders beneath his crisp linen shirt. "Except that Mary knocked the screen over chasing Walker through the house and Carstairs removed it for repairs."

"I thought something was missing." She reached around in annoyance for her cloak. "I should also have realized that something was here that didn't belong."

"Sit down," he said somberly.

"No."

"Sit down on the bed. This is important."

She wavered. Perhaps something had happened during her absence. Perhaps he had an excuse for his presence.

"Does it concern the children?"

He looked directly into her eyes. "Yes. Walker went into hysterics when he discovered you had gone."

Doubting this, she perched on the edge of the bed nonetheless. "What happened?"

"I ran around being his horsey until I wanted to cry. Cook plied him with treacle all day until he felt sick and fell asleep. Mary is convinced you met the man with the pearls. I'm worn-out."

"Oh, honestly," Ivy said, putting her hand over her eyes.

Her heart was pounding. The intimacy between them had built into an inevitable confrontation. It was the end of a trying day; he had granted her no chance to rally her defenses. He looked too comfortable, too confident sitting in her small bed. He should not be here. This was a conversation that should take place between a husband and a wife.

Had no one ever taught the duke that he couldn't behave exactly as he liked?

Why was she not more shocked to discover him lying in wait for her? Had she become completely detached from convention or so attached to him that nothing else mattered? In his presence Ivy felt as if she had taken leave of her senses.

"*Did* you meet him today?" he asked, after an interlude during which her anxiety escalated until she feared her heart would burst.

She felt him uncross his legs, his body leaning into hers. How foolish to pretend that if she couldn't see him, he could not threaten her. His knuckles slid from her ear to her throat, an unsubtle declaration of intent to seduce that she responded to against her will.

"Ivy," he said, his touch dipping boldly into the deep cleft of her breasts. "There was a male visitor today at Fenwick."

She stole a glimpse at him through her fingers. A grave error. His eyes studied her with a wicked fascination that made her wonder what he saw in her that she didn't. "How do you know?" she asked, lifting her hand to his wrist to thwart his next move.

"Carstairs drove by on an errand."

"No one drives by Fenwick on an errand. You sent Carstairs after me."

"I was worried that your coach would not survive the journey. How you traveled in that contraption to London is frightening to contemplate. I half expected Carstairs to come running home with word he'd found a pumpkin and liveried mice on the bridge to your house."

His fingers continued to caress her—soon, she knew, she must object—as he recited what she judged to be a well-rehearsed although not implausible explanation. Sensual instincts and conflicting emotions warred inside her. He was a bewitching man. She knew that at any moment he would make a bolder play. This was no time to engage in a battle she could never win. Her body was defecting to his side, urging her to surrender.

Should she run from the room?

She sensed he wouldn't stop her. Where could she hide wearing a shift and a cloak? She'd be the one who would look mad. Perhaps she could talk reason into him.

"How do you know that my visitor wasn't a male relation?" she asked, reminding herself that one simply didn't push a duke off a bed, no matter how dangerously desirable he made one feel.

His smile provoked her. "If you had any male relations, they would have claimed Fenwick the day your father died." His thumb stroked the shape of her breast through her secondhand cotton shift. "He left you unprotected."

"He didn't expect to die."

"No. I'm sorry for that. And I'm sorry that you've had no one to take care of you."

The cotton abraded her nipple; an intense stab of pleasure pierced her belly. His lightest caress rendered her weak and wanting. She leaned her shoulder back against the bedpost, missed, and would have fallen to the floor had his other hand not lashed around her waist.

He gathered her into the core of his body. Her stomach fluttered in pleasure at the sensation of hard strength that embraced her. "Where is your lover?" she asked in one last bid to distract him. He was breathing unevenly, and she could hardly breathe at all. But it didn't seem to matter as long as he held her in his arms.

He buried his face in her neck. "I wrote her a letter and asked her not to come." His firm lips moved with maddening slowness to meet the hand caressing her breast. Her heart was beating too hard. His touch felt illicit and essential. "It's better that way."

She needed to escape. She needed his kisses. The anticipation of not knowing which she needed more, of wondering what would happen if she chose him, reduced her to nothing. Instinct made the decision for her.

She brought her hands to his large shoulders and felt the deep sigh of satisfaction he exhaled against her skin. "Why did you ask her not to come? I thought you were desperate."

"Oh, I am," he admitted with a laugh. "But not for her."

She wasn't about to ask him to explain that remark, although it tantalized her. "That sounds rather cruel."

"It was a kindness for both of us."

"Won't she be upset?"

"I'll find a way to soothe her feelings. She's fond of jewelry."

She reminded herself that he had just dismissed the woman who was meant to be in his bed. That didn't mean he could sleep in hers. But the words wouldn't come. He had gained the advantage. She wondered what he expected in return. He hadn't given much thought to deciding his mistress shouldn't visit. Ivy surmised that the woman wouldn't view his decision as kindness.

"You realize that I'm about to kiss you?" he asked, as if there were any chance she would refuse when she'd already lifted her face to his and gripped his shoulders in anticipation. "I take that as consent," he said, his eyes dancing with promise.

"I'm not consenting to anything."

"Then let me know when to stop."

"I don't want you to think for a minute that I'm willing to replace your mistress."

"Did I ask you to?" he said with a provocative smile.

Before she could answer, he turned her onto her back and pinned her with his body to the bed. She gasped as if a marble statue had toppled upon her, except that James happened to be gloriously alive, a warm-blooded man to the last angle. His black hair fell across his face and partly concealed the dimple in his left cheek. Beautiful, privileged, on the verge of an arrangement with another lady. What was she doing lying beneath him and secretly reveling in her imprisonment?

The situation felt entirely unfair. She might have been his had it not been for the war and her father's missteps. But then an innocent debutante could not have kept the heart of a dashing heir to a dukedom for long. He would have broken hers.

He still could.

"Why did you send her away?" she asked, the heat of his body spreading through hers, draining her will to resist him. She might have been naked for all that the unfastened cloak and shift protected her against his hardness.

"It's difficult to explain. I want to kiss you all over. Do you mind?"

"Yes." But she didn't. Quite the opposite. She wanted the kisses he had asked for. She parted her lips the moment his mouth covered hers. His tongue stroked hers, gently at first, and his fingers walked down her throat to her stomach. He was kissing her face and throat, and repositioning his body so that she lay snugly beneath his right arm.

"Ivy," he said starkly, giving her an instant to breathe before he kissed her on the mouth again, and his fingers slipped inside her shift to rub across her tender nipples. Her breasts swelled. "I want to do more than kiss you."

"Why am I not surprised?" she said, slipping deeper under his spell.

"This is what desire does to a man." He lowered his

head to her breasts and caught a nipple between his teeth. Her back arched. "Believe me, it doesn't always happen like this. I don't think I've ever felt this desperate. I'm mystified by what you've done to me and completely at your service."

Desire did inexplicable things to a woman, too, she thought, closing her eyes. She couldn't look at his face and follow what he was doing to her body. His hand drifted down her side and eased beneath the hem of her shift. A pulse began to throb in the place between her thighs. His fingertips brushed her hidden flesh and instead of flinching, she felt herself dampen, open to his possession. She inhaled as he probed her folds with his thick fingers.

"Have you ever been touched here before?" he asked, stroking her so slowly she wanted to cry with pleasure.

"Of course not," she whispered, afraid of what he would ask her next. Or what she would ask of him. She was aware of a mounting tautness in her belly, a need that he appeared in no hurry to alleviate. How had he stolen her composure so completely? She managed to lift herself an inch before subsiding at the rasp of his voice.

"One day I'll do more than touch you, Ivy. I'll make you mine."

"Will you dismiss me if I deny you?" she whispered, opening her eyes.

"I don't think you understand what I just said. You won't deny me. I think you want this even more than I do."

She felt his shoulders tense and realized she was holding him so tightly that her fingers had gone numb. He stared at her, his eyes unfathomable, before he lowered his gaze to the juncture of her thighs where his fingers played her. She should have been ashamed that he would see her unraveling bit by bit, but her pleasure only mounted, a tautness inside her that he seemed to control.

"Tell me how badly you need this," he said in a low wicked voice.

She bit the inside of her cheek.

"Tell me or I'll stop."

"I need . . . you—you—"

He laughed in delight. Her hips twisted, and then they both lost control. Her belly clenched, and a power rose from inside her that plunged her into oblivion before she broke into fragments and knew vaguely that when she was put back together she would never be the same Ivy Fenwick again.

She swallowed a sob and felt the pulsations of pleasure ebb from her body. The duke did not say a word. He merely withdrew his hand, sighed deeply, and rolled to his feet. Ivy drew up the shift and cloak to cover herself, still shaking from what he'd done to her.

He paced at her side, debonair to her tousled muss despite his disheveled fine linen shirt and black pantaloons. She hoisted the cloak over her shoulders.

"That was quite bad of you, James," she said with a broken sigh. "I don't ever expect to find you lying in wait for me in my room again."

He hadn't expected her to find him, either. How could he explain that an attack of nerves had ambushed him when he'd searched her room and realized she hadn't returned? And then, because the children had exhausted him, he had stretched out on Ivy's bed, intending to rest his arm, and had fallen asleep?

"I would have been fine if you hadn't taken off your clothes," he remarked as she picked up the dress she had discarded.

"Then it's *my* fault that you brought the children in here and broke the screen? That you didn't announce yourself to me as soon as I walked in the door?"

"I didn't say I wasn't at fault for that." He frowned. "I hope you don't go to supper, looking that—that disarrayed."

She bent at the washstand, talking again to his reflection. "Well, who disarrayed me, James?"

He watched her pat water on her cheeks and wrists. He was beginning to feel like a damned fool. He'd never touched a servant in his life, and she wasn't acting anything like one now. Still, he wanted to kiss her sweet mouth and punish her for her ability to bewilder him with a show of power. He had always believed himself to be above such abuse.

But his body was pulsing with intense urges he had never known. He wanted to throw her onto the bed and fill her with his cock. "I don't know what happened to me just now," he said crossly. "I was asleep, susceptible to you."

She splashed a little arc of water back his way. "As if it's never happened before."

"Not like this. I told you."

"Susceptible? Tell me more. You said I didn't understand what you meant. Well, explain."

He couldn't. He wasn't sure now what he meant. An arrangement with a governess? Never. Set her up as a mistress? Unlikely. Marriage? His mind evaded an answer.

She patted her face and décolletage dry with a second towel that hung on the washstand and retreated into her small dressing room. When she returned, he could see that she hadn't correctly laced her gown. The imperfection would bother him all night, not due to any obsession for neatness on his part, but because he knew how beautiful she was underneath her clothes. He would look at her and remember how her soft body had cushioned him when he should not be thinking of her at all.

Her voice underscored his lapse in attention. "Am I going to be dismissed, James?"

"You will if you refer to me by my first name outside this room. Not that *I* mind. But the servants will think it peculiar."

"Since we will not be alone together in here again, I will only use your title from now on. Or perhaps I shall refer to you as 'His Disgrace.' "

He narrowed his eyes. "Of course I won't dismiss you."

"Then I won't resign."

"You can't resign. Our contract is binding. Besides, I understand you need the wages."

She brushed around him. "I'll go about my duties now if I have your permission."

"You might want to look at the front of your gown before you do," he said smugly. "You haven't laced it correctly, and that wouldn't have happened if you'd asked for my help."

The following day Ivy stayed true to the pact she had made with herself to let nothing distract her from her work. Her charges, in turn, appeared to have made a pact with each other to drive her to distraction. At the start of their morning lesson, she motioned to Mary, whose wide-eyed innocence Ivy was soon to discover hid the strategical genius of the ancient general Hannibal.

"Come to my desk, dear, and read aloud this passage pertaining to the Reformation." She cast a pained look at the row of mounted plaster busts representing the English monarchy that sat in the front of the casement windows. "Master Walker, please don't dance around those busts with that letter opener. You're liable to scratch one of our monarchs with your reckless play or, worse, knock a king or queen out the window."

"I'll do more than that. I'll—" He paused before the bust of an austere-faced Queen Anne. "She's ugly. I'll execute her first."

Ivy swallowed a gasp. "You shall do no such thing in my presence."

"He will, Lady Ivy," Mary said with certainty. "That's why our father won't allow him near a foil yet."

Walker leveled the letter opener to his chest and wheeled on Mary. "On your knees, Mary, Queen of Scots. Your head will roll like a turnip when I'm done!"

Mary hopped up onto her chair, clenched her hands to her chest, and bellowed at the top of her voice. "I am betrayed by the fickle Elizabeth, blackhearted witch of England!"

"Good gracious," Ivy muttered. "You'll have everyone thinking there's a murder being committed up here." She sprang from her chair and strode forward to take possession of Walker's weapon, Mary shrieking the entire while.

"Give me that opener right now," she said, sprinting around the globe after Walker. "You'll kill one of the gardeners if a bust goes out the window and lands on his head."

"Catch me!" Walker taunted.

Mary jumped off her chair. "I'll catch the traitor for you, Lady Ivy."

"Master Walker, sit down this minute!" Ivy shouted.

And to her amazement he did.

Mary pursed her lips. "He won't stay."

"He will."

Mary stared at her. "Uncle James told us that you lived in a house as old as the king who chopped off heads."

"I still live there," Ivy replied, feeling a prickle of apprehension. Were Mary's words a foreboding that the house would be sold off, after all? "The king your uncle was speaking of wasn't the only monarch to order a beheading. My house was built during the reign of King Henry VIII."

"*That* king!" Mary said, snatching the heavy ruler from Ivy's desk. "He's the one who lopped off his wives' heads."

"He didn't do the lopping—the chopping—an executioner did." She went down on her knees to gather the papers Mary had sent flying from the desk. When she stood up, the girl was charging across the room toward the bust of Henry VIII. The schoolroom ruler rose in the air like an executioner's ax and then descended to take a sudden swing like a golf club.

"*No.* Stop right now. Stop her," she said in panic to Walker.

Walker set aside the pile of threads he'd begun to pull from the carpet and lumbered to his feet. Ivy realized the burden fell on her to take action. She set forth across the room as if the future of the English monarchy hung in the balance.

"Mary, don't," she said, dodging the globe.

But Mary did.

And Ivy extended her arm from its socket as far as it could reach, her fingers glancing Henry's plaster beard, her hand shattering glass and making history as it did. She felt a stinging pain in her wrist and found herself curiously detached from the events that followed. Rivulets of blood the color of poppies flowed to her fingertips. A distressing sight, really.

The plaster bust crashed down to the garden below and by great fortune did not take another victim in its descent. She rested against the windowsill and wondered absently why she felt giddy and why the duke was standing in the doorway, his face frightening to behold. She felt Mary tugging at her skirts before she closed her eyes and sighed, floating into darkness.

James was passing through the hall when he heard the commotion from the upstairs drawing room where Ivy was giving the children their lessons. His pride urged him not to interfere. He believed enough in her abilities to handle his niece and nephew without his interference. She hadn't hesitated to put him in his place. She could take care of Walker and Mary. Besides, if he did interfere, she would only accuse him of seeking an excuse to see her again.

But the sound of glass shattering could not be ignored. And when one of the gardeners came running into the house with a decapitated bust under his arm, James didn't wait for an explanation.

He raced upstairs and took one look at the scene in

the drawing room before he went into action. Ivy sat upon the windowsill like a picture in a broken frame. Everything about the moment seemed distorted. She was sickly white, and there was enough blood trickling from her wrist that he might have feared her dead had she not turned her head toward him. Mary had a tight grip on her other hand.

"Ivy," he said, approaching her as calmly as he could.

"I broke the window," she said, turning her head away. "Did you know you can tell the age of a house by the depth of its windowsills?"

He rushed forward and gathered her up in his arms. He would deal with her complaints at a later time. He knew the children were watching. Their attention did not deter his instincts in the least.

He bore Ivy through the door to his bedchamber with a humanitarian purpose he convinced himself elevated him above his earlier earthly desires. He might even have believed his good intentions had a sweetly mocking voice not spoken over his shoulder as he laid the slowly reviving governess on his bed: "Ivy?"

A disbelieving silence, then the same voice continued with, "Ivy Fenwick? One of my oldest friends?"

Ivy sat up from the bed as if reanimated. James was so relieved to see her return to her former self that he finally turned to acknowledge the woman who had shadowed him into his suite. He hadn't been paying attention to her or the children at all. But the rubies around her neck blazed so brilliantly that even if James had managed to disregard her dramatic entrance, he couldn't ignore her presence entirely, much as he would have liked to.

He took her by the arm. "Elora, I sent you a letter asking you not to come," he said in a low voice.

"I didn't receive it," she said, pulling her arm free. "Why is Ivy Fenwick bleeding in your bed?"

"She's the governess," he said, wondering which of his servants had given her Ivy's name. "And she needs a physician. She's had an accident, in case you hadn't noticed."

"How could I fail to notice? There is a trail of blood from the drawing room to your door. Do you like my necklace?"

"Does the Tower of London know the Crown Jewels are missing yet?"

"That would be quite the theft, wouldn't it?" she asked with a grin.

James did his best to politely pretend she didn't exist, but when she started to help settle Ivy into the bed, he realized that erasing Elora from the scene was an impossibility. Ivy was the only one who mattered right now. He had bound her wrist with a bed tassel to stop her flow of blood. If he could, he'd lie down next to her to rest his throbbing head.

"I feel better," Ivy murmured, her head bobbing back against the pillow. "I left the drawing room in a mess. Your Grace, please forgive me. Are the children safe?"

He nodded at her from the foot of the bed. "We rang Carstairs for the physician. Never mind the mess." *Or the mistress,* he thought. *Talk about bad timing.* The situation appeared too suspicious to explain it as anything but the truth.

Elora moved to the other side of the bed. "You don't remember me, do you? It's been a long time, and we didn't part during what one would call an enchanted evening."

James felt as if he should do something to interrupt the conversation, but what? "Despite what it looks like, this isn't what either of you are thinking."

* * *

Elora's red hair had darkened over the years, but she had retained the slender figure and verve that Ivy had admired during their boarding school years. Unfortunately it appeared that she had also remained true to her penchant for misadventure—and it had brought them together in the duke's bedroom.

That was a sobering thought.

"What it looks like, James," Elora said, "is precisely what the servants told me to expect—that the governess cut her hand on a broken window and that you brought her here to await the doctor's arrival." She smiled down at Ivy in sympathy. "He did a decent job of bandaging it, but then James is good with his hands. How did it happen? Are you in pain?"

Ivy scooted over to make room for Elora on the bed. "The children misbehaved during a history lesson. It was an accident. Your Grace, I hope that nothing in the garden was damaged. I feel fine now, but I am embarrassed for putting you to all this trouble."

Elora laughed. "We've had our share of troubles, haven't we? I suppose you know that James and I were on the brink of an arrangement, unless he was hoping to be discreet—in which case I have ruined any chance of that."

The duke shook his head, seemingly perplexed, and slid his hand in his pocket. If Ivy's wrist weren't stinging like mad, she might have started to laugh at the absurdity of the situation. But she could see blotches of her blood on his pristine white shirt and bedcovers, and she felt responsible for losing control of the children's lesson.

"So," Elora continued, "I became a fallen woman because of that one wretched night at the masquerade ball, and you, who should have been the toast of London, are now a governess."

James exhaled. "Would you like me to leave? There is an adjoining chamber through that door where I can wait. I could have tea sent up for you so that you can reminisce until the physician arrives."

"I don't need a doctor, Your Grace," Ivy said, slipping from the bed onto a chair. It was true that she felt a little faint, but who wouldn't after a beheading and then being carried off in those strong arms? Ivy doubted there existed a medical remedy for her attraction to the duke. Undoubtedly her hand would heal. Her heart would only break little by little until she accepted the fact that he wasn't meant for her.

"You need stitches," he said unequivocally. He leaned down to move aside the chair he had kicked over during his heroic effort to bear Ivy to the four-poster. "Don't argue, Elora."

Elora shook her head. "I agree. I told you I followed a path of blood to the door. Ivy, please get back into bed."

"But I'm ruining the bedding."

"The damage is already done," Elora said. "All the way around, by the look of things. James, may I speak with you alone in the other room while we wait for your physician?"

He seemed to hesitate before he acquiesced to Elora's request and followed her from the room.

It wasn't only the loss of blood that depleted Ivy. It was the indignity, her inability to manage the children, and the reminder that once upon a time, she and Elora had sparkled in the same elegant society. Ivy had an indistinct memory about the act that had precipitated Elora's exclusion from the *ton*, from grace, but she hadn't heard the entire story.

She would like to think that the duke had been at war most of the time in the intervening years and that Elora had traveled after trouble alone. But, really, how could it be so?

Elora joined James in the other room only a minute or so later. "She ought to rest," she whispered so that Ivy couldn't overhear. "I think losing all that blood gave her quite a shock."

"Not to mention your sudden appearance." James craned his neck to see past her lithe figure. "Leave the door open. I want to keep an eye on her."

He had known Elora practically all his adult life and wondered now how he could have considered her a potential bedmate. She felt like a cousin or sister to him. She *acted* like a sister, pushing his coat and newspapers off his chaise to make herself comfortable.

"Elora," he began, taking a tactical position by the door to his bedchamber, "I think an explanation is necessary."

"It's all right." She untied her bonnet and reclined on the cushions. "I thought at first that you'd found another woman, and I was insulted, but then I heard about Curtis. I realized that you had to think of the children. I never liked his worthless excuse of a wife. I'll tell Cassandra so if I see her again."

James glanced toward his bedchamber. Was Ivy trying to tidy the bed? Why couldn't she stay where he'd left her? And why had Elora arrived here, now, of all times? He had enjoyed playing Ivy's hero. It was the first gentlemanly excuse he'd had to settle her in his bed. He doubted another situation like this would arise in the near future. Not that he wished any harm to befall

Ivy. His heart still felt like it was somewhere in the vicinity of his knees.

"Why did you come to Ellsworth, Elora?" he asked, scowling at her. "Didn't you get the letter I sent you?"

She waved the glove she had removed in his direction. "Yes, I did. I'm not here as a potential mistress, James. I came to stand for your family."

He stared blankly at her. "What do you mean?"

"Isn't it obvious? Curtis has been dealt a severe injustice."

"Excuse me a moment." He walked across the room to his bedchamber door. "What are you doing, Ivy? Leave the pillows alone. Can't you hold still for a moment?"

"I don't wish the physician to see these stains, Your Grace," came the faint reply.

He *tsk*ed. "Do you think he has never seen blood before?"

"Not mine, Your Grace."

Was it a particular shade of blue? he felt like asking. Instead, he turned back to Elora, who had interrupted her explanation to look at him in surprise. "I've never seen you behave this way," she said, removing her other glove. "You've become a stranger, but then I suppose that's the children's influence. I could strangle Curtis's worthless baggage of a wife."

James frowned. "How do you know about this?"

"It's all over London. Poor Curtis. I hope you're arranging for a divorce."

"When the time comes, of course, I'll help him with the proceedings. It isn't a matter of merely closing a door. I imagine he'll have a say in the matter."

Her eyes flashed. "You aren't going to encourage him to keep her?"

He realized then what it was that he had sensed was missing between them and could not name. Elora had attended every one of his family's functions since he could remember. Conceited donkey that he was, he'd assumed she loved him and had been willing to settle for being his mistress when she secretly wanted to be his wife. "Does this mean that you have loved Curtis all this time and demeaned yourself with me because he was married, and you couldn't have him?"

She sat up, sighing, and pushing a comb back into her hair. "He wouldn't have married me, even if he'd never met Cassandra."

James grunted. "It would have been a blessing had they never met."

"Except for Mary and Walker. She did give Curtis beautiful children."

James mulled this over. In his opinion the children had become little hellions, but he didn't wonder why. Unsupervised, left to their own devices. It was a wonder that they hadn't caused an accident before today. Or perhaps they had. The servants who'd cared for them wouldn't tell. Even Ivy had begged him to spare them punishment.

"I don't understand anything, Elora." He forced himself not to look into his bedchamber again. "Why didn't you at least give me a hint of your feelings for Curtis? I might have furthered your cause."

"You might be the finest lover in London. You might be the duke of every woman's dreams, but you're selfish and see only what affects you. My reputation was ruined years ago, James. If you weren't so self-absorbed, you might have noticed."

"Well, if I didn't know about it, then I'm sure Curtis

didn't, either. We were at war, Elora. Who in the *ton* was hopping from one bed to another like frogs on so many lily pads was the last thing on our minds."

She heaved another sigh. "Then it would only be a matter of time. How did you think that a lady of my background fell into the half-world? One day I was a debutante, the next I was consorting with rogues and actresses. Didn't you ever wonder what happened to me?"

"I suppose I did, once or twice. But the war changed everything, and I wasn't sure it was polite to probe into what might have been a distressful subject."

"But it is polite to sleep with me?" she asked, rising from the chaise to approach him. She reached out her hand.

He shook his head. "Don't do that now."

She smiled and lifted her fingers to his disheveled jacket. "Do what?"

"Touch me," he said in an undertone, turning from her hand. "What do you suppose is taking that physician so long?"

She lowered her hand. "There could be a hundred reasons," she said, smiling tightly. "But it won't matter when he arrives if your patient has run away."

"What?"

He brushed past her to the door in time to hear the precise click of heels echoing through the outer hallway. Ivy had made his bed. And abandoned it. He should have guessed by that mutinous look on her face that she wasn't going to obey him. Neither was she about to sit there listening to him and Elora discuss the death or resurrection of their arrangement.

"I was only trying to restore your appearance before anyone else sees you," Elora said, breaking into the bedchamber after him. "Really, James, I think you're overreacting. She's injured. She was embarrassed by what happened. I don't suppose my turning up helped. Where could she have gone? To the kitchen, or the garden?"

"Home," he said, afraid he'd driven her away. "She could have misinterpreted the conversation you and I had and taken offense."

Elora laughed. "Aren't I the one who should be offended by finding a woman in your bed?"

He disappeared into the hall, scowling, and stared down the empty staircase. "You're the one who admitted being in love with my brother and using me as second-best," he said without looking around. "This isn't a good time to talk about it."

"Did you love me, James?"

"Of course I didn't love you," he said in exasperation. "That was understood." He spied a figure at the bottom of the stairs. "Mary! Have you seen your governess?"

"She didn't come down this way, Uncle James. What's wrong with her?"

"Her hand is deeply cut."

Mary clung to the banister. "She would use the back stairs, wouldn't she?"

"You're right, Mary," he said in relief. "You and Walker go to the kitchens or to your rooms."

"She didn't mean to break the window, Uncle James," she called up to him. But he didn't respond.

Elora had already anticipated his next move, and hastened down the stairs to talk to Mary.

James wondered what was wrong with him. He might have felt more shocked at Elora's admission had he not realized himself that even a sexual arrangement between them wouldn't work. Thank God he had never slept with her. A steamy hour here and there, yes. But he needed a woman soon or he would lose his sanity. Not just any woman, either. Not for an uncomplicated affair.

He couldn't simply seduce the governess, as much as he wanted to, because she wasn't just any governess. He realized a solution existed, and he thought he was ready to explore it.

He had waited five years for the perfect woman. He could wait a little longer to repair the poor impression he had made. For now he could keep Ivy under his roof, his guard, and he saw no reason why she would resist him once he proved that he could be redeemed. There wasn't any question of an "arrangement" with Ivy, except for the contract she'd signed. He was grateful for that, as devious as it sounded. She was bound to him for a year.

Neither of them was to blame for losing each other the first time. She'd come back into his life for a reason. He wanted her more than he had on the eve of war. But this wanting went deeper than anything he'd known. A half decade of waiting, lusting, and dreams hidden away for the right woman.

She wanted him, too.

All he had to do was to persuade her of the obvious.

Chapter 13

Ivy had no intention of remaining in the duke's bed while he and his lover quarreled in the next room, even if—especially since—his lover was one of her oldest acquaintances. To be fair, Ivy couldn't accuse the duke of pushing Elora onto the path of ruin. Obviously, however, he had led Elora further astray.

But their affair wasn't any of Ivy's business. Furthermore, from what Ivy could glean from their conversation, the duke's brother had played a pivotal role in Elora's life. Had he been at the masquerade ball on the night that Ivy's world had collapsed? She found that she couldn't remember. One man's kiss had taken precedence over everything else that evening, except her father's disgrace and subsequent death.

It was possible that the same fate could have befallen Elora, too. Until now Ivy had always thought that she and her sisters had been singled out for their wretched destiny.

The moment she sensed that the duke wasn't watching, she slipped from the bed, drawing up the covers as neatly as she could, and sneaked into the hall.

She'd taken only four steps toward the staircase before he emerged from another door and strode forward, his frown so wrathful she froze in her tracks.

"How dare you disobey me," he said. "Do you realize that you could faint and fall down the stairs from the amount of blood you've lost?" And he swept her up once again in his arms.

Ivy could well have fainted, but more from the sinful thrill of those wonderful arms embracing her than from any loss of blood. Besides, her fate was sealed. Elora had left the sitting room to close ranks in case Ivy made another attempt to escape. That seemed an impossibility considering the physician loomed at the bottom of the stairs, looking harried and self-important.

How strong James was. She let her cheek rest against his shoulder. "This is very heroic of you."

"Isn't it?"

Her hip brushed his groin with every stride he took. Heroic and hard, she thought. "I've failed as a governess already."

"Those children could take down an entire army." He paused outside his bedchamber doors, boosting her up higher in his arms. "When I saw you sitting in the windowsill like that, I admit I felt—well, I don't want to ever feel like that again."

And she wanted to feel his arms around her forever and make him forget any other woman existed.

Night had settled over the house and things were finally quiet. Ivy heard the rustle of unfamiliar sheets and felt a weight across her ribs. No. She didn't want to remember what had happened with the children and the shattered window.

She was in his bed again. With him? She couldn't seem to fully awaken. "Your Grace . . . please." She reached out beside her and her fingers touched soft hair. Was it Lilac? Was she home?

"It's me, my lady. It's Mary. I'm ever so sorry."

"It was an accident." Her eyes refused to stay open. Minutes or an hour passed. She couldn't tell. She drifted.

"It wasn't an accident," Mary whispered, and Ivy jolted awake again. "I always wanted to behead Henry."

"So did Rosemary." Ivy's wrist throbbed. Now she recalled that the physician had given her eight stitches and a dose of laudanum. She managed to pull her hand to her chest. "She's one of my sisters."

"May I meet her?"

The bed-curtains parted, and Ivy felt another presence in the room. A husky voice said, "What are you doing in here, Mary? Haven't you caused enough trouble today? Go back to your own bed."

The pressure lifted from Ivy's ribs. A cool hand stroked her cheek. She wanted to rouse, but then the caress would stop. "Does it hurt?" he asked her gently.

"Mmm, no. It feels wonderful."

He laughed, his face close to hers. "I meant your wrist. But I'm happy to act as a substitute to ease your discomfort."

He kissed her lightly on the lips. She floated away again, compliant, lost, her last sensation one of contentment until later in the night, when she stirred again, her hand aching, and realized she was alone.

James sat with Elora at breakfast the next day, feeling like a simpleton for not realizing the obvious. She had loved Curtis all her life. She might have considered him as a suitor if a married rake hadn't ruined her the night of the masquerade ball. Of course she hadn't advertised the news in the papers. She would have done everything in her power to hide her disgrace. But she was discovered by a pair of debutantes, and their malice had marked her for life.

Elora considered herself only good enough to become a man's mistress, and the man she had chosen was the brother of her true love, who presumably was as oblivious to this imbroglio as James had been.

"How did Ivy help you?" he asked her over the plate of buttered toast the butler passed across the table.

"She was the only debutante at the ball who stood beside me. We knew each other from boarding school. I never met her again after that night."

He tried to hide his sudden eagerness to see Ivy and casually pushed back his chair. "She should be awake by now. It's only courtesy that I check on her. After all, she could have fallen out the window."

"She's been up for hours, James. You'll find her upstairs with the children."

He attempted to look detached. "Well, that's fine, then. I don't see what I was worrying about."

"You worry about everything. I know your secrets. Do *you* still suffer that terrible pain in your arm?"

"Do I act as though I'm in pain?"

She stared at her toast. "Not at all. But before you escape, I would like your permission to take the children to my sister's house for a few days. She has two sons of her own, and it would be good for Walker to play with the other boys. I'd like the chance for the children to know me as something other than the woman you were considering to be your bedmate."

He flushed. "Now that everything is out in the open, the idea sounds a little obscene."

"What we had in mind certainly was."

He laughed at her teasing tone and left the room, in the best mood he could remember since he had returned to Ellsworth. It was a fine house, he thought, large enough in which to lose one's way. It took an eternity to cross through the corridors to the staircase that climbed upstairs. On the way he passed so many Ionic columns and Greek statues he could have been in Athens.

At last he reached the stairs, only to be flagged down by Perris, the butler. "Your Grace! Your Grace!" Perris said, bending over to catch his breath. "A letter has arrived."

"It can wait. No. It can't. It might concern my brother Curtis."

The butler handed him the letter. James tore open the seal before realizing it was addressed to Ivy. "Perris, this is not for me."

"I never said it was, Your Grace. It was sent to our poor Lady Ivy, who went through such an ordeal yesterday. A footman from Fenwick Manor delivered it only a minute ago. I wonder if her family has heard of her horrendous accident. . . ."

James looked first to the signature to verify that the message hadn't been written by Ivy's admirer. He quickly scanned the letter while Perris, the biggest gossip in the house, droned on. He felt like a kitchen girl for reading it. But then word could arrive any day from Curtis or his faithless wife.

How innocent Ivy's life was in comparison to his. Or perhaps not. His brows knotted at the enigmatic note.

Dear Ivy,

I know your employer will not allow you another day off, but if there is any chance he might grant you a few hours of freedom, I shall be forever grateful.

I need to confess to you what I did in London. Until I share this burden with you I cannot sleep or eat. I am so full of morose thoughts that I burst into tears when even a leaf falls.

I had an interview yesterday with a viscountess who is seeking a companion. She has promised me the job. And I have accepted. I expect to start work soon.

There are great changes afoot at Fenwick. I'm sworn to secrecy, but be prepared. It seems to us that you found love in London.

By the way, today is Lilac's natal day. I wish you could be here. For the first time in years, we are celebrating in grand fashion, and all because of you.

Your loving sister,
Rue

James refolded the letter and handed it back to the butler. Ivy would never forgive him for reading another of her correspondences. "Have Carstairs reseal and deliver it to Lady Ivy upstairs. I should never have opened it."

The butler bowed. "An understandable mistake, Your Grace."

"Yes."

Understandable. But James wasn't sure he understood the contents of the missive.

It seems that you found love in London.

Could Rue be referring to that long-ago incident between Ivy and James at the masquerade ball? It was possible Ivy had told her sisters how she and James had met. That pleased him, to think he was important enough for her to speak of in those terms to them.

It was also possible that Rue was talking about another man. She could have been alluding to a poet who enticed a woman with her own pearls and words that promised everything and meant nothing at all.

Ivy saw the duke propped against the doorjamb and felt like she was falling again. Not out of a window, it was true, but into a different kind of danger, one that could only end with a pain worse than anything she'd ever imagined. But when he smiled at her, ignoring the children's cries of greeting, she didn't care how or where she landed. She could only hope he would be there to catch her.

"Your Grace." She stood, edging around the globe, and curtsied. "We were studying the correct forms of address when one is presented at court."

"Elora is taking me on a visit," Walker said, sliding off his stool.

Ivy noticed the duke glance at the letter on her desk. She was positive the rogue had read and resealed it. He had no compunctions about uncovering her secrets. And he wasn't subtle at all about his desires.

"How is your hand?" he asked.

"I would never have known I'd injured it if not for this cumbersome bandage. It does make writing difficult."

His smile vanished. "I understand."

"I've been a bother," she said, held hostage by his stare.

"I see that you received the letter," he said, as if Ivy weren't perfectly aware he had knowledge of the contents. "Is everything well at home?"

"To be honest, I'm not sure. I forgot that today is my sister's birthday."

Mary barreled around her and anchored herself to the duke's side. "Don't make me go with Elora. I want to stay here."

He stroked her hair. "Why?" he asked gently. "Are you that attached to your governess?"

"Well, I am," Mary answered. "But I want to be here in case my father sends you a letter or my mother returns for us."

His eyes darkened. Ivy doubted he would surrender the children, even if their mother did come home. "Fine, Mary," he said, but he was still staring at Ivy. He added in a hesitant voice, "Your governess must take the afternoon off. I think we've worn her to tatters in the short time she's been here."

Ivy studied his stern face. "Are you giving me permission to go home?"

"Only for a few hours. And I shall have my footman escort you and remain on guard outside Fenwick until you are ready to come back."

So he *had* read her letter.

She sighed. "I don't need guards. There haven't been any highwaymen lurking in the hedgerows for decades."

"I'm not worried about highwaymen," he replied. "It's the scoundrels who have been attracted to the area lately that are of concern."

Ivy almost retorted that it took one to know one. But then he gave her a smile that could have melted iron, let alone a lady's heart. She wasn't about to admit to him that when it came to scoundrels, he had no competition. She was grateful for the consideration he'd shown her yesterday and again now.

Even if she was becoming hopelessly entangled in the strings that were attached to his generosity.

"Thank you." She curtsied low. When she rose up, his eyes met hers in a questioning look that threatened to buckle her knees again. *Scoundrel of scoundrels,* she thought. He didn't even have to try. He undid a woman with a glance.

"Be back on time," he said, and his smile told her he knew she would obey.

"I will," she said even though she had not a clue what awaited her at the house. "I promise."

"I might discipline you this time if you're late. Come, Mary." He took the girl by the hand. "Why don't you run out into the garden and pick some flowers for Lady Ivy's sister?"

Chapter 14

Ivy walked toward her family's residence, unable to believe her eyes. A pair of masons teetered on ladders, filling in the turret's stone trim. The huge crack above the front door had been repaired. And the garden—it had been denuded of its protective thorns and laid naked to expose row upon row of young rosebushes that only experienced gardeners could have planted.

She swallowed. The duke must have done this. He had rendered Fenwick elegant again, romantic—and vulnerable to all who passed. He had begun the work of restoration.

Was this why he'd insisted she take the afternoon off? Perhaps he felt guilty that she had injured herself. Had he planned a birthday surprise for Lilac and tricked Ivy into coming home? Her throat tightened. Persuasive, calculating, he seemed unwilling to waste time between mistresses. Elora had indicated that she was no longer game. Ivy was the logical next choice. She wouldn't be surprised to find that he plotted her seduction down to the last move.

The front door stood open.

She stepped into the house, hiding her flower bouquet behind her back, and made her way to the great hall in trepidation. She expected the duke to be hiding in a corner somewhere. The guests seated at the table gave her guarded smiles. In attendance sat three gentlemen, and two ladies whom she had never met. She looked uncertainly first at Lilac, whose smile could mean anything, and then at Rue, whose averted gaze said this was not her doing. She glanced at Rosemary, who shrugged as if to detach herself from the entire scene.

She stared at the covered silver dishes on the table, at the glittering candelabrum, the bowls of imported fruit and wheels of white, crumbly, blue-veined cheese. A place had been set at the end of the table, the empty chair where her father had presided over the festivities. It was the seat of honor, reserved for the master of the house, and Ivy's heart missed a beat.

She'd held out hope until the last moment that it was her arrogant duke who had arranged this surprise. She waited for him to put in an appearance until another man entered through the screen's passage, looking only at her.

She was so disappointed she could have thrown the flowers in his face.

Sir Oliver might be an attractive buck, with scads of admirers in London. To judge by the cheers that greeted him, he had already taken over the house. But as Ivy gave him a restrained smile, she decided that she preferred her scoundrels dark and masterful. The type who unmasked their passions in private.

"Welcome home, Ivy," he said warmly. "I'm glad that your gaoler released you for the day."

* * *

James paced his study. He climbed the stairs to Ivy's room a half-dozen times and turned back before reaching her door. Dusk stole over the park. At last he heard the porter opening the gates, carriage wheels churning the gravel drive.

He walked back into his study. He was determined not to show how his anxiety had mastered him. Indeed it was later than he expected. But it wasn't yet dark. He wouldn't chastise her when he had given her permission to go in the first place. He stared at the letters on his desk, listening for her footsteps. He hadn't heard from his brother. He had written Curtis to tell him only that Mary and Walker were staying at Ellsworth, not the reason why.

Where was their governess?

Sharing the company of her sisters, telling secrets, laughing, perhaps even confessing that she and James had grown close? God, what was he thinking? Committing to Ivy would mean he'd be responsible for marrying off a brood of beautiful and independent women. He would never know a moment of peace again in his life. Or of loneliness. What a compelling if untidy fate.

He waited another half hour before he rang for Carstairs. "Is she here?" he demanded the instant the steward walked through the door.

Carstairs hung his head. He didn't pretend to misunderstand. "The carriage has returned, without Lady Ivy, Your Grace."

The muscles in his shoulders tightened. His arm ached. "Why?"

"The footmen only know that a gentleman said he would return the lady in his own vehicle. Do you want to ride there to fetch her yourself?"

"Most assuredly not. Let her pay the consequences. I granted her a privilege. I felt sorry about the injury to her hand."

Carstairs coughed lightly. "Perhaps there's a reason why she is returning with this other person. Her sisters might have wanted to come along for the ride."

"Or the gentleman might not have wanted my servants to witness what he had planned during the drive here."

"All will be well, Your Grace."

"A dalliance in a carriage? Who would be so brazen?"

Carstairs chuckled. "You would—" He broke off at the lethal stare that James leveled upon him. "Most disappointing, Your Grace. She seemed like such a fine young lady."

"And he seems like such a piece of dung."

"Ah, yes," Carstairs said carefully. "Well, do not fret. All will be well."

James shook his head in disgust. "Not if my suspicions are correct."

Chapter 15

By the end of the birthday luncheon Oliver decided that he might have fallen in love with Ivy were he capable of the emotion. There was something different about her since she'd gone into service for the duke. Her skin glowed with a sensuality that Oliver had not noticed during their first encounter. Of course one didn't expect a woman to exude vibrance when she was lying in the street.

He had invested heavily in her heritage. He'd borrowed money he could not repay and made promises he could not keep, unless he found the treasure hidden inside this house. He had also written and sold more poems during this last fortnight than he had the entire year. She and Fenwick had inspired him, and that inspiration was in itself worth a fortune.

That Ivy treated him like a distant cousin, and that Fenwick's treasure might turn out to be a myth, only whetted his appetite for his quest. He thrived on uncertainty. The day Oliver's life became predictable would be the day he crawled into his own coffin and closed the lid.

"Ivy," he said when the guests began to drift from the table and he finally had the chance to be alone with her. "Would you walk with me in the garden before you leave?"

She glanced wistfully at Lilac; Oliver thought her reluctance to accept his offer was rather insulting considering what he'd done to impress her. "It's Lilac's birthday," she said in a voice that put him in his place as if he were one of her charges. "I have to spend some time with her. And Rue. Besides, the duke's carriage is waiting to take me back to the park."

That was what she thought. Oliver forced a smile and picked up a half-empty bottle of wine from the table. "I understand. Family comes first. We'll have our tête-à-tête soon enough."

Five minutes later Ivy and Rue had retreated to the orchard at the back wall, seated amidst the sun's waning rays and the bees that swarmed around a cluster of lavender. "I don't have much time." Ivy searched her sister's face. "Tell me everything. I am gone only a few days and a man sits at Father's place? Why have you allowed Sir Oliver to act as if he were one of us?"

Rue frowned. "Lilac thinks well of him. Rosemary doesn't. I don't have an opinion at all. We thought you'd be pleased about the pearls and the repairs. We hoped he might save you from the duke."

"I beg your pardon."

"If Sir Oliver is a genuine suitor for your hand, your *only* suitor in England, and is willing to wait a year to marry you, provided you can fend off the duke for that amount of time, then you'll be the first of us to have a husband."

Ivy leaned back. "I'm stunned."

"The duke hasn't already forced himself upon you, has he?" Rue asked, biting her lip.

"What if he has?" Ivy swatted crossly at a bee. "What if I admitted that I'd forced myself upon him?"

"You—you wouldn't?" Rue said, smothering a laugh.

Ivy laughed. "I don't believe that the three of you, four counting Oliver, have decided my entire future in a matter of days. How could you allow him to change Fenwick?"

"He's madly in love with you."

"He's mad."

"Ivy, the duke has a certain reputation."

"So does Sir Oliver."

Rue's humor faded. "But he wants to court you."

"A romance based on an accident in London," Ivy mused. "We weren't ourselves that day, were we, Rue? Are you ever going to tell me what happened in the hotel? You haven't been the same since." She waited but Rue said nothing. "It can't be all that horrible or we wouldn't be sitting here together as we've done hundreds of times."

Rue turned her face to the wall. The bees had started to disappear. The sky turned a shade darker before she spoke again. "I'm too ashamed to tell you."

"You can tell me or Rosemary or Lilac anything. *Anything.*"

Tear after tear slipped down Rue's face before she worked up her courage to speak. "I went out into the hall of the hotel because there was a party being held in several rooms. I wanted to find a servant to ask the guests if they could please make less noise."

"I must have been dead to the world."

"You needed to sleep. I took care not to wake you. But I never found a servant, only a group of young men who mistook me for a woman of the night."

"And you corrected them?"

Rue nodded. "Eventually. They offered me money."

"Please, Rue . . ."

"That's all I can say right now. One gentleman took me into a private room and—we, oh, I can't say what happened. We talked. It's over, and the problem is that I thought I'd be able to forget him. I never believed in love at first sight. Do you?"

"I might."

Rue sighed. "I'm afraid I don't have time to explain everything before I leave."

"Leave?" Ivy said in bewilderment, wiping her sister's face with her fingertips. "Because of what happened?"

Rue gave her a watery smile. "Have you read the letter I sent you this morning? I've accepted a position as companion to an elderly viscountess. She's taking the waters with her niece, and I'm to start when she returns."

"Well, congratulations, then. It's a relief, I suppose. At least you'll be safe with an older woman."

"Bored to tears, too. Oh, dear." Rue nudged Ivy's hand. "Oliver is walking towards us, and it's getting late. Don't you have to leave?"

Ivy shook herself. "I should have gone an hour ago."

"It was good to talk," Rue said.

Ivy rose from the bench. "All you've done is give me more to worry about."

"What about your duke?" Rue teased.

"What about him?"

Ivy met her sister's gaze. Sooner or later Rue would reveal everything. Ivy knew there had to be more to her tale. The sisters couldn't keep secrets from one another, even though some took years to share. In fact, Ivy had never confessed that she'd kissed a rogue at a masquerade ball, years ago. Or that the duke was that man.

And that she had kissed him again and craved his kisses too much for her own good.

"Dearest."

At the sound of Oliver's voice, Ivy turned and she and Rue came to their feet. Within moments he managed to insert himself between them. Ivy sighed and grudgingly took the arm he offered. Rue pretended to shake out a stone in her shoe and ducked the forearm that hovered above her head.

"I'm afraid it will be dark soon," he said, bearing Ivy toward the house with an impressive show of urgency. "I wouldn't want to cause you grief. I've informed the others that we're leaving."

The sky darkened with every step they took toward the manor. Ivy hoped the duke would understand. "At least his carriage is swift," she muttered.

Oliver slowed. "Whose carriage?"

"The duke's, of course."

"Didn't I mention it to you? I sent his carriage home."

She unhooked her arm from his, feeling the blood drain from her face. "You did what?"

He shrugged. "I wanted a little time alone with you and it seemed the only way. How else am I to court you?"

Ivy shook off his arm and said nothing. She decided it would be best to save her wits to answer the duke when she returned to the park.

Chapter 16

James had his spyglass focused on the light carriage stopped outside the park's gates. He stood motionless, but inwardly his temper burned like a bonfire. So did his old war wound. He didn't give a damn that a duke should be above prying into his governess's personal life. If there was any immorality to take place on this estate, James would be the responsible party, thank you.

Then again the governess should not conduct her love affair on her master's property. There was little doubt that James was witnessing a clandestine romance. Before his very eyes she had just kissed the bastard who had brought her home. Now she appeared to be running away from the goat, leading him on a merry chase through the garden maze. What was she going to let him do when he caught her? Nothing if James moved fast enough.

"Hellfire and damnation," he said through his teeth. "I'll tear the little satyr apart hoof by hoof."

"Not Lady Ivy?" a shocked voice said at his waist.

He nearly dropped the spyglass out the window. Sliding off the sill, he turned to the small girl who had caught him during his embarrassing display of emotion. "Mary, what are you doing out of bed?"

She shrank away from him. It did not take much for him to guess why. He knew he reeked of brandy. His shirt was half-tucked into his trousers, and he was muttering to himself about committing murder.

"She's only a little bit late, sir. Don't make her leave. I don't like being alone."

He knelt before her. "I don't like it, either. But surely you know I would never hurt a woman."

"I heard you say you would."

"I wasn't referring to your governess. She doesn't have hooves, does she?"

"Well, then, who were you talking about?"

"That's none of your concern, Mary." He squeezed her arm. "Go back to your room, and don't come out again tonight, even if you hear a row. I promise you that she will not come to harm from me."

She pulled free, her eyes welling with tears. "Don't quarrel with her. I love her, Uncle James, and she loves—"

He sighed, his gaze strained back to the window. "She what? She loves you?"

Mary nodded uncertainly.

"I'm sure she does, darling."

"She might love other people in the house, too, Uncle James."

"Other people?" he said distractedly. "You mean like Walker?"

"I mean you."

James turned to her again. "What makes you think that?"

"She has a funny look on her face when she sees you. And she forgets what she was doing when you come into the room."

"That could simply mean I make her nervous."

"Be nice to her tonight."

"Yes, Mary. I will. Now go—"

"I know. I know. Go back to my room. That's all I ever hear."

Chapter 17

"To be a writer is to suffer an incredible melancholy," Oliver intoned, stroking his thin beard in contemplation. "It is as if I dangle from a frayed thread between life and my own tomb. I look up. I look down. I perceive neither light nor darkness, but a perpetual gloom. I ask myself, 'Is this twilight state my fate?' Do you have the slightest idea what it is to suffer for art?"

Could Oliver's carriage have traveled any slower? Could she stand another moment in his company before she committed an act of violence? The duke would be livid. Ivy would be looking for another position. Without character references. Did she know what it was to suffer for art?

"No, I don't, Oliver," she said, breathing an enormous sigh of relief as the carriage approached the private road to the park. "And quite frankly at the moment I don't give a fig. Your artistic suffering will have to wait for another evening."

For an instant she saw a glimpse of malice in his eyes. But then his prattle had so benumbed her brain that she supposed she could be wrong. In the next moment the carriage jolted to a stop. She slid forward and he caught her, holding her even as she struggled to open the door.

"You've tempted me all day. The least you can do is give me a kiss to hold me through the night."

"Kiss you?" She laughed in disbelief. "You'll cost me everything, Oliver. Let go of my arm."

"Not until you kiss me."

She would have clouted him with her other hand if not for her stitches. The door opened, whether from her efforts or those of the footman, who'd become alarmed at the raised voices inside the carriage, she had no idea. There wasn't a servant at hand when she and Oliver tumbled down the steps together in an inelegant and accidental embrace.

"Behave yourself, Sir Oliver," she said in frustration, and gave him a push against the carriage door. "I almost broke my ankle because of your antics."

"I can't behave myself," he said in a stricken voice. He pressed his pale hand to his heart. "I love you. No, really. Don't look at me in scorn. It's true. I can't quite believe it myself. What a hideous surprise. Marry me, Ivy. Let us be miserable together."

She nodded and crept back from the carriage. He might be proposing to one of the garden statues for all she was paying attention. She'd stopped listening to him five minutes into her return journey to Ellsworth. "Good night, sir," she said, and turned, only to discover him standing directly in her path. "Thank you for everything. And move out of the way. The duke will challenge you to a duel if he catches you misbehaving on his property. He was an officer in the infantry—an expert shot, I'll have you know. He'd put a bullet in your heart without losing a wink of sleep afterward. He isn't a person to cross, I promise you."

"I've shot a couple of men myself, I'll have *you* know. Now tell me that you love me back or I will bay at the moon and run circles around the carriage."

She gasped in horror, convinced he was conceited enough to carry out his threat. Had a light appeared in the salon window? Had that porter been standing against the wall during this entire wretched display?

The duke's manservant sent her a searching look. She shook her head, silently begging him not to make matters worse. He coughed, loudly enough to signal his disapproval. Sir Oliver glanced around and Ivy shot off into the darkness of the garden maze before he turned back to her.

Her heart sank when she heard the thud of unpoetic footsteps at her back and realized Oliver had followed her into the labyrinth. How he could see her was a mystery when she hadn't a notion where she was fleeing herself.

A moonless night eclipsed the estate. Perhaps fear made her faster, but it hadn't sharpened her instincts. She caught her heel on a gardener's spade. When she recovered her balance, she realized that she'd lost Oliver.

She had also lost her way. She slowed, took several hesitant steps, and collided with a hedge. How humiliating to think she might still be wandering through the maze at dawn when the dogs scented her.

An indefinable sound penetrated the tall yews that separated her from the next turn. Was she about to confront Oliver, the porter, or an animal? She rounded another boxwood with caution, breathless, her hair half undone. She wasn't much of a match for man or beast right now.

"Stop."

The low intimidating voice rooted her to the spot. She couldn't make out where it had come from until the duke emerged from what must have been a secret path. How long had he been there? What must he think? She appraised his unsmiling face in disquietude.

Sanctuary or banishment?

She shivered at either possibility and waited for James to decree which was to be her fate.

"Who are you running from, Ivy?" he asked, slowly walking toward her. "Is it necessary for me to search the grounds for an unwanted visitor? Do we have a prowler in the park?"

She remained still, even though her heart was beating harder than when she had been evading Oliver. Despite his show of concern, the duke's shadowed face showed no sympathy at all. She had taken advantage of him today, and not the other way around.

"I was late," she said, seeing no reason to lie. "I didn't realize that my—my companion had sent your carriage home. As soon as we reached the park, I rushed toward the house and ended up here, going in circles."

The duke considered her explanation for a few moments. "This is a maze." He surveyed her disheveled hair and flushed cheeks. "It is meant to deceive and delude. Perhaps my garden is taking its revenge on yours. Do you understand what I'm saying?"

The lambent heat in his eyes wilted the remnants of whatever composure she'd salvaged from her tussle with Oliver.

She held firm under his scrutiny. "Not really." All his cold manner conveyed was his displeasure. He wasn't anything like the playful scoundrel who'd interviewed her for the job. Still, he was perfectly within his rights to admonish her.

"This maze is designed to lead one astray," he said.

"Did you draw the original plans?"

He seemed to grow taller. "Do I look to be over a century old?"

"It's difficult to judge your age without decent lighting."

"It is rather dark, isn't it?"

"What is it they say about the devil on a moonless night?"

"I haven't a notion," the duke said with a smile. "But I have a feeling you're about to find out."

Her lips parted at his words. His knowing smile promised sin and punishment. And it lit a spark within her. In fact, Ivy was certain that invisible flames jumped from his wicked spirit to hers.

He wanted to engage her in a dangerous battle, one she might never win. The female in her rose to the war cry all the same. "I would have thought the maze was for children," she said.

"Certain adults like playing games with each other, too."

She reminded herself that it wasn't appropriate to show disrespect to one's master. Nor was it proper for a governess to secretly desire him, and yet she did. "I wouldn't know, Your Grace."

"You are very cool for a woman who could be discharged for breaking the rules of her employment."

Ivy braced herself for the inevitable. She might be dismissed before midnight. She pictured herself trudging home in the dark and Rosemary saying, "You had to lose your head, didn't you, Anne Boleyn? All these years you were supposed to be the sensible one. How could you, Ivy?"

"Don't you have anything to say for yourself?" She started at the duke's voice. "I'll have you know that I was worried sick about you when you didn't return on time."

She examined his face. Had anxiety been one of the dark emotions lurking behind his anger? The duke worried sick over her? "I apologize, Your Grace. Is—" She blinked in surprise as he grasped her by the shoulders. "Is something wrong with one of the children?"

His answer flayed her with guilt. "Mary was beside herself. I did my best to comfort her. But she wanted you." He paused to allow time for emphasis. "Not her mother. Not me. Not Cook. She wanted Lady Ivy, and Lady Ivy wasn't here."

Ivy shrank inside. She *had* been derelict in her duty. "Your Grace, I'll go to her right now."

He wasn't finished. He wanted to flog her conscience one last time. "Lady Ivy was playing peekaboo in the maze with a man."

Ivy cringed. "I'll explain to her that it wasn't what it appeared to be—that it was nothing."

"Good. Because even though I sent her off to bed, I thought I saw her peeping down through the curtains a moment ago. I don't believe she can see us from where she's standing. But just in case, you might explain to her when you go upstairs that *this* is nothing, too."

He lifted his hands from her shoulders and cupped her chin. Ivy stood motionless, mesmerized by the intensity on his face. She couldn't move. She couldn't raise a finger to resist. He bent his head to hers and when he kissed her, the invisible moon could have fallen out of the sky, and she wouldn't have cared. He swept his tongue across her lips, slowly penetrating her mouth. Desire like steam enshrouded her. She didn't understand how a man's kiss could feel wondrous and wicked at the same time, or how she could want something when reason argued it would only fade to ashes.

And yet—it had to be her imagination—she felt a shudder go through him, too, as they kissed.

Perhaps he couldn't control himself any better than she could. Where was the consolation in knowing he was also at the mercy of this lust?

"We can't stay here," he murmured, locking one hand around her waist to draw her against him. "Let me take you inside."

How melodious his voice sounded in the darkness of the maze. "You mean us—together?"

His hand pressed against her spine until she felt the heat and hardness of his body. "Yes. In private."

His next kiss sought to subdue her, to remind her that domination could be sweet and gentleness could feel like torture. Her knees trembled as his tongue entwined with hers. His hand stroked the contours of her hip until her heart pulsed through her body.

When he broke away, breathing hard, she was bereft, too dazed to disagree to his request. "Come inside the house. It's time to revisit the rules."

She hesitated. "Shouldn't I see to Mary first?"

He didn't even pretend to consider her suggestion. "You can look in on her later." He reached for her good hand. "How is your wrist?"

"It's all right, thank you."

"Stitches didn't get torn from slapping someone in

the face?" A cynical grin crossed his features as he guided her through the hedge with unerring expertise.

"Not yet, Your Grace. Where are you taking me?"

"To the Chinese Room."

She pictured furnishings with a Far Eastern influence, perhaps even a peacock motif, and said, "That sounds pleasant." If she could make it there. His kisses left her feeling shaky. Hurrying through the labyrinth with his hand grasping hers gave her little chance to compose herself. "I must say, you know this maze rather well."

"As well as you know Fenwick's gardens."

"It's all different now," she said softly, breathless to keep apace. "You could ride a horse to the door and nothing would stop you."

"What do you mean?" he asked, clearly distracted, too intent on their destination to understand what she was trying to explain.

They didn't talk again until after they had sneaked through the house and he opened the door at the end of a long hall onto the Chinese Room. Dragons writhed and breathed fire on the scrolled panels covering the wall. But Ivy's gaze went immediately to the room's central decor—a startling replica of a pagoda that enclosed a blue silk couch that would have comfortably seated five people. Or a pair of recumbent lovers.

He closed the door and caught her in his arms again. At an indistinct point between his dizzying kisses and her tentative attempts at questions, he led her to the couch. She sat for only a few moments before he lowered himself beside her and bent her backward, stroking her cheek. "Ivy."

"It's so dark in here. So quiet. Is this the room where you bring your *friends*?"

He shrugged out of his jacket. "Would you believe me if I told you that I've never been in here with another woman?"

"No." She gave a firm shake of her head. "I'm sorry, but I would not."

He arched his brow. "Then I won't bother to confess that right now I can't remember the name of my last lover."

"How romantic." She rolled onto her side. "Why don't I leave you here alone to see if your memory returns? I'll ask Carstairs to bring you some writing material."

He bracketed her inside his arms. "I don't want Carstairs. And I don't want to be alone. I want to be with you. Alone with you." He threaded his fingers through her hair. "You broke a rule tonight."

"We're breaking one of mine now."

"Then why don't we make a pact to abandon all rules while we're in this room?"

She frowned. "What does that mean?"

He dipped his head, whispering to her as he kissed a path from the corner of her mouth to her neck. "We do whatever pleases us."

She went still. He waited, afraid he'd moved too fast, frightened her. As soon as he felt her body relax again, he grazed her collarbone with kisses. Then he traced his hand down her side and lifted her skirt to her knees. She tensed again, her eyes seeking his, and he murmured, "I'll only do what you want."

She bit her lip. "What if I don't know what I want?"

"Then give me what I want."

She glanced down at the skirt he was slowly raising to her waist. "Is that a quote from the Book of Scoundrels?"

He almost laughed. "It does sound like it, doesn't it?"

"Don't tell me," she said, drawing a breath as his fingers skimmed the inside of her thigh. "You've never said that to a woman before."

"I can't recall everything I've ever said," he admitted. "But I swear I've never felt like this and I'm not entirely sure it's a good thing for either of us."

But he couldn't stop touching her. He was breathing too hard; his blood ran too hot and wild for him to care about right and wrong. She was a confusing and intoxicating force, a bold woman, both sensitive and strong. He wanted to linger over every inch of her skin that he uncovered, indulge his desires in her body at his leisure. He nudged her thighs apart. His gaze searched her face.

At last he touched the folds of her sex. "Damn the darkness," he muttered. "I want to see what you look like there."

"That's improper," she said in a faint voice.

"It is for other men to look." His voice was thick. "But not for me."

"Why is that?"

He sank his finger into her core, probing his finger as deeply as he could. The knob of his shaft throbbed against his pantaloons. She was soft and wet. He pushed a second finger inside her sheath.

She gasped and lifted one leg at an enticing angle. That artless move practically forced James to his knees. He clenched his teeth and considered the consequences of replacing his fingers with his cock. His belly quivered in readiness. She moved against his hand, needing a release as desperately as he did. He could feel her excitement grow. She laced her arms around his neck, panting, closing her eyes.

"Soon," he whispered, and applied his thumb to the hood of her sex. She gave a soft groan and his erection jumped. If she weren't so damned sweet and innocent, he'd unfasten his trousers and burrow between her thighs before she could draw another breath.

For now, it was enough to pleasure her and savor every helpless shiver that coursed through her seductive body.

His senses reveled in her unguarded sensuality. He looked at his hand, his fingers snug between the folds of her sex, and he felt a rush not only of passion, which he knew well, but of possessiveness. He belonged inside her. She *would* be his.

Her heel slid down across the couch. "James," she whispered, her essence glistening on his hand. He swallowed. The fingers she had curled around his wrist tightened. She wanted to know she was safe. And he wanted to assure her.

Still, he teased her, brought her to the edge again and again, ready to break himself. He stroked her faster until he knew she couldn't last another moment. When she reached her peak, she writhed with a sensual wildness that was beautiful and delectable to behold. As the tremors subsided from her body, she opened her eyes and gave him an unfathomable look. We she inviting him to continue or simply too dazed to express what she felt?

It took him almost a minute before he withdrew his hand from her warmth. "I promise you," he said, "this isn't going to be the last time we're together."

She surprised him with a cynical smile. "You led me here under false pretenses."

He watched in regret as she drew her skirt down over her knees. "And what about the man who brought you here? Were you leading him on a chase?"

She frowned. "No, not intentionally."

"How long have you known him? Where did you meet?"

She slid back against the couch to sit upright. "I met him in London when—oh, I might as well tell you the truth."

"I'd prefer you did. In fact, considering what's happening between us, I expect you to."

"It's rather embarrassing, but not as unsavory as what you're thinking."

"You don't know what I'm thinking," he said with a frown.

"Yes. I do. You're jealous."

"I'm not. All right—perhaps I am a little. I am still insulted that you didn't ask me for an advance."

"How? There were scores of other applicants for the job. It didn't seem a good way to start work by asking for a loan." She looked away. "I wanted to make a good impression."

"Oh, you did," he said quickly.

"Not that sort of impression. I almost died when I dropped my door knocker and ended up on the floor with you."

"Forgive me."

She looked back at him. "I'm every bit as guilty as you."

"That must have been quite an accident," he mused, drawing a handkerchief from his pocket to wipe his hand. The scent of her body still tantalized him. He didn't want it to go away.

"There *wasn't* an accident." Her frown deepened at the memory. "The incident alarmed the bystanders more than it did me. I was so preoccupied, I never saw the phaeton coming."

Preoccupied. James understood that. It took enormous effort for him to carry on this conversation while his carnal self was still making demands. His blood had barely cooled to a simmer. How easy it would have been to persuade her to give him her innocence. How complicated their lives would become afterward. But apparently another man also desired her.

Did this man have a conscience?

Was it any of James's business?

He decided, wisely or not, that it was.

He realized that Ivy was staring at him, awaiting a reaction. "Why were you preoccupied?" he asked somberly, just to show he was paying attention.

She sighed. "I can't tell you. It's personal."

"What?"

"It's a family matter."

"Are you saying that I'm good enough to dally with in the dark but not to entrust with a family secret?"

"Do you want to know what happened with Sir Oliver or not?" Ivy asked him in a mildly annoyed tone that reminded him she was an earl's daughter.

"Yes. Go on. I want to know everything."

"He apologized profusely for his reckless driving. I would have been content to leave it at that."

"But he wasn't?"

"Evidently not."

"He's a scoundrel. Take it from one who knows. You shouldn't see him again."

Ivy wriggled to the far end of the couch. "He asked me to marry him."

James scowled. "All scoundrels propose in the heat of passion."

"Do they?" she asked archly, her eyes widening at this helpful information. "I shall have to keep that in mind. However, in the interest of fairness, I should explain that what he attempted to do to me was nothing compared to what we just did."

James nodded. "I see. It's a good thing, too."

"And no one has asked for my hand in five years."

"That long?"

"Furthermore, as grateful as I am for this position, I must be truthful and confess that I am like any other woman who wishes for a husband and home of her own."

He stood abruptly as she lifted herself from the couch, waving aside the hand he extended to help her. "Those are normal desires," he said after a pause. "I don't understand why they haven't been fulfilled."

"I'm not asking you for sympathy."

He shook his head. "I wasn't offering it. In my opinion the only reason your desires weren't satisfied is because you were locked away in a manor with a moat of thorns to discourage callers."

"My name was ruined."

"Nonsense."

She drew a breath. "I'll say good night now, Your Grace. I'll look in on Mary before I go to bed. Do we act as if this never happened?"

"That will be easier said than done."

"Then—" She half turned, then stopped. "May I confess one more thing?"

His gaze drifted over her becoming silhouette. "Of course."

"I know I shouldn't have done it, but Sir Oliver became rather persistent and I panicked. Not because I dreaded having to kiss him. He's rather handsome if one is drawn to brooding self-indulgent men, which I am not. But I panicked because I was afraid of having to face you after I came home late and in a different carriage. And—" She trailed off, leaving him in suspense.

"And?" James gestured with his hand.

"And in order to discourage him, I said that you would challenge him to a duel if you knew what he was doing and that everyone knew what an expert shot you had been in the infantry." She paused to catch her breath. "I had no right to say that, but I did. I'll understand if you dismiss me."

She curtsied and rushed from the room before James could comment or even sort out what she had said.

Dismiss her? Not after tonight. Not ever, if he had the last word in the matter. He didn't know what part she would play in his future, but he wasn't about to lose her because she had bragged of his skill in order to defend herself against a persistent jackass.

Fight a duel in her honor? He was furious enough at the bastard who'd upset her to tear him apart with his bare hands.

But fight a duel?

Everyone knew what an expert shot you had been in the infantry.

But only four people knew that James could no longer hold a gun steadily enough in his right hand to shoot with any accuracy at a phaeton, let alone at an opponent on a dueling field. Carstairs, his physician, Wendover, and his commanding officer.

James would disgrace himself in a duel. He would be forced to forfeit or be killed. But he would defend Ivy no matter what the personal cost.

He just didn't know how.

Chapter 18

Rosemary felt guilty that she had applied for a position outside the house—who would care for Lilac if she was left alone at Fenwick? Ivy held the family together and Rosemary supported her efforts as best she could. Poor Lilac still believed that her childhood friend would return to marry her. Rosemary could no longer even remember his name. He had gone off to school and allegedly from there to war. His parents had died in the interim.

Rosemary wandered through the house, tired from helping the servants restore order to the great hall. No one could recall the last time a birthday had been celebrated in style, and despite the fact that Oliver reminded Rosemary of a fox in a henhouse, she *had* enjoyed setting a good table, surrounded by young ne'er-do-wells who knew how to laugh, if nothing else.

Cheer. Warmth. Laughter.

How long it had been since Fenwick had known a revel?

Oliver and his friends had departed in an excess of

high spirits and promises to return. Rosemary had been waiting for the house to settle before she sat down to write into the night.

Now she mounted the stairs, not bothering with a candle. She knew her way in the dark. Everyone had already retired for the night. Perhaps she would go to her mother's room for inspiration.

But someone in the house appeared to have had the same idea. She entered her mother's musty bedchamber without making a sound at the exact moment that a figure disappeared into a panel inside the fireplace.

"Rue?" she whispered before she noticed the gray frock coat and notebook that had been placed on a stool by the wall.

She wished now for a candle to read what Sir Oliver had written in his notebook. Perhaps another of his idiotic poems to commemorate tonight's party.

Why had he pretended to leave and then returned? He was already acting as if he were the master of the manor, and as far as Rosemary knew, Ivy hadn't accepted a proposal.

"Dammit," he muttered, banging something—his head, she hoped—against the wall. "Where the hell did I put my tinderbox?"

Rosemary rushed forward, pressed her hands against the panel, and said into the airless void, "Perhaps you left it under your coat. Why don't you have a little think in the dark to refresh your memory?"

His face popped into view as the panel started to close. "What the blazes are you doing, woman?"

"I should be asking you that."

"How am I supposed to see in the dark?"

The panel slowly ground back into place. "You're a writer," she said, looking down at his shadowy form. "Use your imagination."

"How—"

She backed away from the fireplace and sat on the edge of the bed. An hour in the passage might teach him not to assume he could act as lord of the manor without permission. After several minutes she curled up on her mother's coverlet, wishing she hadn't drunk that last glass of wine. Spirits made her drowsy, drained her of the energy to write.

She closed her eyes. Oliver would wake up the entire house with the racket he was making. If he had half a brain, he would find the tunnel leading to the solar. The manor walls concealed a number of cavities in which the girls had played as children until Lilac had fallen through the rungs of a rotted ladder.

She'd broken her leg in several places, and it had never healed properly. The girls had been forbidden to explore the hidden passages of Fenwick after the accident.

When they were younger, they'd listened to the noises inside the walls at night and sometimes still did.

"They're ghosts," Rosemary always insisted.

"They're rats," Ivy would counter with all the authority of her one advanced year in age.

Rosemary kicked off her shoes. Tonight Rosemary was forced to agree with her sister. That was definitely a rat in the wall. And he was still scratching. She pulled a dust-laden pillow over her head and tried to remember where she had left off in her story, the revision of Anne Boleyn's tragic life.

* * *

Mary's bed looked like a shipwreck, even without benefit of a visit from her unruly brother. Ivy tucked the girl in snugly and escaped to her room without incident. Then she took her time washing and changing into her nightclothes, feeling not the least bit tired.

She wanted to stay up all night savoring the memory of the duke's every caress, the silly conversation they had shared.

She wouldn't have slept even if her conscience let her; just as she had blown out the candle, the loudest thunderclap she'd ever heard blasted from the back fields of the estate.

She waited for rain to fall.

She waited to hear Mary call for her.

She waited to hear one of the servants in the house rouse or the dogs bark, but there was no other disturbance until, at dawn, she forced herself to stir from her chair to face the day.

And the duke—as lovely as the prior evening's intimacy had been, it had also been illicit and could only lead to unhappiness. Ivy certainly could not allow such liberties to continue.

Determined, she recommitted herself to resisting any other advances he made. Despite how she might feel toward Sir Oliver, at least the man had offered her marriage.

What a beautiful dream. Anne Boleyn stood on the brink of her revenge, watching as Henry was led to the scaffold, his head to lose. Beside her Rosemary heard the taunts and jeers of the spectators, the cries of treason from courtiers who jostled against her and pulled her back by the arm to squeeze in for a closer look.

"Don't," she mumbled, one insistent hand reaching through her dream to drag her across the bed. "Leave me alone. He deserves to die, and I shall be witness to justice served."

A shrill voice assaulted her eardrum. "Thanks to you, he might well have died in there! What came over you, Rosemary? How could you be so unkind to a man who brought food to our table? One of these days you and Rue will murder some innocent who comes to our door."

Rosemary groaned and buried her face in the pillow, but the tirade continued. "How could you mistreat the man who hopes to marry Ivy?"

Rosemary turned her head to avoid meeting Lilac's baleful stare, only to look across the room into the smirking face of the man she had enclosed in the wall last night. And completely forgotten. She sat up in a swelter of guilt and resentment.

"He doesn't look dead to me."

"He was practically unconscious when I found him," Lilac said, darting to Sir Oliver's chair to dab his wrists and throat with the damp towel in her hand. "What if I hadn't woken up in the middle of the night to check in on you? This is what happens when you overimbibe."

"What if," Rosemary mused, stretching her arms in the air. She narrowed her eyes. "What if that man who scribbles nursery rhymes hadn't broken into the house and sneaked into Mother's room, doing who knows what?"

Oliver surged from his chair. "Nursery rhymes?"

"Oh, I'm sorry. I misspoke. Nursery rhymes convey political messages and contribute to social improvement. Your poems are written to impress wealthy tarts and flatter flatulent old lords."

"Oh!" Lilac's hand flew to her mouth. "Rosemary, how can you speak such awful words?"

Sir Oliver glanced in the old looking glass to straighten his stained cravat. "She speaks the same awful words that she writes. She hasn't the talent to become a success and so she despises those who have."

Rosemary stilled. The smile that spread across her face felt like ice breaking in a frozen pond.

"Where is my gun, Lilac, dear?"

Lilac shook her head, disregarding this threat. "He wants to be our friend, Rosemary. The only friend we've had in years. What has he done to earn your distrust?"

"Ask him why he was in the passageway." Rosemary's anger surged to the surface. She'd never wanted to pummel anyone in her life as much as she did Oliver, not even the most ruthless of debt collectors who had hounded the sisters without mercy for months on end. He'd gotten under her skin, and he knew it. "Ask him the reason why."

Sir Oliver glanced at Lilac and shrugged helplessly, the handsome prince confronted by an evil witch. "I tried to explain to her last night, but she wouldn't listen. You are my witness. She won't listen to me now."

"Rosemary, I'm truly ashamed of you," Lilac said in an undertone.

"He's a snake," Rosemary said in an incredulous voice. "And he's crawled into your good graces. Lilac, you're a bumpkin and I shall tear my hair out by the roots with despair of you."

Lilac calmly took her by the arm. "He went into the passageway because the carpenters had warned him that the interior structure of the house showed signs of decay. He was afraid the manor would collapse in on itself like a house of cards. He was concerned about the safety of the workmen and that we might witness an accident."

Rosemary remained unmoved. "And his solution to this imaginary tragedy was to sacrifice himself? How noble."

"I thought so," Lilac said, frowning.

"Noble deeds can be performed during the day," Rosemary exclaimed. "Wouldn't it have been safer to explore in the morning with someone standing by with a light? And to ask permission?"

Sir Oliver looked sheepish. "I had a little too much wine last night and got carried away. I never meant to frighten anyone. Rosemary is right. I should have told someone what I was up to."

"Do you see, Rosemary?" Lilac said. "This is what happens when one is cut off from society for five years. One loses perspective."

"One loses one's mind," Rosemary muttered, walking straight past Oliver to the door with her pen and notebook in hand.

Lilac stared after her. "Don't you have something else to say?"

"Yes. I have a pounding headache and I'm going to lock myself in Ivy's room for the day. Aside from the delivery of a pot of tea and an apple tart, I would appreciate not being disturbed again."

Sir Oliver studied Lilac's generous curves from the chair in which she had forced him to sit and let her fuss over him like an angel of mercy. He had come close to asphyxiation in that passageway, and revival by a woman with a fine pair of bosoms and glittering blond curls had helped restore his temper.

She didn't seem to suspect a thing, which made him wonder if he had chosen the wrong sister to pursue and whether it was too late to change tactics without looking like a complete bounder.

Lilac was lovely. Lilac was also lame. But he hadn't intended to take his heiress wife to London, so in that regard her appearance mattered less than her fortune.

All the sisters appeared to be enamored of the manor house. He didn't foresee a problem leaving his bride to rusticate while he carried on his usual affairs.

He reached around the chair for his jacket. "Lovely angel, it would be wrong of me to allow anyone else to catch us alone together in this bedroom and assume the worst."

Lilac sighed. "That's thoughtful of you, but there's no one in this house to care anymore, Sir Oliver. I don't know why my sisters think you're up to no good."

He pulled down his jacket sleeve. "Sisters? You mean Rosemary is not the only one?"

"Rue doesn't much care for you, I'm afraid," Lilac admitted.

He feigned a smile. "But you do?"

"Is there a reason I shouldn't?"

"I can think of none, Lilac."

Chapter 19

James didn't see Ivy in the morning. His first instinct, which happened to be his basest instinct, urged him to seek her out. Inquiring about the condition of her hand was a plausible excuse. However, since he couldn't trust himself to face her with the memory of last night's interlude fresh in his mind, he went to the last place he'd seen her—the Chinese Room. He knew she wouldn't come here again of her own volition.

But no sooner had he entered the darkened chamber than he heard the provocative whisper of silk. His heart pounded in anticipation. Had his unworldly governess sought him out to make sense of last night's passions?

He waited until he heard the door close before he turned—only to see Elora crossing the room with a grimace. "What an appalling room. I know chinoiserie was the fashion when your father built this house, but, eh, James, what excess. A pagoda. I'm embarrassed on your behalf. Who would ever sit on that couch? It looks for all the world like a courtesan's bed. Whatever are you doing here?"

"I was thinking."

"About—let me guess. About Ivy?"

"I can't believe I ever considered an arrangement between us," he said, laughing reluctantly. "You aggravate me to no end. Why would you presume to know what was on my mind?"

"It might have been that lost look on your face when I came in."

"My back was turned to you. For all you know I could have been sticking out my tongue at the water carrier on the wall."

"But you weren't," she said, approaching the couch. "You were thinking about her."

He sighed.

"It's all right as far as I'm concerned," she went on conversationally. "But you must remember that whether she's fallen in position or not, she was still born a lady."

"So were you," he said, arching his brow. "Even if I can't recall a time when you acted like one."

Elora stared at him in speculation. "And that remark, James, is one I would expect from a brother teasing a younger sister."

"Which would explain why we never became lovers even though we had ample opportunity."

"A blessing, isn't it?"

"Perhaps," he said. "But allow me to defend myself for a moment. *I* had nothing to do with Ivy's unfortunate circumstances."

"As far as I can tell, you're not offering her redemption. I did see the look on your face when you carried her to your bedroom after her accident."

"The sight of that much blood is always distressing," he said, turning his face from hers.

"Did you carry off the wounded soldiers in your regiment on the battlefield with such solicitude?"

"Possibly."

"Did you stroke their foreheads and turn hysterical when one of them pricked a finger or required stitches for a wound?"

"I thought she was going to fall out the window. Did that scare me? I won't deny it. Furthermore, I did not 'stroke' her face. I merely wiped away a streak of blood to make sure there wasn't a gash on her head from the broken glass."

Elora studied him with her lips compressed as if she didn't believe a word he'd said. She knew him too well, he realized. He might delude himself, but it was damn hard to deceive someone he had trusted.

"Head injuries can be dangerous," he added as an afterthought. "So can falling from a window."

"Falling in love with someone who has no defenses against the world is dangerous, too." She picked up a twig from the couch and examined it from several angles. "Are you in love with her?"

"Don't be absurd." God help him. Elora couldn't have any idea where that twig had come from; she had been miles away from here last night. "I've only known her for—"

"—five years?" she said, flicking the twig in his direction.

He deflected it with his left hand. His good hand, as he'd once thought of it, lifted a second too late, feeling as if it belonged to a puppet he was still learning to work.

Silence passed, and James felt compelled to speak, if only out of fear of what Elora would say next. "How was Walker during your visit? Did he behave?"

She plopped down on the couch. "Walker is a little beast. But what can you expect?" She laid her head back on the cushions and studied the pagoda. "I took him straight to his governess. She didn't seem at all herself this morning."

"Perhaps her wrist is causing her discomfort."

"This room is quite secluded, isn't it? Did you bring her here last night for a rendezvous?"

He almost choked.

She lifted her head. "Sticking out your tongue again? You should be careful. My grandmother always said if you did it often enough, it would freeze in that position. Imagine how painful that would be."

The only pain James felt in the next few moments was the deep sting that radiated down his right shoulder and his arm to his fingertips as he grasped Elora's hand and hauled her to her feet. He'd attempted to hit a target on a tree before dawn and had narrowly missed Carstairs instead.

Some duelist he was.

And since he suspected he would probably not make a good liar, either, he decided to ignore Elora's impertinent remarks, neither repudiating nor confirming what they both knew to be true.

As they reached the door, Elora balked and pulled out of his grasp. "Allow me to give you a little advice. You do *not* want to be seen by the woman you desire with the woman you supposedly desired before you realized who was the true object of your desires."

He glanced down the hall. "If I hadn't known you half your life, I wouldn't have understood a word you just said."

"Another thing, James—Oliver Linton might act like a fop but he can be quite deadly when he's crossed."

"How the devil do you know—"

"Mary isn't the only one with big ears. I know Oliver. Don't underestimate him."

Ivy had taken a solemn oath at daybreak that she would never be caught alone with another man again—unless the duke appeared before her, in which case she doubted her vow would hold up to his charm. Still, it was better to be prepared.

Mary dragged through her lessons that morning, and if Walker hadn't whirled around the room like the four winds, Ivy might have dropped her head on the desk and slept from sheer exhaustion. The duke had depleted her emotional reserves.

"Walker, sit in the corner and finish your arithmetic. Mary, come to the globe and put your finger on India."

Mary trudged to the desk, yawning all the way. "I think it's here, my lady."

"That isn't even the correct continent. It isn't a continent at all. It's the sea."

Mary rubbed her eyes. "Sorry. I didn't sleep well last night."

Ivy softened her demeanor. She needed to bear in mind the turmoil in the children's lives. "Neither did I."

"Because of my uncle?"

"His Grace had nothing to do with it. I heard thunder, and it woke me up."

"He was furious at you," Mary whispered. "Especially after what he saw you doing through his spyglass."

Ivy felt blood rush to her face. Indignation chased away her fatigue. "He used an instrument to spy on me?"

Mary nodded slowly. "He had a proper fit, too."

Ivy glanced at the longcase clock standing against the opposite wall. "Look at the hour. It's fifteen minutes until luncheon. I'll ring for Sally to help you wash and change."

"It's twenty-five minutes to the hour," Mary corrected her, craning her head as Ivy ushered her to the door. Walker hadn't needed another prompt. He'd already bolted into the hall.

"That clock is slow." Ivy crossed her fingers behind her back and renewed her oath. After her upcoming confrontation with the duke, she would *never* be caught alone with a man again.

James had just sifted through the post in his study when he heard Ivy and Carstairs outside the door. Carstairs spoke in his usual polite monotone while Ivy's voice rose to a crescendo that signaled a problem in the house. He wondered what the children had done now and wished he could appease them with a letter from their father.

The instant Ivy stood before his desk, he realized that she had come on a personal matter. He should have been focused on her consternation, but instead he was stricken with an insensible desire to take her in his arms and make right whatever had caused the distress in her eyes.

Until he realized that *he* was the cause of her distress.

"You wicked, unscrupulous duke."

He stood and came around the desk, grateful that Carstairs had closed the door. "I knew you would have misgivings about what we did last night, but I visited that room this morning, and felt no regret."

She banged her good fist down on the desk. "I'm not

referring to what we did. It's what *you* did I cannot forgive."

"Didn't we do it together?" he asked cautiously. He reached for her, reconsidered at the glare she gave him, and lifted his hand to rub the back of his neck. "What did I do?"

"You spied on me."

"I told you I was anxious about your return."

"You spied on me and Oliver with a *spyglass*."

His eyes narrowed. "That's what I get for trusting an eleven-year-old girl who's already beheaded her first king."

Ivy gasped. "You don't deny it?"

He shook his head. "How else was I supposed to keep watch for your arrival? In another few minutes I would have been on my horse and galloping to Fenwick. I told you I saw you through the window."

"Do you watch the other female servants with your spyglass?"

"What other female servants? The maids who are married to the footmen? Cook, who is old enough to be my mother? Or the housekeeper who once changed my nappies?"

"Are there peepholes in my bedchamber?"

He laughed impolitely. "Not as far as I know. I can have some holes bored in your wall if that's your pleasure."

"It isn't," she said, her voice almost as deep as it had been in the dark last night. "I can't believe that you let Mary catch you in the act."

"Is that right? Well, I wouldn't have been at the window with the spyglass to be caught by the child if her governess had been home on time. As agreed."

Ivy looked taken aback. "It won't happen again."

"Good."

She swept up her skirt in her hand. "Not *any* of it."

James realized he'd just been snared in a trap of his own making. "What precisely does that mean?"

"I shall henceforth maintain a professional demeanor and distance from you at all times," she said, raising her chin.

He made the dreadful mistake of laughing again. "Ivy, we both know that maintaining a distance between us is impossible."

Her mouth thinned. "For you, perhaps."

His blood flared. She couldn't be serious. "Is that a challenge?" he asked, his gaze flickering over her as if they were opponents in a tournament.

"If it strengthens your will to think of it that way, then yes. It's a challenge."

He blew out a breath. "You're challenging *my* will? For how long?"

"I doubt you can survive a week without trifling with a woman. You kissed me while you were waiting for Elora to arrive."

"That's different. Elora is in love with my brother."

She walked sedately to the door. "You didn't know it at the time."

"But I did know that Elora and I were wrong for each other. Why else would I have written advising her not to come to Ellsworth?"

"Good day, Your Grace."

He darted around her to the door she had just opened, placing his arm against the panels. "I don't think we've established all the rules yet."

Ivy tried to open the door all the way. "What good

would it do? You would only override them. Your Grace, kindly remove your person from the doorway. I'm afraid I'm going to hurt you."

"Do you see me trembling in my boots?" he asked, his voice evocative of last night's pleasures.

"Do you think me incapable of resorting to violence to escape you? It isn't something I'd enjoy doing, but if you drive me to it, you might see a different side of me."

She pulled a little harder at the door. He ignored the pain and grinned.

"If I didn't fall for Sir Oliver's silly poetry,' she said, "I'm assuredly not going to be swayed by a man behaving like a bully."

"Bully? You think this is bullying you?"

"Well, you aren't letting me leave."

"Only because I hadn't finished talking. But since you are intent on breaking my elbow, I wonder in truth who is bullying who. Just don't bring up that poet in my presence again."

"As you wish. Should I meet him again, it will be in secret."

He felt his anger rising. "That is *not* my wish. I showed you last night what I wished for you to do."

Her cheeks turned red. "What you really want is my property," she said, pulling at the door with every word.

"Correction," he said, realizing he should have the sense to move before she broke the door. "What I really want is you as my property."

"Subtle as a sledgehammer, aren't you?"

"I didn't exactly try to hide how I feel toward you."

"It's impossible."

He shook his head, smiling at how easily he could

fluster her. "It's inevitable. Do you think I couldn't court you if I set my mind to it?"

All of a sudden she looked more than flustered. She looked furious. "It isn't in my nature to be cruel, but in my opinion you deserve a setdown, waste of time as that will probably be."

"Criticizing one's employer is not part of a governess's job."

"Satisfying said employer's unspeakable desires are not, either, unless I missed that in the contract."

"You didn't *read* the contract."

"No. I was desperate and I trusted you. But right now, well, let me just say that Sir Oliver is famous in London for collecting hearts. If I didn't fall for his nonsense, why should I fall for yours?"

He snorted. "I wasn't the only one with unspeakable desires last night, and do not ever compare me to that jingle-maker again."

"Poet. He is a poet. Women love his poetry. They swoon at his feet."

His lips curled in derision. "Then why aren't you swooning at his feet instead of attempting to shatter my bones?"

"Because I have work to do, and if Your Grace would be so kind as to release me, I shall go about my duties."

He shrugged, lifting his arm. "There. You are free."

She reached for the doorknob. "Seven days, remember."

He stared at the back of her neck. What he remembered was nibbling past her shoulder to her plump breasts. And her voice, urgent, low, when she had climaxed.

"Your Grace?" She turned her head. "On second thought, maybe we should establish a few rules to follow."

"Follow where?" he said absently.

She closed her eyes briefly as if asking for help from above. "Are we to speak to each other? If I accidentally walk into a room and you are present, am I to leave immediately? Shall I raise a fan to shield myself from any lascivious glances you cast my way?"

"What lascivious glances?"

"The ones you give me when I bend over to pick up an object one of the children has dropped."

"Can you pick up objects and hold a fan to your face at the same time?"

"I've never had reason to try," Ivy replied. "Are you saying that you can't control the way you look at me?"

He gave a droll laugh. "Let's agree we shall not remain alone in a room together nor seek out each other's company for the week. That should remove all temptation."

She smiled up at him. "I should have no trouble obeying those orders. I'll be as inconspicuous as a speck of dust."

That, he thought, would be impossible. "Then we will have no further problems."

The rest of the day proceeded smoothly in Ivy's view. Her irritation at the duke's supercilious attitude buoyed her until evening. During the night, unfortunately, she fell prey to thoughts of him and by morning, she realized she showed signs of weakening. She would stand firm, however. She would not admit she looked forward to that baritone voice booming at the children to stay out of his study or at Carstairs to stop disarranging his desk.

She would submit to torture before confessing that she missed the dark eyes that followed her across the room and engendered sensual images in her mind, sometimes at the oddest moments, as today, when she was scolding Walker for putting a piece of cake in his pocket and sitting on it.

How unseemly to be wiping cream cake from a cane chair while picturing herself half-naked in the duke's arms. Or worse, wondering what he looked like in the buff. Outwardly she might be holding up to his challenge. Inside, she was on the verge of surrender.

"The cake is gone," Mary whispered in her ear.

"What? Oh. So it is."

She glimpsed a flash of black tails at the door and sighed. The duke had left the room without a word.

She could not allow him to keep affecting her in this way. She felt flushed. She suffered chills. She stole glances at him like a fool. Then when he looked up, she looked away, drawing his notice to her disconcertment. He must be thoroughly enjoying himself.

On the third day she decided to give him a dose of his own medicine. She absolutely refused to look in his direction as she was leading the children to the lake with their sketchbooks and he, from what she could guess, was on his way to fish with Captain Wendover on the dock.

She clasped her pencil box and book to her chest and held her head so high that the sun momentarily blinded her. And she tripped over one of the dogs accompanying the duke.

The box and book went flying. So might have Ivy if

quick-witted Mary hadn't grasped the sash of Ivy's gown in time to slow her momentum. The friendly dog entangled beneath her feet yelped.

Ivy pitched forward, preparing to meet the grass chin-first when a powerful arm lashed around her waist and arrested her fall. The duke straightened and stepped back before she could catch her breath.

She looked at him.

He looked at her.

And he said in an expressionless voice, "Did you tear your stitches?"

And in a detached voice she replied, "I don't believe so. They are to be removed soon, anyway. How good of Your Grace to save me from my clumsiness."

He nodded. They broke apart. Ivy knelt with the children to collect her pencils. The duke rejoined his friend on the path to the lake.

Chapter 20

That might have been a frustrating enough start to James's day without Carstairs bounding across the lawn after him and shouting, "Sir Oliver Linton of London is in the reception room and wishes to see you on a matter of utmost urgency!"

James glanced over his shoulder to gauge Ivy's reaction to her other suitor's name. But she and the children had walked out of earshot, and he was glad for it.

At least now he had a person on whom he could take out his exasperation. Finally he could meet this brash fox and put him in his place. It took nerve, he thought, to call upon a duke uninvited. It required sheer gall for a caller to leave the reception room and settle himself in the study.

He didn't bother to disguise his contempt when he walked into his study and discovered Sir Oliver reading one of the books on his desk. "Would you mind not prying into my personal belongings?"

Sir Oliver dropped the book on the desk as if it had burned his fingers. "Bad habit, I'm afraid. I tend to judge a person's character by the books he reads. Ovid's *Epistles*. I'm quite impressed."

"Don't be." James took his chair, ignoring the hand extended over the desk. "It belonged to my father."

"I see. Well, I hope this is not an inconvenient time to call."

"It is. I was in the middle of an important meeting."

"Ah. Then I shall be succinct. I've come to discuss the matter of Ivy Fenwick."

James smiled. "Do you have a complaint to lodge against her? If so, I suggest you put it in writing so that my estate manager can review it at his leisure. Now if that is all," he said, rising.

"Dash it," Oliver said forcefully. "I am seeking your permission to court the lady, not complain about her."

James leaned forward as if Oliver were a fly he were about to flick off his desk. "What?"

"Hasn't she mentioned me?"

James widened his eyes. "I do not engage in personal conversations about members of my staff with strangers."

Oliver tapped his finger on the arm of his chair. "No," he said. "I don't imagine you would. But I just introduced myself."

"Unless, of course, she came to me with a problem that required my intervention. That would be a different matter."

Oliver nodded in understanding. "A problem such as a recalcitrant child?"

"Or the unwelcome advances of an admirer."

There was a pause. "I imagine it is a common problem inside a house this large."

James waited for another moment to pass. "It is a

problem outside this house, too, I fear. Not even a week ago my governess was accosted on the park grounds."

Oliver's eyes glinted; he'd raised his guard. "She told you this?"

James shrugged. "She didn't have to. I witnessed the offense with my own eyes."

It was Oliver's move. He gave a soft laugh. "Perhaps the scene you witnessed looked incriminating, but I assure you it was innocent. We'd had too much wine and were overcome with high spirits on the ride here."

"My governess did not appear to be in high spirits when she was running from you through the maze."

"Man-to-man, Your Grace, isn't 'offense' an exaggeration? She resisted one last kiss outside my carriage. It was only mischief."

He scowled. "Man-to-man, Sir Oliver, I consider Lady Ivy to be an essential person in my household and any offense against her will be regarded as an insult served to me."

Oliver crossed his knees. "Do you mean that if I want to court her, I'll have to court you, too?"

"Don't play with words."

"It's what I do. I am a poet. I write pretty words."

"Keep this up, and the next thing you'll be writing is your eulogy."

"She's only a governess to you, but to me—she is everything. Please give me your approval, and share whatever advice you believe might help my cause. I'm still encountering resistance from her."

"I'm not giving you my approval because you annoy me, and I have no advice to share on the subject except to say it will have to be a very long courtship, almost a year, so that she can fulfill her obligations to me."

"But there must be other governesses."

"Oh, there are," James said. "The reception room was packed with them. Carstairs might have even retained their names if you'd like to select another one to court."

"I mean governesses that *you* could choose from after letting Ivy go."

James stared at him. "Now why would I want to go through all that rigmarole of interviewing another governess when the children have grown so fond of the one we have? The entire household is passionate about Lady Ivy. We are so passionate about her that we are no longer allowing her a day off."

At this point James forced himself to stop before he revealed his own passion for Ivy to the presumptuous coxcomb. He rose from his chair, indicating an end to the conversation.

"I have no advice to share, I'm afraid. I am no Casanova. But I do have a steward named Carstairs who will see you to your carriage."

"Well, I'm not quite finished. I—"

James strode from the room before Sir Oliver could complete whatever irritating statement he had been about to make. If he wanted Ivy so desperately, and she wanted him, then James wouldn't stand in their way.

Yes, he would.

As he reached the front door, he realized that he couldn't afford to deceive himself. He would stand against this man like the Cliffs of Dover against a French invasion, and obviously he didn't have the luxury of the year in which to win her over.

Subtle overtures and regard for propriety would fall by the wayside in this war.

It took a scoundrel to trump another scoundrel.

James would not lose. Ivy would be his no matter how many strategical battles, for her, and against her, he would have to fight.

Ivy sensed brewing trouble in the air, and the stormy expression on the duke's face when he strode past her to rejoin his friend only confirmed her fear.

"What's put him in such a bad temper?" Mary whispered over the drawing propped on her lap.

"I haven't any notion," Ivy replied.

"Do you think Uncle James could have heard from my father?" Walker asked as Ivy put aside her sketchbook.

"I'm sure he would tell you if he had," she said. "What do you say we end afternoon lessons with a game? Please, anything but a sack race. And nothing to do with beheadings."

"How about hide-and-seek?" Mary cried, and Walker clapped with such enthusiasm that Ivy was forced to conceal her chagrin. There went the remainder of the day, but the children deserved a diversion from their worries. "Fine. But inside the house. I'm not climbing any hills or trees. Wash up first and we shall meet in the entrance hall in twenty minutes."

The house provided two hundred or so hiding places where a normal governess wouldn't think to look. But Ivy hadn't been the eldest of four sisters for nothing. After she counted down against a marble column, she opened her eyes and spotted her charges careening toward the corridor of the west wing. Several doors slammed as she set off at a leisurely pace.

She passed through the ballroom with no success,

and from there to the gold drawing room, so glorious in the waning light that she almost forgot her purpose.

At last, in a darkened anteroom to the music chamber, she closed in on her prey.

A muffled sound rose from the depths of a huge armchair that faced a tapestried alcove. She trod softly across the carpet and swung around to confront the culprits in the chair before they could flee.

"Aha! I've caught you fair and square and you're not getting away from me again!"

James looked up in dark amusement, slouched in the depths of the armchair as if he'd been half-asleep. From his bare left hand dangled one glove. His other hand, encased in the black leather of another, lifted to rest at her side, the pressure it exerted deceptively light. "And why would I want to flee from anyone as fetching as you? Especially when you've gone to so much trouble to find me."

Her shocked brain failed to cobble together a coherent response. She managed to straighten an inch before he reacted. The glove dropped to the floor. The heel of his left hand slid down her spine. The next thing she knew, she lost her balance and landed with her chin buried in his cravat and her hip trapped between his groin and upraised knees.

For a moment neither of them moved. But she wasn't as light as air. She'd fallen hard and at an off-kilter angle. The chair tipped backward.

She gasped.

"Oh, God," she heard James mutter before they toppled over in a tangle on the floor. Something hard hit the floor. The back of the chair or what sounded like a large pumpkin.

He made an indecipherable noise. Mortified at their undignified descent, she hoisted herself up to examine the man she had imprisoned. It seemed that strange paroxysms gripped his strong frame. Had he been dealt a blow to the head?

"Are you conscious, Your Grace?"

Alarmed by his failure to answer, she crawled over his torso to determine whether he was merely winded from the weight of her, or in the throes of a serious affliction. His face lay hidden in the crook of his arm . . . all the better to smother the snorts of silent laughter he evidently could not control.

"You find it amusing to frighten me?" she asked, forgetting her place and gripping a handful of his cravat to—well, she had to force herself to refrain from strangling the rogue.

"Yes." He turned his head, his eyes warm with triumph. "You lose. I knew you wouldn't last a week. It was worth a cracked noggin to win."

She reared back. "What the devil are you talking about?"

He tapped her chin with his gloved fingers. "This is a forbidden act under the terms of our recent agreement."

She stared down into his sinfully handsome face. "You don't think for a moment that I came in here looking for *you*?"

"No?"

"No. *No.* I was playing hide-and-seek with the children."

He grinned. His hand stole down her arm, black leather on bare skin. "You can use any excuse you want, darling. My door is always open."

"Then let me get up and shut it."

His hand lifted to her chin again. "Let's renegotiate, shall we?"

"In this position?"

"Not close enough?"

She rocked back on her heels and pressed against the arm of the overturned chair to push onto her feet. There wasn't time for her to even turn around. In one lithe move, James sprang upright and walked her into the wall.

She stood against the ancient tapestry she'd admired only a minute ago. "You promised me this wouldn't happen."

"But you made it happen," he said, loosening his cravat. "I'm only a man, after all. How can I resist when you throw yourself in my lap? I was almost asleep, and vulnerable to your wiles."

"My wiles, indeed."

"You're full of them."

She pursed her lips. "Are you accusing me of *attacking* you?"

"That's what it felt like. Mind you, I'm not complaining. I just wanted to keep our facts straight."

"If it didn't count when you caught me falling over one of your dogs," she said, "then why should this?"

"I came to your rescue. Again. And we weren't alone. I didn't throw myself at you in a moment of weakness."

She could feel a vein throbbing in her temple. Perhaps she was the one who'd hit her head on the floor. "I thought you were Mary and Walker."

He raised his brow. "Do I look like Mary and Walker?"

"Not in the least." She leaned her shoulders back against the wall. "And if you don't believe that I was playing with them, then I suggest we find them together and you will discover the truth."

The dark intensity in his eyes mesmerized her. A moment later his mouth slanted over hers and Ivy decided she didn't care if he thought she had broken their pact. He was kissing her again, and she was kissing him back as if it had been months and not days since they'd sworn never to be together again.

She succumbed to his expertise.

He rewarded her surrender with kisses that unwound her like a skein and slowly drove her wild. He bit her neck and blew gently on it to soothe the sting. His hands shaped her breasts and he ground his body against hers until her blood pulsed in need. Her muslin dress proved no hindrance to his quest. She doubted a coat of armor could safeguard her from his talents. And she wished—oh, how wicked of her—she wished for each of them to be standing naked against the other.

"James," she whispered, one hand hooked around his neck, the other motioning to the scarlet damask couch across the room.

"Hmmm?"

"Why don't we—" The deep thrust of his tongue inside her mouth made her forget she'd meant to suggest they sit down together. He grasped her bottom in his hands and drew her into the hard ridge of his arousal.

"Why don't we what?" he asked hoarsely, sucking hard on her lower lip.

"I can't remember—oh, yes, I can. The couch."

He lifted his head, his eyes hooded. "Would you like me to carry you to the couch?"

She struggled to recover from his kiss. "It's either that or we return to decency and go about the rest of our day."

He shook his head, leaned down to lift her as his answer, then froze.

A peal of children's laughter chimed from the door of the music room. Ivy smoothed her dress and looked into the duke's disgruntled face as he straightened.

"She'll never find us in here," Walker crowed above the muted sounds of furniture scraping across the wooden floor.

"She will if you knock over that harp," Mary cried. "And why are you blocking all the doors? How will we get out if we hear her coming?"

Ivy gave James an I-told-you-so stare. He subjected her to a long hard look, put a finger to his lips, and pointed to a second door beside the fireplace. "I'll go out through the anteroom. You can leave through the main door."

"But I'm the one who has to catch them," she whispered.

He brushed a kiss against the back of her neck before he bent to right the overturned chair. "Our pact is broken. We might as well become partners. Between Mary's penchant for beheadings and Walker's for building fortresses, we're liable to need each other as allies in the future."

She drew away in reluctance, still under the influence of his powerful masculinity. "I believe I can manage the children, Your Grace."

"As well as you manage me?"

This was neither the time nor the place to prove herself to the grinning blackguard. Ivy hoped, however, to have improved her management skills before their next encounter. At minimum she must come to terms with her own expectations. Would she be content to become the duke's mistress? She knew the answer. But was she prepared to lose him?

* * *

James's melancholy had lifted. He still felt a dark threat in the air, but through it a few rays of light had penetrated so that the rest of his life did not seem as bleak as it had an hour before, when he realized he had serious competition for Ivy.

If he had to fight a duel to prove his manhood, then he would fight a duel. Even though it meant learning to use a gun with his left hand. Time was his true rival.

Time, and whoever was at his study door as he sat contriving excuses to seek out Ivy to apologize for his behavior. Or to resume where they had left off. He hadn't imagined that she'd fused her sweet body to his and kissed him like a sorceress who had just discovered her own power. He was still as hard as steel. In fact, he should check whether it was her at the door.

No. Ivy wasn't privy to Carstairs's secret code of knocks. His *rap-rap-RAP* meant an important person had come to call, a person James knew.

He rose from his desk and scowled at the door. It wouldn't be Wendover, annoyed that James hadn't returned to the lake to fish. Wendover would not bother knocking.

"What do you want, Carstairs?"

"I regret interrupting you again, Your Grace, but there is another gentleman here from London who claims you are acquainted and insists on speaking with you."

"It's not that rhyme-maker again?"

"Oh, no, Your Grace. But—I've a sense there might be a connection to our governess."

"Is this 'sense' grounded in fact, Nostradamus, or is it a message you received from another world?"

Carstairs chuckled. "He mentioned Fenwick Manor, Your Grace."

"Dear God. Send him in."

James returned to his desk. Now what? A confrontation with another suitor for Ivy's hand? Who could blame the woman for hiding inside that house for so long? No wonder the gardener had let the thistle and thorns grow roof-high to conceal the Fenwick sisters from the world.

But a wall of thorns hadn't protected Ivy from James.

He glanced up in surprise at the gentleman Carstairs ushered into the room. He was in his late sixties, with tousled gray hair, jacket too short in the sleeves, and a high-quality coat that needed a good cleaning.

"Don't you remember me, Ellsworth?" he asked, dropping into a chair without waiting for an invitation.

James narrowed his eyes. Where in the world would Ivy have met this person? "Have we met?"

"You lost a hand of cards to me at the club."

"Did I?"

"Then I lost three to you."

"I don't doubt your word, but I'm afraid I still don't remember."

"A crowd of us went out after your victory to celebrate and ended up sailing down the Thames on a barge with several amorous women. I fell off, and you saved me."

James expelled a sigh. "Now I remember, Ainsley Farbisher. What brings you here?"

"I understand you are managing a property I would like to acquire."

"A . . . property?" James felt the muscles at the back of his neck tense in forewarning. It was one thing for

James to covet Ivy as a treasured possession. It was quite another for a gin-soaked old gent to sit across his desk and echo the same sentiment. "I hope you are not referring to a person in my employ."

Ainsley's eyes bulged. "Good heavens. I was speaking of the attractive parcel I passed on my way here. The house that stands beyond the stone bridge."

"You mean Fenwick Manor?"

"Yes, that's it. The Tudor estate in the oak wood."

"And you don't wish to marry any of the ladies who occupy the house?" he asked, scowling in suspicion.

Ainsley contemplated the question. "Is that a condition of acquisition?"

"Have you ever seen the inhabitants of the manor?" he asked pointedly.

"No, I haven't. Is it in use as some sort of an asylum?"

"Excuse me?" James asked, masking a smile.

"I was told by a tavern keeper that several men who'd visited the manor had disappeared inside the house and that their remains were never found due to tragic circumstances or—" He wavered, appearing afraid to continue.

"Or what?" James asked, completely enjoying this legend of the Fenwick sisters.

"—or else the house is currently in use as a country brothel and the men who enter would rather die than leave."

James did smile then. "Ainsley?"

"Yes, Your Grace?"

"Come here and take a look at my boots."

Ainsley obeyed, withdrawing a handkerchief from his coat to dab at his brow. "Handsome, they are. The height of fashion."

"I'm glad you approve. Your head will be pinned beneath the sole of one if you make another ridiculous remark about asylums or brothels."

"I won't."

"Good."

Ainsley returned to his chair in relief. James leaned back. This was no coincidental offer. Had the acquisition of Tudor manors become the latest rage among London's aristocracy? Or had the mystery of four beautiful sisters sparked interest in another type of procurement? All James knew was that he felt compelled to guard their privacy from young poets and old fools and probably everyone ill-intentioned who fell in between.

"How did you hear about Fenwick?"

"I can't remember," Ainsley said, blinking at the change in James's tone. "Must have been at the club."

"Odd topic of conversation for gentlemen gamblers in London, don't you think?" James asked, his eyes boring into Ainsley's.

Ainsley slid to the edge of his chair. "No. No, we're always boasting about who has inherited or won the largest acreage. Distressed properties with that much potential don't land in one's lap every day."

"Perhaps you read about it in the news," James suggested.

Ainsley's eyes lit up. "That's it, of course. I'm always dipping into papers that passengers leave in their coaches. My wife brings them home by the basket when she takes the stage to visit her mother."

James started "Your wife?"

"Yes. Alvina."

"Why the deuce are you asking about marrying vulnerable young ladies when you have a wife?"

"I only asked if the marriage were a condition of sale," Ainsley said, clearly miffed. He came so swiftly to his feet that he knocked his cane across the floor. "On second thought, perhaps it would all be too much for me to manage."

"What? The manor house or the Ladies Fenwick?" James picked up the cane and handed it to the gentleman, who seemed in a sudden rush to leave.

Ainsley backed out the door, bowing awkwardly. "Good to see you again, Ellsworth. Hope we meet soon at the club."

James followed the man to the hall to demand further explanation, but the instant Ainsley slipped outside, another visitor approached, commanding his complete attention.

Ivy had scraped her lustrous hair into a lopsided knot and changed into a bleached white dress with blue ribbons banded beneath the modest bodice. Her mouth looked dark and swollen from their kisses, a sight that immediately emptied his mind of everything but lustful hope. Or hopeful lust. She turned him inside out.

"I want a moment of your time, please, Your Grace," she said. "If it is not inconvenient."

He ignored the crispness of her voice, the rigid lift of her shoulder when he stepped closer to her. "Would you prefer we spend this moment together in the Chinese Room?" he asked, his smile impudent. "And it's no inconvenience at all."

"That will not be necessary."

She moistened her bottom lip. Right then he could have handed her the keys to Ellsworth Park. She was the woman that had eluded him all his life. "No? You mean—do you want our encounter to take place *here*, *now*?"

Her eyes met his. "Not that sort of encounter, you single-minded knave. I'm not going to let you deceive me again."

He studied her. "*I* deceive you?"

She was breathing fast, her skin shone, and her hands were clasped behind her back, not in modesty, he realized. But in restraint. She wasn't aroused at all. She looked ready for a bout of fisticuffs.

"I didn't lose fairly," she said.

He grinned. "It doesn't matter. I won, and I don't care whether it was fair or not. You fell into my arms."

"I won't fall that easily in future. I don't like losing to a cheater. I was only doing my job. That incident shouldn't have counted. You'll have to be at death's door for me to make a mistake like that again."

James frowned as if listening intently to every word she said. Which he wasn't. Her message, however, he understood. She was angry at him, and it wouldn't last. He adored her. That was enough for a man to assimilate in one day. He wasn't ready to admit it to her. But he couldn't deny the truth to himself.

"At death's door," he said. "That is an unkind sentiment. I am hurt to the quick. What did Shakespeare have to say on the subject, 'How sharper than a serpent's tooth it is to have an ungrateful governess'? To think that I saved you from the windowsill."

"And I appreciated that."

"You don't sound appreciative." As a matter of fact, she sounded as if she wanted to murder him. And he wanted to keep her in this house for the rest of their lives. He saw the future clearly: Ivy arguing with him in the doorway and him giving her orders afterward that had nothing to do with domestic affairs. Ivy, in his bed, inviting him to take pleasure in her body. Ivy, reading to *their* children.

A footman passed through the hall.

Ivy turned her head. "That's all I wished to say. I was only trying to do my job the day you rescued me from the windowsill."

He realized he shouldn't tease her. Yet how could he resist? "Do you know what my job is?"

"To taunt every woman you meet?"

He took the hit, reminding himself not to underestimate her. "That was also unkind, Lady Ivy."

"How remiss of me. I forgot that Your Grace is such a tenderling who must be mollycoddled."

He smiled. "The worst sin I have committed is to find you irresistible."

She stared at him in disbelief. "I'm not certain where you have acquired your religious instruction. Perhaps at the Hellfire Club. But if you are curious about the definition of the sins we have both committed, I'm sure the parish church would be pleased to provide you with a Bible."

"Thank you for the advisement," he said after a pause to imply that he'd taken her warning to heart. It wouldn't do a damn bit of good, but he'd play along.

She eyed him narrowly. "My conscience has been bothering me all afternoon."

He looked at her without blinking. "Mine hasn't."

"Well, that's all I meant to say."

"Then I'm glad you said it."

"You're not taking this seriously, are you?"

"I won't touch you again unless you beg me. You won't touch me unless I'm about to be lowered into my grave. If that's what you want."

She swallowed. "I think that would be for the best."

He folded his arms across his chest. It wouldn't be the best for *him*, but he could wait, knowing that she'd be worth every damn minute of suffering until he held her in his arms again.

"Then thank you," she murmured, and dropped a curtsy as if she had read his thoughts and hastened to leave before temptation got the better of him.

It almost did.

But somehow he was able to nod, feigning compliance, and watch her walk away, pretending he had conceded to her wishes, which weren't unreasonable.

There were times when a man had to toss a lady over his shoulder, give her a good smack on the behind, and master her until the next morning.

This wasn't one of those times.

But it wouldn't be long now.

And his blood clamored for the day.

Chapter 21

Ivy had been reading from *A Midsummer Night's Dream* to the children before bed. Walker refused to settle down unless Mary stayed until he fell asleep. The one night that the duke had insisted he go to sleep by himself, the boy had been seized with night terrors and was found wandering about in the hall, oblivious to his surroundings.

At last he nodded off. Ivy closed the book. "You may read in your room for fifteen more minutes before you go to sleep, Mary. You know I'm in the next room if Walker wakes up. Heavens, I'm so tired I can hardly move."

No sooner had she closed her eyes to take a momentary rest than thunder boomed from the fields beyond the house. Five minutes or so later a series of blasts drew her—and Mary—to the window.

"Walker hates thunderstorms," Mary whispered, wide-awake and scornful.

Ivy studied the clear starlit sky. "I don't see a single cloud."

"Isn't tomorrow your day off?"

"Yes, but I have work to do here. And I'm having my stitches taken out."

"Did Uncle James forbid you to see your lover?"

Ivy turned to the girl in exasperation. "No. He forbade you to discuss adult concerns. I do not have a lover."

"I'm sorry."

"Run off to your room before you disturb your brother. The thunder seems to have stopped now, anyway."

Another boom resounded from the fields. Walker sat bolt upright and bellowed, "The French are coming! Papa! Uncle James!"

"Dear me," Ivy muttered, and gave Mary a nudge toward the door. "It's only thunder, Walker," she said, drawing the curtains on the starry night before she left the window to console him.

He had dropped back off to sleep before she reached the bed. Mary stared at him from the door. "You told a lie, Lady Ivy. It wasn't thunder at all."

"Well, whatever it was, it's over now. Perhaps there are poachers in the woods."

"My mother would thrash Walker for wailing like an infant."

Ivy tucked in the covers and joined the girl at the door. "If your brother asks, which I doubt he will, you are to assure him it was thunder he heard—unless you wish to stand in the corner tomorrow."

"I shall tell Uncle James."

"Go ahead."

"What if he dismisses you?"

"Then you will soon be arguing with another governess."

Ivy heard the girl's apology but did not linger to acknowledge it. She hurried to her room and from the window witnessed the duke canter into view on his gray. His cloak billowed out like a black sail. The two heavyset men riding in his wake enhanced his dashing, devil-may-care appearance.

Ivy felt an irrational urge to open the window and demand to know what he had been doing at this hour. Perhaps it was at this unguarded moment of emotion that the green-eyed monster of jealousy crept into the chamber and, finding a disquieted soul, offered to keep her company into the night.

She would have been better off with Mary's precocious honesty or Walker's fears. Her uninvited guest tormented her with sly dialogue.

Where would the duke have gone so mysteriously, in the middle of the night?

He could have gone to visit a neighbor, Ivy reasoned. Or a tenant who had taken ill after supper. That was a decent landlord's duty.

He could have gone in search of the sexual gratification you refused him. Do you not remember how his reception room overflowed with women on the day of his interview?

Ivy could hardly forget.

But he had chosen her—as a governess.

He kissed you at a masquerade ball five years ago. Twice you have let him go now.

Ivy stood firm. He'd probably gone hunting. She had heard gunshots fired.

Indeed, the voice mocked her. *And his prey begged to be caught. What do you know of the games that sophisticated lovers play?*

Ivy drew back into the curtains. As James drew nearer, he swayed unsteadily in the saddle and then slid to the ground without his customary agility. One of his companions dismounted and hastened to his side.

Ivy's heart raced. Had he been shot? It didn't seem possible that anything could diminish his vitality. He had been injured at war and survived to return to the ruling class. Still, he was mortal, no matter how everyone had come to place him on a pedestal.

He's been fighting over a woman, the voice taunted in glee.

"You wicked man," she said, wanting to pound her fist on the window and run to his aid at once. The sinner. Risking his life over a woman who wasn't Ivy or even the lady from London he invited to sin with him in his exquisite home.

Fickle, the voice said in the silence.

Amoral.

Passionate.

She wished she could ask her sisters' opinion instead of listening to this plaguesome voice in her head. Her sisters might try to confirm her first suspicion, that the duke had merely been out hunting.

But for what at this time of night? Or whom? And why did he need assistance to dismount? Was he drunk?

Rosemary would advise her to ask him in the morning and not lose any sleep over what was only speculation tonight. But Rosemary had never been kissed by a charismatic duke at a masquerade ball or swept off to his bed in what would have been a romantic moment except for the hideous gash on her wrist and the presence of Elora in the adjoining room.

Ivy wasn't going to question him in the morning

about his late-night rendezvous. He would only consider her curiosity a sign that she could not stop thinking about him if put to another test, which was obviously true. But Ivy needn't give him another reason to gloat.

She said her prayers and went to bed, resolved to find out discreetly from the other servants what mysterious activities the master had committed during the night.

Except he looked so haggard the following day she decided she would rather remain in ignorance. His eyes brooded with secrets. Deep lines of fatigue drew his face into a forbidding mask.

Evidently the duke had exerted himself to the brink of physical exhaustion in some nocturnal mischief. If his dissolute appearance was the result of an assignation, Ivy doubted she would survive a love affair with the scoundrel.

Still, in her heart she believed that his ominous deportment had less to do with romance than it did with an issue infinitely more dangerous.

For the next four nights the disturbing pattern continued. Elora had left them before Ivy could ask her if she heard anything unusual after she retired. Ivy moved Mary and Walker to rooms across the hall and they slept fitfully from the moment she settled them into bed. The duke no longer appeared for evening prayers at all, and Ivy thought this was for the best.

He was short-tempered with the staff. He avoided Ivy. And when he walked through the house, an indelible darkness followed in his wake.

Even his appearance had changed in the past week. He'd lost weight and his elegant clothes hung on a chiseled frame that was strangely beautiful to behold. As far as Ivy could tell, he spent most of his daylight hours fencing, boxing, and in archery contests with Wendover and his two younger brothers, who were soon to join the navy. If Ivy hadn't known better, she would have sworn the duke was preparing for battle himself

Finally, on the fifth night, as she waited at her window for his return, he slid off his horse, and for once, his attendants weren't quick enough to catch him.

She raced from her room, not caring whether the stupid man was in league with the devil, a smuggling ring, or Wellington's spies. He was clearly engaged in some activity that put his safety at risk, and it must be stopped.

She needn't have worried about anyone noticing her. The house was in an uproar when she descended to the first floor. She shrank back as Wendover and the gamekeeper helped the duke up the stairs.

"I am capable of walking myself," he snapped.

He looked dreadful, pale, his cloak hanging at an odd angle from his neck like a broken wing. He leaned heavily against the balustrade, and it seemed that the flock of servants below held their collective breath until he turned his head and shouted, "Go!"

Carstairs ordered two footmen to fetch His Grace's physician. Wendover and the gamekeeper remained behind the duke in the likely event that he would miss a step and fall.

Ivy was grateful the children had gone to bed.

She knew that she must discover the duke's secret. And she would do so tonight.

Chapter 22

"I warned Your Grace," the physician said to James, who lay reluctantly in his bed with every Tom, Dick, and Harry at his side. "If you continue to strain your muscular organs, they will dilate and weaken beyond what your blood supply will be able to repair."

James grunted. "And that's why you just removed a bucket of my blood, is it?" He ground his teeth as the dark-coated figure applied another steaming cloth to his arm, blistering his skin.

"The wet heat brings comfort," the physician said with a sigh. "I encouraged light activity, as I recall."

"Well, I can't weave a shawl to save my life. I haven't the dexterity to play marbles with the children. It takes me a half an hour to bait a fishing rod."

"Read a book. Soak in a hot tub."

"Can I challenge a man to a duel to see who finishes his book first before his bathwater turns cold?"

"A duel?" Dr. Buchan peeled off the cooling cloth and applied a thick coating of green ointment to James's skin.

"Yes. I can punch a hole in a wall. I can lift this bed.

But I can't pull a trigger or hold the gun steadily enough to blast the door behind you."

"Perhaps you should start practicing with your other side."

"Brilliant. Do you think I'll be able to compete with an expert duelist in a fortnight?"

The physician gave a rude snort. "No."

James swore. "Neither do I. Isn't there another surgery you can do?"

"Not in a fortnight. Not ever, I'm afraid. You're a lucky devil to have survived the first without developing gangrene. No doubt you still have bone chips and bullet fragments that are causing you distress. Whoever splintered you did an excellent job. I might chance severing the adhesions with a fine scalpel, but there's a risk of damaging your muscles and atrophy."

"What was your field of expertise in Antwerp?"

"Obstetric physician."

"Great God."

"I am leaving you with a tincture of morphia for the night."

"Take everyone with you."

James closed his eyes. The door opened and shut. "I am not taking that swill," he said between his teeth. "I was addicted to it for six months." He sat up as he heard the door of his dressing closet swing open.

"Whatever you have forgotten, sir, take it quickly or I shall growl at you."

"Growl at me all you like." He opened his eyes and saw Ivy beside his bed.

"What are you doing here? Gloating?"

She stared down at him, shaking her head in dismay.

"No. You can't believe for a moment that I enjoy your suffering."

He lay on the bed with his shirt undone. He just realized that if she had been sitting in his dressing room, she had heard his conversation with the physician. "I thought you weren't going to come near me again."

"Not unless you are at death's door," she said quietly, looking at the bandage, pair of scissors, and bottle of medicine on the table beside his bed. "Are you?"

He sat up, cursing under his breath. "As a matter of fact, I am. I'm fatal. Have you come to give me comfort?"

She didn't move.

"You're beautiful," he said.

She sat down beside him. "I heard every word."

"Good. Then you know that I need you and I'm not willing to let anyone else take you from me."

"Are you practicing every night in preparation to fight a duel? Over me?"

"That's right."

"Then it all makes sense now, the midnight gallivanting and shooting in the fields. Why by day you were short-tempered, like a man who expects an enemy to attack from out of nowhere. You gave Walker nightmares."

"I thought it would be worse if I came home in the afternoon looking like a corpse." He reached for the bandage on the table beside the bed and wiped the ointment that the physician had plastered on his arm.

"My father died in a duel, James. It is a male ritual that I will always associate with death and unhappiness."

"I wish I could go back in time and prevent your father's death. Perhaps he felt he didn't have a choice but to stand up for himself. I'm sure he didn't intend to hurt you and your sisters. The best I can do now is promise to protect you."

She sighed. "Men and their honor."

"Will you stay the night with me?"

"Yes," she said, without even pretending to hesitate.

He pulled off his shirt and with difficulty unfastened his trousers. "I don't think I'll die tonight, but if I do, I'll be a contented man with you at my side."

Ivy knew perfectly well the duke was an uninhibited man. A sexually practiced man. A completely naked man who had undressed her and tossed their clothes between the bed's posters before she could hang them over a chair.

They rose together and faced off without a stitch, studying each other's nude bodies in ardent silence. He was masculine to the marrow. How well made were the wide shoulders and arms that she knew from the day of her accident to be capable and protective. Indeed, she felt more faint now at the thought of belonging to him, of touching the heavy member between his legs that proved he wasn't anywhere near death's door.

"I could stare at you all night, Ivy," he said, his dark eyes traveling over her with a heat that penetrated the secret places of her body.

She clasped her hands together. "I could say the same of you, but I'd have to sit down to do so. The nearness of you in such a state overwhelms me."

"I haven't even touched you yet," he said with a confident smile, and stepped forward.

"James," she said, staring past him, "don't you think we should pick up our clothing from the middle of the floor?" Not that she could move when she was melting from the inside out. Her female soul was ready to submit.

"Why bother?" he asked in amusement.

"What if someone opens the door? It looks—I don't know. It looks untidy, disorderly."

"Sex is untidy and we shall shortly become so disorderly that it won't matter where you put your shoes."

"Oh." A wave of light-headness overcame her. His words flooded her with anticipation. He was the first man, the only one, she would ever love and want. She'd learned that he was an honorable man who cared for his wards. She knew he was highly sexual and to please him challenged her innocent upbringing.

As further evidence of his vitality, he walked her against the bed, framed her face in one hand, and kissed her deeply. His other hand found her breasts, his fingers twisting her nipples until her blood sang in her veins. She was mad for this duke who had taken up midnight training to fight for her.

She would forbid him to do so and divert him by indulging his every other desire. Although it seemed he would not hesitate to take what he needed from her without asking.

"Ivy," he said. "Don't go anywhere."

As if she would run out into the hall completely unclad.

"Wait," he said unnecessarily, backing away from her with another dark smile that promised her obedience would be rewarded.

He extinguished the candles burning in the wrought-iron wall sconces. She stood for endless moments, enveloped in smoky darkness. The moment she dared to turn, a pair of sinewy arms hoisted her into the air and deposited her on the bed.

She waited, breathless, searching his face and finding within its shadows a reassuring warmth and indication of wicked intentions. "No games this time," he said. "No boundaries."

His body hovered over hers. "You cheated before."

"I know. I couldn't help myself."

"You're deplorable."

"Am I, darling?"

"At times."

"At this moment? Am I deplorable or am I deluded? Did you not seek my bed of your own will?"

"You know I did. I think you know I love you."

"I think you know that I want to marry you."

"How would I know that?"

"I didn't steal kisses from you at the masquerade ball. You stole my heart."

"And you've only realized now it was missing?"

He reflected on this for several moments. "The world is full of heartless men. Few of them are given a chance to have their hearts returned and allowed to feel happiness again."

His lips met hers. His fingers stole down her throat to her belly. She started to shiver, to feel her hips lift against him. "I thought you were supposed to rest."

"My arm. I should have been resting my right arm. If you're going to eavesdrop, at least listen attentively."

A doubt entered her mind and swiftly exited as he began to scatter kisses everywhere he possibly could. From one corner of her mouth to the other. To her throat, her breasts, and in between her ribs until he paused. She raised her head. His face had disappeared.

"James. You're not . . ."

He was. He slid his hand under her buttocks and gave her a good push that brought her into the middle of the bed, spreading her legs apart as he did. He licked between her folds and at the pearl of her cleft. She subdued the urge to sob. This was an act that should only be performed in darkness. She couldn't see what he was doing, but she could feel every lap of his tongue to her core.

"James."

He didn't respond, too intent on caressing her belly and teasing the hollow of her womanhood with his mouth. She felt his fingers replace his tongue, working deeper, stretching her pliant flesh. The more he gave her, the more she needed. Her nerves knotted. She couldn't stay still. Her body demanded relief and she was past caring how disgraceful she looked.

He rose up again and lowered his lips to her breast. His fingers sank deeper into her sheath as he sucked hard at her nipple. She felt his erect penis against her stomach. That was what she wanted. "Oh, please," she whispered. "What have you done to me?"

"Nothing yet."

"Then . . . do it."

He laughed softly. "I'll take my sweet time. You aren't in bed with a schoolboy."

"I never imagined for a moment that I was."

"Do you know how beautiful you look right now?"

He pushed her legs farther apart, exposing her damp curls and the crease below. He shifted and positioned his shaft at the entrance of her body. She gasped at the contact.

"Keep breathing, Ivy," he said. "Put your legs around my back. It might hurt a little."

"Only a little?"

"I'll do my best," he said in a thick voice.

"I trust you, James."

"Remember you said that."

She made out the angular shape of his face in the darkness, the width of his shoulders. *Take me,* she thought. *I don't care how much it hurts.*

She was both a goddess and place of worship. And he was as dedicated to pleasing her now as he was to protecting her when they stepped outside this room. Twice she attempted to clench her thighs together. Calmly he pressed her legs apart, braced himself over her, and concentrated on sliding his shaft between the engorged seams of her sex. A slow torture for now.

He was on fire, imagining the moment when he would sink his cock into her heat. Not all at once. She was still quivering, his beautiful virgin. Stretching her took restraint. Readying her for the moment required that he wait and let her pleasure build. She raised her hand as if she wanted to touch him. The gesture inflamed him. He flexed his back instinctively.

"May I?" she whispered.

"I beg you," he said in a hoarse voice. He felt so hot. *Could* he wait? Her hand strayed over his chest, finding the demarcations of his ribs, his abdomen. A woman's touch had never thrilled him and left him aching like this. He was the only man she would ever know.

He pressed another inch inside her, his penis throbbing, his blood smoldering. She moaned and shifted, restless, and he leaned lower to kiss her, his aggression mounting.

"I can't stop now, Ivy."

"It's all right. I want this, James."

He withdrew slightly, his prick coated in her moisture, and thrust inside her harder this time. Her eyes widened, and he felt her inner muscles close around him, forcing him to drive in farther to breach her maidenhead.

"Ivy," he said on a moan like a man with a fever.

He slid his hand between their joined bodies and rubbed her nub. He felt her shiver helplessly. Her legs tightened around his hips. She cried out something he could not understand. Blood roared in his head.

Then she arched and lifted upward with a desperation that pushed him to the edge. His elemental side took charge. He grasped her arse in one hand and embedded himself inside her fully. She gave a soft cry, and for a moment she didn't move. But it was done. She was his. There would be time for tenderness later. For now he surged into her again and again, aware that she had climaxed, her body shuddering beneath his.

And still he wanted, needed more. He'd waited so long for her that he was almost afraid what would happen when he finally let go of his control. Nothing but instinct. Nothing but her.

He gave himself to pure sensation and wondered for a moment if he would die from the intensity. He found release in their fierce mating and attempted not to crush her beneath his weight as he collapsed. He thought he would come forever. His heart pounded erratically in his chest. He was stricken with a gratitude he could not express, a concern that made him fear his unbridled desire might have been more than she'd expected. It was more than he had hoped for. If ever a woman had been worth waiting for, it was her.

"How do you feel?" he whispered, kissing her softly on her shoulder.

She rolled up against him. "Wonderful. Broken. Worldly. What about you?"

"I think love has given me a fever," he mused. "You are indeed a woman of the world."

She sat up and placed her fingers against his forehead. "And you are warm."

He laughed. "Aren't you, after what we just did?"

She didn't answer, but through his half-closed eyes he noticed her gaze travel the length of his nude body. Her interest gave him another erection, which he intended to put to good use after he rested for a moment. He turned onto his right side, smothering a groan.

"What is it?" she asked in alarm. "Are you in pain? Did we do something we weren't supposed to?"

"Damn me." He laughed again, drawing a deep breath. "You're already acting like my wife."

"Open your mouth, James."

He narrowed his eyes. "What for?"

"Let me give you a dose of that medicine."

He looked at her with gratitude and perhaps envy. Here this goddess sat with her steady hands and voluptuous body sticking in his mouth a brimming spoonful of the soporific before he could seize the moment.

He shuddered. "Why did you do that? I shouldn't have let you force it on me."

"How does it taste?"

"Like a dead toad's spleen."

He wasn't sure how she managed it, but she brought him a glass of water, reapplied the ointment and bandage to his arm. Then, with no cooperation on his part, she rummaged in his wardrobe for a nightshirt and dressed him in it like an oversized doll. If he didn't adore her, he would never have tolerated such humiliation.

"Ha," he said. "You're still naked."

"You're still impossible."

He grabbed her around the waist, aroused and possessive even as Morpheus worked his insidious magic. What a feeling. James wanted to throw the bottle in the fire. "I've never killed a toad," he said. His eyelids felt like lead. His body felt relaxed and still aroused. "I'd kill to keep you, though."

"I hope that is the medicine talking."

"No." He laid his head against the pillow. "It's the aristocrat."

She wriggled out of his arms. "Do you love me, James?"

"I must." He closed his eyes. "I asked you to marry me and I let you dose me with poison."

She slid off the bed. "You need to stop playing and settle into bed."

"I've only started to play." He frowned. "You're the one who needs to settle into bed."

"Would you be quiet for a moment? I'm very upset. There's something wrong with you."

"There's nothing wrong with you," he said admiringly. "That was the best f—"

"James."

"I was going to say it was the best fun I've had in my life."

She looked at him in vexation. "Well, it won't be the best moment in mine if anything happens to you as a result of what we did."

"You have severely underestimated me if you think I will expire from a single act of sex."

"And you've overestimated me if you don't think I'll die of shame explaining this to your doctor."

"I'll be fine."

"Promise?"

"Hmm."

"What—" The woman had pulled the carpet out from under his arse. No, the counterpane. They weren't on the floor this time. God, his brains felt addled. He opened his eyes. She was dressed and bent over the bed, smothering him in covers.

"What did the physician tell you that I missed?" she asked sharply. "Obviously I didn't hear everything he said."

"He ordered me to stay in bed for two days straight. He didn't specify what I could or couldn't do while I was here. By the way, I don't need a governess. Did I disappoint you?"

"Perhaps I should call him back."

"Oh, my God. Do I look ill to you? Allow a man his pride."

She didn't understand, but he was too tired to explain.

The least hesitation of instincts, an uneven skill, would prove fatal during a duel. It didn't matter that her father had died as the result of a challenge. He had cheated and paid the cost.

If James could not win a duel over her now, then he did not deserve her.

Chapter 23

Oliver had played the role of invalid for over a week and Ivy still had not returned to Fenwick. Initially he'd enjoyed Lilac's attention to his imaginary malaise, but boredom, along with Rosemary's disapproval of his person, had conspired to bring about a complete cure. He took glee in using the duke's candles for the light he needed to compose poems to Ivy.

He glanced up as Lilac entered the room with his supper tray. "Hungry yet, Sir Oliver?" Lilac inquired with a cheerfulness he didn't know how she could maintain.

"And what is on the menu this evening, my dear?" he asked from the couch in the drawing room where he posed in languid discontent. "Ragout of duck and asparagus points washed down with champagne?"

She cleared away his papers and set the tray down on the table. "Carrot broth, stewed cabbage, and raspberry trifle. Oh, and tea."

"Ye gods," he said, hoping his reflexive grimace passed for a grin in the poorly lit chamber. "I mean, you spoil me. I don't deserve your continued kindness."

Lilac plopped down in the chair on which she had placed his papers. He thought to protest, but then she pulled them out from beneath her derrière and placed the pile on the end of the couch. "I'm enjoying taking care of you, really. I never thought I had it in me."

He stared down at his broth and swore he felt his nose twitch and sprout whiskers. "How could you enjoy it?"

"Well, it isn't every day that Rosemary traps a man in the tunnels and forgets about him."

"How would anyone know?" he asked with a morbid sniff. "There could be dozens of lost souls down in those—tunnels, did you say?"

"Yes. The passages are attached by tunnels. We explored them every summer when we were girls."

He was appalled, both by the soup and the thought of little girls crawling through cobwebs and who knew what else. "Your parents allowed you to do this alone?"

"Sometimes Mama accompanied us. But usually it was Quigley or Terence who came along as guard."

Quigley, the gardener, had yet to succumb to Oliver's charm. Quigley had lived at Fenwick since before the sisters had been born. He might know a thing or two about hidden treasure. "Who is Terence?"

Lilac blushed a becoming shade of peach. She was a golden-pink-complexioned girl, lovely in her own way, if eccentric, as were the rest of the quartet. "Terence is my best friend. He sailed off somewhere for the East India Company, Morocco or— "

"Malacca." He grinned. "How long has he been gone?"

"Six or so years." Lilac put down the soup spoon. "Don't give me a lecture, Sir Oliver. Everyone else has. It's my affair if I choose to wait for him."

"Well, have you heard anything from him?"

"Perhaps."

He didn't ask her how long ago that had been. There was no reason to embarrass her, but Oliver couldn't imagine waiting six months for a woman, never mind six years. A week had strained his patience. "When do you think Ivy will come back?"

Lilac had picked up his notebook and was moving her lips as she read his latest rendering to herself. He watched her face, forgetting what he had just asked her. She appeared to be lost in his most recent poem. He was entranced, aroused, her opinion suddenly all that mattered in the world.

"What do you think?" he asked softly.

She blinked. "It's enchanting. I've never read anything like it."

> A thousand stars shone upon you like day
> While I stood alone in the dark
> That night in Bulgaria when you went away
> With a stranger you had met in the park

He winced. "It's Belgravia, Lilac, not Bulgaria, and the way you read it, it sounds awkward and lacking cadence."

"It's not the way she read it," an amused voice announced from the doorway. "It's how you wrote it. 'Stars shining upon one like day.' I think, Sir Oliver, it would have been more enticing if you had written a poem about a stranger in Bulgaria."

His mouth tightened. He set aside his tray as Rosemary pushed the door open with her shoulder, a handful of dried thistles in her hands. "And your obscure novels are blazing a trail across the Continent, are they?"

She tossed the thistles in the fireplace. "I could have been a best seller in Bulgaria for all you know."

"I *was* a guest at one of Lord Byron's house parties last year. He declared one stanza of my work to be practically excellent."

"How cruel of him," Lilac said after a long pause.

"It could have been worse," Rosemary said, plucking a burr from her skirt.

Oliver gave her a negligent glance. "Oh?"

"He could have declared you to be practically awful."

He laughed reluctantly. She was a bold Amazon whose face became breathtaking when she smiled. Oliver was quite unprepared for the impact. Whatever the Fenwick sisters lacked in reputation they atoned for in allure. "When do you think Ivy is coming home?" he asked her, uncomfortable with his thoughts.

"I honestly don't know. Is that raspberry trifle?"

"Yes," Lilac said. "You might as well have it. He hasn't touched it. And, Oliver, I'm afraid if you want Ivy, you'll have to go after her."

"What do you mean?" he asked, expelling a sigh.

"Obviously she isn't about to chase you," Rosemary said, squeezing in the chair beside Lilac.

"It's almost as if she's forgotten you exist," Lilac said with her typical candor.

Oliver tapped his spoon against the bowl of tasteless broth. "I realize that all of you are the victims of circumstance, and that owing to events over which you had no control, you withdrew from society and have during the period of your involuntary ostracism—"

"You think we're ill-mannered," Lilac said as Rosemary calmly devoured the trifle.

"I wasn't being insulting."

"It's all right," Lilac said. "We are social exiles and do not care for convention."

He glanced at Rosemary. "So you think *I* should pursue your sister?"

"I said nothing of the sort," she replied, and set her empty bowl back on the tray.

"You did," he insisted.

"No. I said she would not chase you. If you go to Ellsworth and the duke catches you, you shall get whatever you deserve."

Lilac nodded. "You didn't see the way the duke looked at Ivy. Perhaps there's a reason why she hasn't come home. Sir Oliver, I'm afraid you might be too late."

Chapter 24

Ivy lightly traced the creases in his beautifully sculpted face with her fingertip. She wished she could stay the night, watching over James, if only to hear him tell her that they belonged together as man and wife, and that was that.

There was a chance he would change his mind by morning. But he must have been brought into her life five years ago for a reason—perhaps so that her heart would hold a place for him.

She poured another glass of water to leave at his side and debated whether to add a few coals to his fire. He still felt hot. She decided that she would check him again in half an hour and slipped from his room, hoping that no one else in the house spotted her. Of course he would be well. As he'd pointed out, it wasn't likely that a man could make love with such intensity and succumb to a grave illness hours later. Not that she was an expert on the subject. But she was the one who should be running a fever. She felt both exhausted and exhilarated.

Her mind kept returning to the offer he had made her. His wife. The duchess. A title that implied dignity and rulership. No more trysting in the Chinese Room. Or knocking over chairs. And if they ever needed a governess, Ivy would conduct the interview and would not kiss any of the applicants on the floor.

A fine example the two of them had set for the rest of the house as well as for the children.

Of course Ivy could not have foreseen that one of the little mischief-makers would be waiting in her room, tonight of all nights.

"Walker, what are you doing in that chair and wearing on your head? And is that your uncle's cane? Are you sleepwalking? Or is that you, Mary? Answer me. This has to stop."

She gasped as the shadowed figure rose from the chair and stepped into the moonlight. It was—she wasn't sure *who* it was at first. It appeared to be a footman dressed in a maid's frilly mobcap and apron. Had the servants been using *her* bedroom for their antics? She nearly laughed until she took a closer look at the agitated face under the cap and realized it belonged to Sir Oliver.

Her heart jumped in alarm. She hadn't believed any of his nonsense about rescuing her from the duke. "Oh, no, Oliver. Not in here. Have you gone daft?" Which was a question she realized didn't need an answer. He was wearing a cap and apron in the house of a man who had decreed he would kill Oliver if he set foot on this property again.

"I might well be daft," Oliver said. "I can't think of any other explanation for the risk I'm taking."

She was so upset the words tangled in her throat. "It's rash and dangerous for you to come to this house, let alone sneak into a private room. How did you find your way inside?"

His lips thinned. "I waited for hours outside the garden walls. I hoped I would see you in your window."

"The duke will fly into an understandable rage if he catches you here."

His gaze drifted over her with a sly knowledge that felt like a violation. Her hair needed to be brushed and bound. She had not bothered to refasten the buttons at her nape. She was relieved that he did not remark on her unkempt appearance.

"The duke is ill, isn't he?" he asked, his voice mildly taunting.

"What makes you think that?"

"I saw a physician leave the house."

"The children often beg treats from the kitchen and suffer for it."

"The children were playing in the summerhouse in the dark. Without their governess."

"Leave this room right now, Oliver." She couldn't control the quiver of panic in her voice. "If the duke discovers you here, he'll kill you and I don't think anyone would blame him."

He looked down at her bare feet. "Why would the duke come to your room this late at night?"

"That is not your affair. Nor did I say he would. The issue is that *you* are here, a trespasser and intruder."

He gripped her by her upper arms. "I want to marry you. Don't you feel anything for me at all?"

"At this moment exasperation is the kindest emotion I can muster. Let me go."

"Let me kiss you. Or at least arrange to meet me tomorrow."

"What if someone sees you here? He won't tolerate

an insult, Oliver. You're the most stupidly impulsive man I have ever met."

He laughed. "I was half-mad before I met you. When are you coming back to Fenwick?"

"Aren't you listening to me? No, you are not. I might as well be talking to the wall. Fenwick will belong to a stranger before long if my sisters and I can't scrape together enough money to pay its upkeep. You aren't plump in the purse, and we don't *know* each other."

He lowered his head to hers. "We could save Fenwick together. I know you won't believe me, but in the short time I've been living there, I have fallen under its spell."

"You've been *living* there?"

"If you had *read* my letters, you would have already known."

"What letters?" she asked in bewilderment.

"Ah. That's what I thought. The duke has intercepted your correspondences. The devil."

The devil, indeed. Ivy wasn't at all surprised. James had made no secret of his possessive streak. "How can you be living at Fenwick? Who gave you permission? It needs to be put to a vote."

"It was. Lilac voted yea, and Rosemary nay."

"Well, I wasn't asked."

"You were. You didn't reply. Nor did Rue. Quigley was the deciding vote, and a hard one to win. The lease on my London lodgings ran out at the end of the month, and I have moved into your gatehouse."

Ivy shook her head, stunned by her sister's betrayal. "Why would Lilac agree to this? I don't believe you."

"She agreed because Rosemary almost killed me. Yes, it's true. She pushed me into a hidden passageway and left me there to rot. If Lilac hadn't rescued me, I would be dead."

Ivy felt as if she were frozen in the moment. Part of her wanted to be back in James's arms. Another part wished she could return to Fenwick with its secrets and her sisters and no problem more complicated than surviving another tomorrow. The familiar, no matter how painful, called for her to return. But the duke needed her, and where or why Oliver stood in the middle of this muddle, she hadn't the patience to discern.

"I'll come to Fenwick as soon as I can." And she would not take Oliver's word on anything until she had talked to Lilac and Rosemary for herself. "Now escape this house before either the duke or I kill you, Oliver. This is a provocation that no gentleman would excuse."

He released her. His mouth quirked in a triumphant smile that tempted her to slap his face. "Just kiss me once."

A cry rent the silence. A hinge creaked. Ivy turned instinctively, half-expecting to discover a naked duke standing in the door. Oliver, for all his high-flown nonsense, had retreated back into the dark. But it was not the duke who darted into the room and flung her arms around Ivy's waist. The diminutive intruder was Mary, loud sobs shaking her body.

The sound of a female weeping penetrated his drugged sleep. Ivy? He ordered his body to act. He preferred the agony of hell to this helpless oblivion. He summoned all his energy to shove the counterpane to the floor. His right arm jerked upward into the air. He swept his hand across the bedside table.

An enemy in the night. Where in God's name were his weapons? A soldier had cried for help. *Curtis.* He thought of his brother in battle. Goddamn Curtis's wife for betraying her family. How could she abandon those beautiful children? He would hunt down her lover and take revenge to satisfy his brother's honor.

He hated this weakness, this fog in which unrecognizable figures loomed and disappeared before he could work out where they stood. He must fight it. *Fight.* Pain jolted him into a twilight clarity. He'd rather suffer then sleep.

He wrapped his reliable arm around the bedpost and pulled himself upright. The poultice on his shoulder slithered down his chest. The drug was still strong in his blood, beckoning him back under black waves of oblivion. He released the post and reached back for the water on the table, taking a deep swallow before he realized it was morphine. Where the hell was his pistol? Not that he could pull the trigger. He grabbed something sharp.

Did he still hear crying? Had he been weeping in his sleep? He staggered from the bed but made it no farther than to the clothes chest before he had to rest.

"Damn, damn, damn." He grasped another post, struggling to remain upright.

From his viewpoint he could look through the window to the garden. Was a deer running through the park? A maid? Was he hallucinating? Why was he clutching a pair of scissors? He glanced up again. He saw nothing in the garden but the familiar blur of hedges laid out beneath the moonlit trees.

His hand loosened from the post.

The crying had stopped, but he heard soft voices in the hall. His instincts told him that his sanctuary had been invaded. He had ruined a young woman and failed as her protector in one single night.

Ivy went to Mary without a moment's hesitation. She had only an inkling of what the child had witnessed in her past, but she vowed it would not happen again. "What is it? Walker again?"

"N-no."

Sweet mercy. "Then what is it, my dear? Why are you crying so?"

"Papa might be killed. Uncle James is sick. And I peeped in on Walker. He's wet the bed, my lady, and I don't know how to tell him that our mother is never coming home."

Ivy was ashamed at how relieved she felt that Mary's distress did not stem from catching her governess in an indiscretion. "Tomorrow we shall make other arrangements. Perhaps I shall sleep in the dressing closet between you and Walker. Come here. I have a handkerchief to dry those tears. I know how sad you must be."

"Have you been sad before?"

"Oh, very."

Mary trailed her to the wardrobe, whispering, "Is the maid still in your room?"

Ivy closed the drawer and then the wardrobe door. "The maid?" she said, turning around woodenly.

"The one I saw you talking to before I came in. I didn't mean to interrupt. Ladies like to talk to each other. She had a funny voice. Was she angry with you?"

Ivy dabbed gently at Mary's face. Was this how it started? A small untruth meant to protect an innocent person? What if Mary mentioned the "maid" to James? Would Ivy lie again to prevent James from challenging

Oliver to a duel? A little lie that grew into a circle of deceit like a serpent consuming its own tail and ensuing self-destruction? Better to say nothing than to deceive.

"You may always interrupt me when you are upset, Mary. That is why I am here. Calm yourself. Sleep in my bed tonight. I'll ring for another maid to change Walker's sheets." And she would peep in on James on the way, allowing the moron in the maid's cap to escape before a servant on the estate sighted him and roused the duke from his bed.

But the duke was not in his bed. And it was Ivy who almost panicked, not Mary, when she encountered James lumbering down the hall toward them in his nightshirt, dripping the poultice she had applied and brandishing a pair of scissors. To be fair, he did look like a mythological monster and her frayed nerves could not be expected to withstand another shock tonight. As soon as she realized he was in a feverish state and had no idea what he was about, she returned to her practical self—she who mopped up messes, tended the ill, called out instructions, and promised herself she could have brandy and a private bellow when it was all over.

Mary came to her senses as most young women eventually do in a crisis. She ran back to her room to ring for help and settle down to read Walker stories in his bed when he woke, while Carstairs and three able young footmen guided the duke back into his chamber. Ivy nearly fainted when she discovered the chaos he had wreaked. The bronze-gold bed tester shimmered against the parquetry floor. Side tables and chairs had been overturned as if swept by a dragon's tail. Whatever had caused him to go into this frenzy?

Even when incapacitated the duke was a power like no other man Ivy had known.

She hung back as Wendover and the footmen herded him back into the bed, Wendover shouting for someone to call back the physician and James, in response, ranting about the insanity of Napoleon Bonaparte and an intruder in the park.

"Doesn't anyone believe me?" he roared.

Ivy stood back from the doors to his room. It was improper for her to be present at all in the duke's extremity. What did it count that he had proposed to her during the height of their pleasure? There had been no witnesses.

He might forget his promise by tomorrow. He might not remember it now.

Despite the uncertainty, she couldn't regret what she had done. She had given herself to him of her own will. Even if she weren't bound to him for a year, she knew she wouldn't leave him by choice. She would love him long after her legal obligation was fulfilled.

For five years she had lived her own life. She hadn't cared what anyone thought—until he had broken through her isolation and forced her to return to the world that existed outside Fenwick. He couldn't simply leave her to manage Mary and Walker on her own. What if she had conceived a child tonight? Had he left a will to cover this eventuality? Why was she letting herself fear the worst?

The duke's roar broke through her reflections. "Why won't anyone believe me?"

"Believe you about what?" Wendover patiently asked with the measured respect of a lifelong friendship.

"England has been invaded by an army of maids,"

James replied, and although Carstairs closed the doors and Ivy heard no more, she knew that this was not the end of the matter.

The duke would live to recover and cause more trouble in her life.

She was still awake when the sun rose. Mary had come back to Ivy's room, where they had held a nightlong vigil, each one taking turns to scout the hall and return with news.

"His valet knocked and was admitted at two," Mary reported.

"The maids brought in boiling water," Ivy announced at dawn.

"You should have seen his breakfast." Mary crawled into Ivy's bed. "It was enormous, and I'm so hungry."

"So am I," Ivy said, sighing in relief. "Sneak back to your room, miss. Try to get some sleep."

Mary turned onto her side. "Do I have to?"

"A good spy can't be caught in her night rail. I shall commend you to the Alien Office for your intelligence work."

Mary rolled off the end of the bed. "You're ever so silly."

"Be sure to take your passport. Beware of iron spikes in the hall."

"Lady Ivy?"

Ivy listened to the clatter of activity outside her room. "Later, Mary. I have to wash and dress and look presentable."

Mary giggled. "Good luck."

"You—"

Mary darted into the hall and closed the door.

Chapter 25

By morning, word had spread through the house that in the physician's opinion the bloodletting had caused the duke to run a high fever, which proved that his body had responded to medical treatment. Dr. Buchan had completed an anatomical examination of the duke and declared him fit.

Ivy was astonished when she was called into the drawing room. Smartly turned out in a white muslin shirt with a steel gray coat and matching trousers, James did not resemble the monster she had met in the hall last night. True, he looked a trifle pale. His cheeks seemed drawn. And she was hesitant to meet his gaze. She was afraid she would find his eyes devoid of any emotion for her. She was too vulnerable to have him dismiss what they shared with a look, or worse, to act as if nothing had changed between them at all. Nonetheless, she had known what she risked.

But then courage compelled her and she looked straight up at him. There was a sexual heat in his gaze that she might have attributed to lingering fever—until he strode from the fire to kiss her on the cheek in front of Wendover, Carstairs, and the two footmen who had just entered the room behind her.

"I've shared the news," he said in a hoarse voice that made her shiver in her shoes. "I hope you don't mind. Wendover is to be my best man. We'll arrange the wedding plans this week."

She glanced around, savoring the smiles and murmured congratulations reassuring her that James had remembered his promise. His smug grin also reassured her he hadn't forgotten the hours of pleasure spent in his bed. She felt as though she'd walked through a storm and emerged in the middle of a rainbow.

How had he managed to return so quickly to his devastating self after scaring the wits out of her? It was a tribute to his unbendable will and stamina and her answered prayers. Now if only she could forget Oliver's surprise visit and hope that Mary had already put it from her mind.

"If you don't stop touching me, James, everyone in the house will guess what we've been doing," she whispered as one of the footmen placed a tea tray on the table.

He led her to a chair, speaking in her ear. "I'm only doing my duty."

"Seducing the governess?"

"Begetting an heir," he said rather loudly.

She glanced around. She was certain she saw one footman grin at another. "Not before the wedding."

"A fortnight or so won't matter. Nor will anything else in the past. It's not as if we're going to stand at the altar after we've said our vows, waiting for the vicar to shout, "On your marks, get set—"

"I hope not."

"Whether we marry here or in London, we'll have to celebrate with our tenants. Do you ride a horse?"

"It's been years," she confessed.

"Can you hold several glasses of apple cider?"

She gave him a strange look. "Do you mean in my hands while I'm astride?"

He grinned. "I'm not asking whether you can perform in a circus. Our tenants will want to toast our well-being, and Ellsworth produces a potent cider."

"That doesn't surprise me in the least. In that case, however, I think several sips will probably be my limit."

"We'll decide on your limits later, shall we?"

"Do you have to speak in such a loud voice about these things?" she whispered.

He blinked. "What does it matter? We have nothing to hide."

He didn't. Ivy did, and she felt horrible. To start things off by keeping a secret from him felt like a betrayal. And she hadn't done a thing to encourage Oliver. He'd brought nothing but trouble into her life.

James straightened, leaving her to blush and meet Wendover's knowing smile. How was she supposed to conduct herself now? Like a servant or a newly engaged lady? Despite James's insatiable appetite for passion and his return to good health, she had to consider what sort of impression she made. As duke he could get away with murder.

He could even make a covert gesture to his best friend, ignore the second footman who brought him the post on a salver, and mumble some excuse about asking Ivy's opinion on whether she preferred that their wedding be held in London or here in the country, and would she mind walking upstairs to inspect the late duchess's suite that she would soon take personal possession of . . . in which the duke, she assumed as he trailed on, was to take immediate possession of her.

Chapter 26

Oliver brushed down and watered his horse. He knew Rosemary had awakened and watched him from her window, so he gave her a jaunty wave on his way to the gatehouse. A gatehouse, for God's sake. Had he remained with his feckless circle of friends in London, no one would even ask him why he'd been dressed as a maid. He wouldn't be sleeping alone. He wouldn't have been rejected by one temperamental woman and had his writing mocked by her sultry sister.

He mounted the gatehouse stairs, took a bottle of wine from the cupboard, and drank its contents so quickly he couldn't make up his mind whether it was Peony or Primrose he fancied most. He stretched out on the uncomfortable trundle bed with his pistol on his chest. He doubted Ivy would tell the duke he'd broken into his house, but the woman did have a mind of her own. Then he fell asleep wondering how he would find a treasure that had eluded discovery for centuries. How did he even know it actually existed? It was certain that he wouldn't find it lying half-drunk in the gatehouse. Was it worth the price of facing the duke in a duel? Oliver had heard rumors that Ellsworth had lost his abilities as a marksman. Except he didn't appear at all incapacitated. Anyway, if Oliver killed him, he'd be forced to flee England, without benefit of an heiress or her fortune. One didn't kill a peer of the realm and resume his activities the next day.

His plan was unraveling. He had to recover something from the time and money he had invested.

He was too perplexed to have come to any decisions when hours later he heard Quigley in the garden catching snails. There was a vehicle traversing the bridge, to judge by the muffled clop of hooves and grinding wheels. Or was that Lilac bringing up his tea? Poor lady. For all her loveliness, she could never make a graceful entrance. Her gait unfairly ruined her worth. The girl needed a prince.

He grunted, pulling a blanket over his head. A moment later Lilac screamed and the clatter of broken china, underscored by a furious roar from Quigley, propelled Oliver down the stairs and out into the glare of a gray morning.

And a vicious assault in progress.

Was he seeing things? A man appeared to be chasing Lilac through the roses, and Quigley had taken a shovel to swing at—God, it couldn't be.

Oliver opened his mouth to call out the man's name. But then the front door opened, and out ran Rosemary, holding a pistol in her hands. Oliver thought for a moment that she might shoot him.

The damned pups escaped and started to bark. He strode out into the garden and shook his head. Terrible mistake.

He saw two of everything.

"What's happening?" he demanded of Rosemary and her blurry double.

She ran past him with a look that labeled him as helpful as horse manure. "There's a man attacking Lilac. Can't you see?"

He realized he had his pistol in his hand. He was also still wearing the apron, but its removal would have to wait. He blinked several times. His gaze picked out Lilac in the garden. She had hefted a crumbling urn full of geraniums into her arms and heaved it at her attacker, whose mask had begun to slip.

And who happened to be the last man Oliver had gambled with in a silver hell in London. "Help me, Oliver!" Lilac cried, reduced to flinging clods of dirt to defend herself.

He snapped out of his trance to obey, the dogs barking as if echoing Lilac's plea. Joseph Treadway had his hands around Lilac's throat, and Oliver raised his gun, aware of Rosemary rushing up behind him. "Please do something," she beseeched him. "He's strangling her. I'm afraid if I shoot, I'll hit her."

"The treasure," Joseph said, spittle and dirt running down his chin. "I want your—"

"Move back, Rosemary!" Oliver said. "Move out of my way now." Strangely, she did. Perhaps it was his voice. Perhaps she was indeed an intelligent woman, for she retreated several paces with only a covert glance at Lilac.

He waited another second, took aim, and said quietly, "Jesus. Joseph, look at me."

The man turned reflexively, his grasp loosening on Lilac's neck, and Oliver pulled the trigger. He hit his acquaintance in the chest; a kill he'd intended and a kill he'd made. He felt Rosemary rush around him. He looked up to find her handing him her gun.

"Help Quigley."

He didn't know if she'd heard him call the dead man by name. There could still be time for him to find a way to cover the slip. Besides, she was too engrossed in pulling Lilac out from under Joseph's crumbled body to argue such a point now.

He turned, sidestepping dogs and geraniums, and took off up the path to help Quigley. But the old gardener had fended off his attacker like a swashbuckler, with a few swings of his shovel.

Oliver raised Rosemary's gun and trained it on the man Quigley had beaten. Good God. Look who it was. It wouldn't be difficult to take down a man of Ainsley Farbisher's age and half-arsed ability. In fact, the old roué was running from Quigley before Oliver needed to intervene. No mask could conceal his lumpy nose and potato-shaped chin.

"Well, shoot him," Quigley said, throwing his shovel at the clumsy figure headed for the small carriage on the bridge.

"I have just killed one man," Oliver said, lowering Rosemary's dueling pistol.

"Aye, a fine shot that. Now do it again."

Oliver considered that option, but Ainsley had reached the bridge, and if Oliver gave chase, he took the risk of the old bugger revealing their acquaintance. "Damnation," he muttered. "He's got away."

"You let him escape." Quigley wheeled back around toward the sisters.

Oliver strode through the neatly weeded garden to

the spot where Lilac stood, Rosemary trying to shield her from the body at their feet.

"Oh, Oliver," Lilac said. "I don't know what we would have done if you weren't here. He was going to—"

"Don't talk about it," Rosemary said. "He didn't do anything."

"Yes, he did," Lilac said. "He choked the breath out of me and said he would kill me if I didn't yield my treasure. We know what that means. How hideous of him. As if I would give up my valuables without a fight to the death."

"We shall talk of it after we're inside," Rosemary said, her face colorless. "You need to come into the house, Lilac."

"Is Quigley all right?" Lilac asked, craning to look around her sister's shoulder.

Oliver wrenched off the apron he was still wearing and dropped it over the face and chest of the man he had just killed. "Quigley appears to be fine," he said, straightening to study her. "What about you?"

"I broke the china," she said. "And the silver tray got dented when I hit this person in the chops with it. What would have happened to us if you hadn't been here, Oliver? It doesn't bear thinking about."

He tasted bile in his throat. "I should never have cleared the garden."

Rosemary put her arms around Lilac's shoulders and dragged her toward the house. "I'll trust you to take care of this," she said to Oliver. "If the magistrate needs my word as a witness, I shall be happy to give it in your defense, Sir Oliver."

"Thank you," he said stiffly.

She stared down at the apron. "Of course."

Chapter 27

James led her through the hall and up a side staircase that Ivy hadn't known existed. A row of footmen bowed to her and James as they passed, and it was dreadful of her, but she wanted to break into giggles. She and the other servants had been playing cards for pennies not three days ago. And now she had to act as if she were their better.

"I'm embarrassed," she whispered, balking at the landing built beneath a domed skylight. The clouds drifted by, a discontented shade of blue.

"Whatever for?" he asked over his shoulder.

"I was one of them and now I'm one of you."

He laughed. "In that case, there'll be more embarrassment in the months to come."

"I don't think so," she said, looking down from the skylight with a prim face. "I intend to set a good example."

"It's too late for that," he said, and pulled on her hand.

She caught the mahogany handrail, resisting. "I dislike the tone of that. I came to this house with the best intentions."

"You couldn't follow any of the rules."

"Not that again."

He pulled her off the railing and into his arms. "Ivy, you and your sisters are the most original young ladies I've ever known. You can't fault me for what happened during the five years I wasn't in England to keep you on the straight and narrow."

She laughed. "And that's why you are leading me to the Duchess Suite, is it? To redeem me from all those years of disgrace and originality?"

He shrugged, a typical man with only conquest on his mind. "I did mention that your sitting room adjoins your own personal library?"

Ivy felt herself falling under the spell of his guileless smile. Typical female, she thought wistfully, encouraging the conquest with her willingness to be led on. "There is a library downstairs, James," she said.

"Not one quite as intimate as this." He smiled into her eyes.

"That's what I suspected." She let him tug her up another three steps. "What do you mean by suggesting we were on a crooked path? I take exception to that."

"Forgive me. I should have known better than to insult the females of Fenwick."

He glanced at her again over his shoulder. To judge by his vitality today, Ivy would almost have believed him to be immortal. She had realized last night that he was not. "What did I or my sisters do to justify that comment?"

His deep laugh pleased her senses. "For one thing Rue threatened me behind the door with a sword like Joan of Arc. For another, Rosemary greeted me with a dueling pistol in hand. In the midst of this hostile welcome Lilac acted as if I had arrived for tea. And, you, my wicked heart, kissed an absolute stranger at a masquerade party. I suppose it is a blessing, considering convents are no longer an option, that the walls of Fenwick sheltered the four of you from the world for as long as they have."

"Ah," she said softly, "then you must see why the fault lies at your door."

"I chased you *to* your door. That was a poor impulse on my part. I've admitted and apologized for it."

"You're to blame for everything," she said, drawing free from his grasp.

He arched his brow. "You look sad. What have I done?"

She shook her head. "Nothing. I was just thinking how different everything might have turned out if you had proposed to me at the masquerade and sought my father out before he got into that fight."

"I've wished, too, it had happened that way." He leaned with her against the railing. "Would you have waited that long for me? And been faithful?"

"How could you doubt it? Of course my father might well have fought another duel. It was his nature."

He laid his hand over hers. "But I would have been able to help. I'll take care of all of you now."

She felt a shadow fall upon her contentment. His chivalry enchanted—and humbled—her. She didn't care if he teased her about what she and her sisters had done to survive. She'd do it all over again if she had to. She'd long ago accepted her past. She had nothing to hide anymore, except for Oliver's visit last night, which she hadn't had a moment to explain to James. Should she tell him now? Should she ruin his high spirits? Would a few hours more really matter?

Moments later, when they left the stairs and he opened the doors onto the octagonal sitting room that was to be her retreat, she was so overwhelmed that Oliver was the furthest thing from her mind.

Sunshine broke through the clouds and into the suite from a bow window that looked out across the lake. The room smelled pleasantly of beeswax and lemon oil. Ivy could not imagine the work needed to maintain the French tapestries and central chandelier on which she could not detect a single cobweb. The walls had been painted a restful yellow hue between the floor-to-ceiling Ionic columns.

"It's charming, James. It's warm and—well, this is so lovely I may never want to leave."

She walked through an arched doorway into an alcove that contained a small library. A coat of arms hung above the fireplace. A game table sat in front of two cozy chairs.

"What do you think of the bedroom?" he asked, strolling into yet another room.

She followed. There was a circular dressing room and a tall chest of drawers, one of which James paused to open and briefly explore, but her eye went straight to the Chippendale bed hung with yellow damask embroidered with pink cabbage roses and poppies. James removed his vest and tossed it onto the matching counterpane.

He turned and took her into his arms. "Well?" He started to kiss and undress her at the same time.

"James, at least draw the drapes."

"I want to see you in the light. No more chasing you into corners or hiding in your bedroom."

"I agree. Our engagement calls for good form."

"Yes—all I'm asking for is a good look at your form."

"Did you untie my dress already?"

"Be patient, Ivy. I'm not as fast as I used to be. Bless you for not wearing buttons today."

"So that's the secret to keeping you under control."

He pulled off his shirt. "Wide eyelets would be helpful. I'll have to hire a personal dressmaker for you."

She dropped her hands to her sides. "I would think you'd be mortified to run upstairs the way we just did after what happened last night."

Her bodice and sleeves fell alongside his shirt. He smiled faintly. "I might have been, if I could remember everything that happened after you took advantage of me and left my room. Surely I can't be held accountable for behavior I don't recall committing."

"I took advantage of you?"

"It's all right, darling. You forgive me. I have forgiven you. I know you were only trying to distract me."

"You do have a distorted memory."

"Not of you. All I remember is a goddess with a beautiful face and a body to match."

She frowned as her shift and undergarments met his trousers on the floor. "James, where is your jacket? And your cravat?"

"I think I left them outside the door." He knelt to take off her garters and stockings.

"You didn't," she said with a gasp.

He laid his cheek against her thigh, smoothing his hand up the curve of her backside. "I've wanted to do this forever." He leaned back, his hands skimming her hips. "Would you take down your hair?"

"Really, James. I need an hour to pin it back properly. People will know."

"Take it loose and hold it up with your hands. Yes. That's nice. Turn around slowly."

"It's not even noon," she said, a flush working up her neck.

"I know how to tell time, Ivy." His dark brows drew into a scowl. "Is this too much for you?"

"I haven't a clue why you would think that, James. It was only last night I believed you were dying and we slept together for the first time. Now, before breakfast, you inform the entire house that we're to be married."

"Why didn't you have breakfast?"

"Do you honestly think I could face the rest of the household across a table after last night?"

"I did. Faced the servants, I mean. I took breakfast in my room as I often do."

"Ignorance is bliss, isn't it?"

"You'll have to eat sooner or later."

She contemplated him in concern. "You really don't remember coming out of your room?"

He grimaced. "God. I didn't run up and down the stairs naked in front of Cook, did I?"

"Not quite," she said, dropping her hair to cover her breasts. "James, please, do we have to hold this conversation in front of the window? I feel extremely uncomfortable."

"I'll close the drapes."

She sighed in pleasure as he strode across the floor without the least inhibition and casually drew the curtains, like a Greek god disappearing into the obscurity of Olympus, to the disappointment of any mortal who happened to be standing below. Who would have thought that she would admire a man's backside? Or that the way his lean body moved could make her mouth go dry?

"Thank you," she said.

"You're welcome." He strode up to her, raking a hand through his hair. "Tell me about last night."

"You had a nightshirt on, with that hideous poultice dripping down your legs. You lumbered down the hall like a wounded beast. Yes, Cook stood guard at the stairs so that you wouldn't break your neck. Mary saw everything."

His gaze turned inward to a self-torture Ivy could feel. She looked away, wishing she hadn't told him. He would despise her, however, if she hid the truth. At last he gave a rueful laugh that broke the tension.

"I apologize," he said. "Wendover tried to tell me this morning, but we were interrupted. Is that the worst of it?"

"As far as I know. I was locked out of your room after that."

She looked up. So much for self-torture. He was sprawled out across the bed in complete disregard for his effect on her senses. Enough light entered the room that she could make out the blistered skin on his right arm, his muscular thighs and the rigid organ that he made no coy effort to conceal. He was incongruously magnificent on the floral counterpane, a lion in a field of roses and poppies. But she was not the least bit easy standing before him with every dimple and flaw exposed. His eyes raked her with raw desire.

He smiled. "You still look uncomfortable."

He looked utterly dangerous while she stood suspended in a sensual daze.

"Ivy, lie down beside me and close your eyes."

She did, her blood quickening at the request.

"Is that better?" he asked, caressing her back until she gave a deep sigh.

"Yes."

"There are three conditions I will require of you from this day on."

"Hmm?" This was certainly the sweetest day of her life. He had survived the night. He wanted to marry her. The past five years of grief, shame, and deprivation would be erased.

"Anything," she whispered. And she meant it with all her heart.

"First, you will never drug me again, no matter what the physician says, no matter that I might be taking my last breath. I want to be aware at all times. Do you agree?"

She sighed. "I don't know that it's a wise choice, but, yes."

"It is a wise choice, believe me. I became quickly addicted to opiates after I was injured. It was hell to break their hold on me. I don't want that to happen again. I'm afraid I wouldn't have the willpower the next time."

"I didn't realize that. I apologize for forcing it on you."

"Second, you will always tell me the truth, no matter how embarrassing or how unpleasant it might be. I should have told you before about my addiction."

She had always given him the truth until now. She would before the day ended. "And the last condition?"

"We take pleasure in each other whether it is dark or light, whether others approve of what we do or not. Do you agree?"

A pulse throbbed deep in her belly, responding to the sexuality in his voice. Her body agreed. Her mind had a few doubts, but they were swept away as soon as he started to kiss her, and all that mattered were the hands moving over her in persuasion and her need to belong to the potent male who was proving to be every bit as dangerous and delicious as he'd looked a few minutes ago.

"One more thing," he whispered, squeezing her nipples until she didn't care if the ceiling flew off the roof.

"What?"

"Don't expect proper behavior from me in the bedroom."

And next he proved exactly what he meant.

Chapter 28

He was in heaven, determined to ignore the pain radiating down his arm. He stretched out beneath her, drawing her down between his legs. She was warm and supple against the desperate hardness of his body. The filmy light played upon the curves of her breasts and generous hips. He wanted to see, to claim every inch of her.

"Come here. Move up closer. You're going to ride me if I stretched you enough last night."

He let her catch her breath before he grasped her bottom and lifted her over his engorged cock. "Ivy?" he said in hesitation. "Promise me you aren't going to faint?"

"I'm not made of china," she whispered, breaking into a smile.

He smiled back, his heart hammering. He was thick and throbbing to push inside her, but he guessed she'd be tender from last night, too tight to use without some restraint. If he could hold back. He slid his hands up to her breasts and teased her nipples again until she shivered and arched her back in supplication.

"I'm right here, sweetheart. You'll feel me very soon."

"I can feel you now." She gazed down at him, her eyes half-closed in expectation. "Why are we waiting?"

Why? Because once he let go, his reflexes would take over and nothing would stop him. All his good intentions would vanish and he would turn wild.

The knob of his erection slipped through her copious moisture and then she was sinking down on him, her spine flexed, her breasts ripe and round. She was his goddess in the garden, a dream he'd lost and then found. She swallowed his prick in her snug body, not resisting even when he drew her down deeper and thrust upward.

She moaned, and he ran one hand up her back, tracing her delicate ribs as he escalated the rhythm of his thrusts. Her hair cascaded down to his damp chest. Lightly he stroked her hip again, encouraging her movements. When she caught her breath, he stroked his fingers across her belly and lower through the curls of her cleft. The muscles of her sheath tightened and he felt the pressure to the base of his cock. She was giving herself to him, and he'd never known sex to turn him feral one moment and gentle the next.

The shape of her body excited him, her full breasts with the silky pink areolas that he could lick for hours, knowing how easily he could bring her to the edge with a lash of his tongue. Her voluptuous derrière put forbidden ideas in his mind—all that sweet flesh, his for the pleasure of taking. The male in him reveled in her climax, his conquest. He waited until he knew she was lost in sensation before he impaled her once more, holding her hips steady as he came.

He clasped her to him tightly and buried his face in her hair as he recovered. His heart was thundering so hard that moments passed before he realized that Ivy was slipping out from under him in panic; it was then he heard someone was pounding at the outer door. He released his breath and reluctantly flung himself off the bed.

"So much for privacy," he muttered, darting around the room to collect their clothing.

"Who is it?" she whispered, and caught the shift that he sent sailing over the bed.

"Open the door, James," an urgent voice said as if in answer to Ivy's question. "It's me, Wendover. There's been a problem at Fenwick."

"Is something wrong with one of my sisters?" Ivy called out, allowing James to redo her corset and laces.

"Your sisters have suffered a fright." Wendover's voice dropped to a gruff whisper. "I can't tell you until you let me in. The ladies are downstairs. I don't give a damn what the pair of you are doing. This is important."

James, his shirt still hanging out, glanced at Ivy to make sure she was decent before he hurried through the sitting room to open the door. "What the hell has happened that couldn't wait another hour to tell us?"

Wendover strode into the room and shut the door behind him. "There's been a murder at Fenwick."

"Who was murdered?" Ivy asked, her hand freezing at the back of her dress. "One of the servants?"

"Apparently it was a stranger who assaulted Lilac in the forecourt outside the gatehouse. A man chased her through the gardens and was strangling her."

Ivy leaned against James. "Who stopped him? Someone stopped him, didn't they?"

"Yes. It was the gentleman from London who is leasing the gatehouse. It appears he killed the man in order to save Lilac's life."

"Sir Oliver," Ivy said in disbelief. "He *killed* a man to save Lilac?"

Wendover met James's sharp look. "That's what everyone seems to have witnessed. He's downstairs, James, for you to talk to. I thought I should come and tell you right away. Ivy, I thought, too, that you would want to be with your sisters."

"Of course. Thank you, Wendover. James was showing me—"

"Let's go, then," James said, clearing his throat. "We'll find out what this is all about. Don't fuss, Ivy. Your hair looks fine. Your sisters have seen it loose before."

Chapter 29

They assembled in the drawing room. Ivy reassured herself that Lilac and Rosemary, aside from their understandable pallor and rumpled cloaks, had survived the attack mostly unscathed. In fact, it was Sir Oliver who looked shaken. He drank both the brandies that Wendover offered him. Really, what had she expected? He had just killed a man to protect her sisters.

Even though he had a reputation as a duelist, it would be abnormal for him to be unaffected by taking a man's life.

Her eyes met his. She turned her head and found James watching her in frowning silence. Guilt flared inside her that she hadn't yet told him about last night. The attack wouldn't have happened if Fenwick had remained hidden behind its thorns. If she hadn't gone to London. *If, if, if.*

She blinked at the sound of Rosemary's voice. "We've left Quigley in charge of the house," her sister said, "which worries me greatly. It's true that he chased off his assailant with a shovel, but only because the man appeared not to carry a firearm. Quigley's getting on in years."

James reached down to straighten his cravat, a unconscious gesture that melted Ivy a little inside. She wanted the solace of his arms around her. "What did they look like?" he asked.

"They wore masks, like highwaymen." Rosemary's voice was reflective. "I did not see either of them as closely as Lilac and Quigley did."

"I'm glad I didn't see his whole face," Lilac said, putting her hand to her throat. "But he had red-brown hair and fine clothes like a gentleman."

"A gentleman he was not," Wendover said from the window in a contemptuous voice.

"Perhaps it was a random robbery," James suggested. "The house looks deserted, and they might have been two thieves who happened upon the place in their travels."

Ivy hazarded a glance at Oliver. "Two robbers wearing masks in the morning?"

"Robbers abound in every part of England," he murmured. "Some men wait for opportunity to prey on weakness."

"The house no longer looks neglected since Sir Oliver had the garden cleaned and the mortar work repaired," Rosemary pointed out. "Besides, the dead man had a disgusting obsession with Lilac."

Lilac leaned from her chair to put her hand over Rosemary's. One would think it was Rosemary whose life had been in immediate danger, and not the other way around. Unspoken anger constricted Ivy's chest. She should have been there, and yet it was Oliver who had saved the day. Why could she not summon more gratitude for his actions? She couldn't bear to think of anyone harming Lilac.

"I'll be fine," Lilac said. "What Rosemary means is that as this miscreant was trying to strangle the breath from my body, he kept insisting that I yield my treasure to him."

James rose from his chair, his face dark with unconcealed fury. "Where is he now?"

"Hopefully six feet under," Oliver said, coming to his feet. "I sent the footman to the magistrate to have his body taken off the premises. The other man escaped."

"How?" James asked.

Oliver wavered. "I'm not sure."

"There was a small carriage on the bridge," Lilac said, looking unexpectedly at Captain Wendover.

"Can you describe it?" he asked her gently.

"No." She shook her head as if she just realized it herself. "I never saw it. I *heard* it. Few travelers cross the bridge. Those who have in recent years only caused mischief." She colored, as if realizing James could interpret her remark as an insult. "I wasn't referring to present company, of course."

James smiled wryly. "I understand."

"I was outside, you see, taking tea to Sir Oliver in the gatehouse. I broke some of our best china on the man's head and dented our silver tray. I even threw an urn of red geraniums at him, which I think only aggravated his rage."

"Good heavens," Wendover said, shaking his head in admiration. "I'd like to have seen that."

Lilac gave him a shy smile. "That's how I was able to fend him off until Oliver shot him. Rosemary frightened off the other one with her gun, but Quigley had done a bit of damage by that time."

"It's a blessing that Rue wasn't there," Ivy murmured, catching Rosemary's eye.

Rosemary nodded. "Yes. We would have had two dead bodies for the magistrates to dispose of then."

Sir Oliver looked up at the duke. "There will undoubtedly be an inquiry."

"I don't anticipate that to be a concern, do you?"

"I shouldn't think so."

"I will, of course, offer whatever help the young ladies may require." He paused, glancing across the room at Ivy. She could see the questions in his eyes, the doubts, and she would be damned if she would let Oliver spoil the intimacy that she and James had built. "Why did you presume to have the garden cleared, Sir Oliver?" James asked.

Sir Oliver did not appear disconcerted at all by the question. "I believe you're aware that due to my carelessness I almost took Lady Ivy's life in London. It isn't a secret that I have developed a tendresse for her."

"Which she does not return," James said evenly.

Sir Oliver's expression did not change. "That remains to be seen."

A dark warning flared in the duke's eyes. "No, it doesn't," James said. "Last night she agreed to be my wife."

"Ivy!" Lilac said with a jubilant laugh, and Rosemary gave one of those smiles usually reserved for the rare times she had written a book that satisfied her impossible standards. Ivy was delighted to see their pleased reactions to the news. If only Rue could have been there, too. If only the gathering had not been caused by such a gruesome event.

And there would be more trouble to come, judging by the tension Ivy sensed between the duke and Sir Oliver. Why couldn't Oliver concede like a gentleman and go on with his life? He couldn't have fallen truly in love with Ivy during a chance encounter outside a shop.

"Last night?" he said in a voice fraught with such doubt she wondered then whether he was possessed of a madness that made him oblivious to the opinions of others.

James didn't appear to care. To look at him now, masterful and brimming with arrogance, he showed no sign of vulnerability, and she knew without a doubt that he would fight to keep her.

"Congratulations," Oliver said with no pleasure in his voice. "I regret I won't be able to attend the wedding. It's time for me to meet with my publisher in London."

"Oh, Oliver." Lilac rose unsteadily from the low sofa. "Are we going to lose our protector and tenant? Is there nothing we can do to make you stay?"

There was another uncomfortable silence. The duke stared at Sir Oliver in naked dislike. "You have taken lodgings at Fenwick Manor?"

Wendover pushed off from his position at the window. "Why don't we leave the ladies to take tea while we finish this conversation with Sir Oliver in your study, James?"

Ivy didn't know whether this was a good idea. She wanted to act as a barricade between James and this man to whom she was now indebted for saving Lilac's life. Was it too much to hope that this turn of events would even out their association? Could he not make a graceful exit?

In fact, much to her surprise, he did just that. First he bowed. "Ladies," he said to Lilac and Rosemary, "your hospitality shall linger always in my heart. I regret that you had to witness the horrendous deed I committed in your defense."

"You aren't leaving us forever?" Lilac interrupted, having regained her balance. "I've come to enjoy the romance of harboring a poet in the gatehouse. And after your heroism today, how can we do without you?"

Ivy stood up, determined to keep James and Oliver apart for as long as she could. "The tea is cold, and I should see to the children. Sit down, Lilac. I shall be right back."

James turned as she stepped forward and took her in his arms. "Dearest, you should stay with your sisters."

"The children might be distressed, James. I should see to them."

"You should stay here," he said firmly.

"Please," she whispered.

His mouth grazed her cheek. "Do what you are told. One of the footmen can find the children."

She could sense Oliver watching them, even though he appeared to stare straight ahead. If she'd thought she could have gotten away with it, she would have feigned a swoon or a case of hysterics. She might fool James with such dramatics. She wouldn't deceive Rosemary and Lilac, however.

"Be careful," she whispered, catching the cuff of his sleeve.

He paused impatiently. "I am walking to the study, Ivy. What do you think will befall me on that perilous journey? Will the statue of Heracles come to life and try to snatch my girdle?"

"You aren't wearing one."

"I might have been this morning," James replied. "The physician was attempting to truss me in bed when I woke up."

She shook her head, about to answer until she realized Oliver was right behind her. She turned as Captain Wendover opened the door.

"These must be your lost cherubs." Sir Oliver gestured with his beaver hat to the two children huddled together in the hall. "Eavesdropping on us? That isn't polite, you know. Your governess ought to pay more attention to her duties."

Ivy slipped out between him and James to confront the children. Sticky red jam coated Walker's cheeks, and he backed up slowly when she reached for him, content to let Mary suffer the consequences of being caught first.

But Mary didn't move, didn't utter a word. She stared up at Sir Oliver, a confused look on her face. "Mistress Mary?" Ivy said, holding out her hand. "Shall we wash up and take tea with my sisters? They're dying to make your acquaintance."

"This can wait until we're out the door," James said behind her, and at the sound of his clipped voice Mary darted around Ivy and Oliver and threw herself like a heroine in a melodrama at his mercy.

"You aren't going to die?"

James frowned, holding her away from him. "Fanciful girl," he said in a tender voice. "Of course not."

"But I had a dream—"

"Just go into the drawing room and let me introduce you to my sisters," Ivy said softly. "The footman can bring some damp towels. Don't touch anything or anyone until you're clean."

"Our mother never allowed us into a tea party," Walker said, wiping his hand on his shirt.

Sir Oliver made a face. "I don't wonder why."

"Were you acquainted with my lady mother, sir?" Mary asked boldly.

Ivy drew a breath. "That's not an appropriate question."

Sir Oliver frowned. "I don't believe so."

Mary gave a shiver and stepped closer to Ivy.

"Are you ill, child?" She grasped Mary's hand and motioned at Walker to follow. "Come. Have a sit-down with my sisters. They always make me feel better."

She whisked the children into the drawing room, aware of the pensive look on Oliver's face. Hadn't she used the children's ailments as an excuse for the physician's visit to the house? Had Mary recognized his voice from last night? It was unlikely but possible.

But if Mary could put Oliver's face to the few words he'd spoken, it would seem as if Ivy were hiding Oliver's visit from James.

The longer she waited to tell him, the worse keeping silent would seem. Should she ask her sisters' advice? No, not after what they had experienced today. She would wait until Oliver had left the park.

The three men sat in the study, taking brandy, the details of the death at Fenwick not a subject gentlemen cared to discuss in the presence of ladies. Wendover had put into words what James was thinking: "It's remarkable to me that those young women can speak of the incident as though it had occurred a decade ago and not today. And how astonishing that they went into action." He shook his head. "I understand now, James, why there could be no other duchess for you in England."

James failed to suppress a grin of agreement. "The Fenwick sisters haven't descended from royalty for nothing. Remarkable, yes, in so many ways. But vulnerable, too." His gaze fell on Sir Oliver. "Tell me more about the attack."

Sir Oliver shifted in his chair. "There wasn't time to think. I was asleep when the men staged their assault. It was early, but the gardener was up catching snails, and Lilac was bringing me my morning tea, despite the fact that she knows I am not an early riser."

"How inconvenient for you." James rolled a golden sovereign across his desk.

"I stay up late to write, you understand."

"And last night?" James said. "The moon was full? It inspired you, and so on?"

"I was up until the sky lightened. I've fallen behind in my work, which is why I must leave now for London."

"What did the men look like?" Wendover asked.

"As I said, I was asleep when they attacked. I ran barefooted down the gatehouse stairs with my gun. Quigley had beaten back his assailant with his rusty old shovel. The second man seemed intent on violating Lilac."

James caught the sovereign before it reached the edge of the desk and tossed it in the air. He reached for it and missed. "Does it not seem strange that he would commit a sexual act in front of witnesses?"

Sir Oliver looked James in the face. "I have long ago given up searching for reason in the irrationality of mankind. My talents are better put to use writing poetry. I might die in poverty, but at least I shall have invented worlds I can understand."

"And their description?" Wendover asked again.

"For the last time, my mind was muzzy. The attack happened too quickly to take notes for a fashion magazine. The men wore masks. Did I not say that? The one who escaped appeared to be less agile and perhaps older than his dead accomplice. Or perhaps he seemed slow because Quigley had rendered him several stunning blows while I went to Lilac's aid. The man I killed was dressed in a gray or brown jacket and trousers. Again, it is difficult to give an exact description as Lilac had battered him with an urn of geraniums before I ended his abuse with my gun."

James looked down at his desk. "And you heard him command that she yield the treasure?"

A pause. Sir Oliver frowned as if he had to relive the memory, word for word, moment by moment, and James understood why. It wasn't every day a man interrupted another man in the act of rape and was obligated to make sure that this would be the last woman he ever assaulted.

"I can't remember the exact order of how everything occurred," Oliver admitted. "I believe I swore. I—I think I said, 'Jesus, Joseph, and Mary.' My voice startled him. He turned to me. I wanted his attention. I needed him to step back from Lilac so that I could have a clear shot. And I—I had asked Rosemary to stand away. I shot to kill, hitting him in the chest. I ran after the other man. Then I came back to Lilac to cover the bloodied corpse."

James was silent. It made sense, and yet he *wanted* to find fault. "You covered him in dirt?"

Sir Oliver grimaced. "I don't remember. It might have been Lilac's shawl or the jacket I'd been about to put on when I ran down the stairs. Remember, I'd been in a dead sleep myself."

"How did the other one escape?" James asked, picturing the garden, the slope to the bridge, the impediments, gone now, thanks to Oliver's intervention.

"He had a small carriage on the bridge. I didn't see it,

but I heard the snap of a whip, the rumble of wheels and hooves."

"You didn't think to run after it for at least a look?" Wendover said in a faint reproach.

Sir Oliver answered him with a cold stare. "No. I thought to draw Lilac away from the dead body that had fallen on top of her. Was that wrong of me? Should I have left her there in shock? You were an officer, Your Grace," he said to James. "You are better trained than me in these matters. What would you have done?"

"No doubt the same thing. But you have killed a man—two men—before, Sir Oliver."

"On a dueling field. There might have been a woman involved, but she was not being assaulted in my sight." Oliver's voice rose. "Am I on trial for protecting a woman's virtue?"

"Of course not." James glanced at Wendover for a moment before speaking further. "I don't think they should return to that house."

"You will have a job persuading them, I fear." Sir Oliver came to his feet. "With your permission I will return to Fenwick and leave for London before it is dark. I might even come across a drunken man in a tavern who is lamenting the death of his partner."

James rose. "Then unless the magistrate requires a formal report from you, we are finished."

"Perhaps." Sir Oliver nodded in Wendover's direction. "Good day."

James stroked his jaw. He waited to speak to Wendover until the footman in the hall closed the door. "What do you think?"

"From what little I know of Ivy and her sisters, the two ladies won't leave Fenwick of their own volition."

"Perhaps we can convince them that a temporary stay in the park is a good idea." James flipped another coin in the air. "Heads or tails?"

"Heads."

James caught it in his left hand. "It's tails. He's hiding something, and I don't know what."

"He's a cocksure bastard. Perhaps he knows more about the other assailant than he's willing to tell. He might even be going after him to make himself more the hero."

James grunted. His arm had started to hurt. He swore it was because he wanted to reach across his desk and throttle the weasel. "This was supposed to be a day of celebration," he mused.

"Which I interrupted," Wendover said.

James released a sigh. "I was showing her the library."

"The hell you were." Wendover shook his head. "I know the difference between the sound of pages being turned in a book and bedsprings."

"I'm not the least bit interested in good manners."

"I've noticed."

They walked toward the door together.

"Come to think of it," James said, "I'll need more than good manners to put her back in a receptive mood. I wanted to give her my mother's diamond and sapphire necklace while we were upstairs. Remind me later to look for it again."

"Offer her comfort," Wendover said. "She'll need it more than jewels. She isn't like Elora."

"I'll have the devil's time taking her mind off what happened to Lilac. No doubt *she* will want to comfort her sisters."

"Allow me to assist."

James grinned. "They are beautiful, aren't they?"

"Why did you hide them from me for so long? You could have invited them to dinner or a picnic at the lake."

"They hide themselves from the world."

Wendover frowned. "Four women of reduced circumstances couldn't keep up a manor that grand forever. What sustained them through the years?"

"Wits, a strong heritage, the revenues from Rosemary's writing, plus a bountiful supply of fruits and vegetables from the back gardens."

"That's all?"

"And, I gather, sisterhood."

They had reached the doors to the drawing room, from which drifted warm voices and laughter. "I hope I don't offend you, James, but your fiancée and her sisters are not the 'usual' sort of gentlewomen one encounters at a country assembly. Or anywhere that I would think to look."

"I know."

He only wished he'd known years ago when he first met Ivy and assumed she was too desirable, too young and vivacious, to wait for a man who aspired to climb the military ranks. He should have wed her before going to war. With luck he'd have left her with his father and an heir to keep them contented until he came home. Perhaps, if he'd had the wisdom to marry her then, he would have had a reason to return home sooner.

Oliver had intended to drive to the gatehouse and collect his belongings before he set off for London. But when he reached Fenwick, its mystery beckoned to him once again. This might be his last chance to search for the treasure, if it existed.

It was definitely the last time he would be able to poke about without one of the sisters inadvertently trying to end his life or requiring that he save hers.

He brought his carriage around to the stables, identifying himself to the nervous young groom, and walked back to the house, where Quigley sat dozing against the door.

"Quigley."

"What? I've got a gun—well, it's you, sir. Why'd you sneak up after what happened today?"

"What are you doing?"

"Standing guard."

"God. Let me in the house, would you?"

"Why, sir? The ladies aren't at home."

He helped the gardener to his feet, wincing as the man's grimy hand left a soil mark on one of Oliver's fawn riding gloves. The urn of geraniums, bruised and missing most of its vibrant red petals, sat as it had before Lilac had hurled it at Joseph's head. The damned idiot. And Ainsley. How had that fool found out about Fenwick?

"No trouble with the magistrate?"

"Not a bit. I told him to go to Ellsworth Park if he had any questions, and that seemed to satisfy him."

"That's fine. Be a good man and let me in."

"Well—"

"Listen to me, Quigley. Trouble comes in threes. I wouldn't be at all surprised if those two varlets hadn't traveled with another man."

Quigley spit on the ground, narrowly missing Oliver's boots. "The servants would have seen 'im by now."

"What if, during the mayhem and confusion, the third villain managed to sneak inside the house and hide? He might be lying in wait for the ladies to return."

"Lying where?" Quigley asked, like a bull about to charge.

"There are hidden passages inside the manor. I know because Lady Rosemary accidentally closed me inside one, and I would surely have expired had her sister not heard my feeble exhortations."

"Feeble whats?"

"Never mind, good fellow. You know of these passageways?"

Quigley swiped his muddied hand across his nose. "I do. In the time of the Pretender Oliver Cromwell, his soldiers traversed these passages searching for the exiled prince who'd long escaped, as the legend goes. But not all of Cromwell's men were as fortunate. They haunt the house."

Oliver was in no mood for a history lesson. "I thought it was Anne Boleyn's ghost who came to play in one of the bedrooms."

"That's true. Her spirit and that of the young lady who lived in the manor at the time are those thought to have trapped Cromwell's men in the tunnels in order for the young king to escape."

"Which he did," Oliver said.

"And lived on to rule merrily over England for a good many years, bless his wicked soul."

Oliver tamped down a surge of excitement. This legend supposedly held the key to the treasure. "Quigley," he said in a grave voice. "You risked your life today, and I cannot in clear conscience leave this house without ensuring it is safe for the ladies to return. I will search the hiding places before I go, but I need you to stand watch so that I am not closed in and forgotten."

"I could go down with you."

"My eyes are probably better than yours, Quigley. Do not fall asleep on me."

"I'll have the footman sit with me."

"Excellent idea."

"One caution, sir."

He curbed his impatience; he had to gather up candles, flint, and tinder. "Yes?"

"There is a passageway below the staircase that no one has ever searched. It's where the soldiers were thought to be trapped. Be prepared for a skull or two."

Chapter 30

Ivy dashed up the stairs to her room. Not to the Duchess Suite, where James had attempted to render her useless earlier in the day, but to the small chamber befitting her station as governess. Walker had smeared his sticky hands all over her skirts. She might be accustomed to wearing worn clothes, but at least her apparel had always been clean.

She jumped when she saw the figure sitting in the same chair that Oliver had occupied last night. There was no mistaking this handsome intruder for a maid, however. Two glasses brimming with champagne and a half-empty bottle sat on the table beside him.

She put her hand to her heart. "I need to say something, James."

He stood, lifting a glass to her mouth. "What did you want to tell me?"

She drank the entire glass in one gulp. "You've shaved. And—"

"And?"

And if his brooding gray eyes didn't pierce her like

an arrow to the heart, she would not have ended up beneath him on the bed a half minute later.

"How thoughtful of you to surprise me," she whispered, slipping her hand inside his shirt to skim her fingers down his chest to his flat belly.

As if to reciprocate, he worked his hand under her gown to the soft tuft of curls that covered her mons. "You're so wet, you must have known I'd be here waiting."

She squeezed her eyes shut as he pinched her taut pearl between his thumb and forefinger. "That's another quote from the Book of Scoundrels. Have you got it memorized from the front to back . . . or did you edit it?"

"All I have to do is look at you and do what my instincts tell me."

"My instincts tell me I'm supposed to be dressing for dinner."

"Undress for me instead."

"James, we don't have time for that."

He bent his head and kissed her into silence, pressing two fingers into her cleft and halting her protests. She stifled a moan. He slid his mouth down the length of her throat, taking small bites of her skin on his wicked way. Her breasts swelled against her corset.

He unlaced her gown and underbindings, rendering her naked to the waist. "I want to suck your nipples again. I know it excites you."

"You're making a mess of me," she whispered to him in dismay.

He brushed his mouth back and forth against the tips of her breasts until her lower body softened and she lifted her hips. "I can't ever seem to get you alone," he mused. "There's always someone interrupting us."

His erection pressed against her thigh. He had an insatiable appetite for sex. "Have you forgotten this morning?"

"How could I? It was only a few hours ago." His hot stare traveled over her wet nipples to the juncture of her thighs, where his hand still played her like an instrument.

"I guarantee that when we are married, I won't be as lenient about your time."

He didn't look lenient now. He looked wild and tantalizing, a man who held her in his power without any restraints at all. "And how do you propose to solve this matter, James?"

"I believe you missed several years of discipline. You're not a debutante now. I might require a few devices to help me keep you to myself. Handcuffs, silk ties. We can poke around some old dungeons and see if you find anything to your liking."

"What if I want to keep you for my pleasure alone?"

"It doesn't work like that."

"Too bad. I—" She lifted her head to see him sliding down her body. He pried her legs apart, and when his mocking face disappeared from view, she dropped her shoulders back on the bed and struggled to find her voice. "You can't do that with other people in the house."

"Why not? Do you think they'll feel left out?"

His laughter warmed the naked skin above her stockings. He pressed his face into her cleft and ate at her without mercy. She went absolutely still, except for a shiver or two that she couldn't control. "James," she whispered in utter helplessness.

He paused for a moment. She reached down to stop him, recovering only to submit again as his tongue penetrated her sex one slow stroke at a time. Her nipples tingled, rigid with a tension she felt deep in her stomach.

She rolled onto her side, but his hand promptly turned her back against the bed where he wanted her. "I'm not finished," he murmured.

"Twice in one day." She wanted horribly to move against his mouth. "It's not even dark."

"Yes. Hmm. We still have the night."

His mouth closed over the most sensitive part of her body; his tongue teased her nerve endings with his merciless talent. Afraid she would cry out, she raised her hand to her face and bit her thumb. The pain failed to counteract the pleasure he was determined to inflict on her susceptible body. Her hips undulated with abandon.

She gasped. "If you keep this up, James, I won't be able to walk to our wedding."

"I'll carry you, darling."

He rose up briefly to kiss her. He must have sensed she was on the verge of breaking; he held the power to withhold or give her release, leaving her suspended, willing to beg. "Please," she whispered, and he went down again, his mouth resuming its deliberate torment. "One day," she said with a soft moan, "I'll take my revenge."

"I can't wait. Maybe you'll be able to write your own book on the subject."

He caught her bud between his teeth and nudged her thighs farther apart with his elbow. Her hips rose. His hand stole across her stomach to bunch her skirts up higher and subdue her restless movements.

She was frantic, shaking with desire. He knew what she needed, how to arouse her basic nature as he satisfied his.

"Do you want something from me, Ivy?"

She heard the bed creak and felt a coolness against the bare skin of her thighs. James stared down at her with a hunger that matched the intense longing she felt for him. He unfastened the flap of his trousers and took his penis in one hand. Her belly clenched in anticipation. The next thing she knew, he had positioned his hands under her bottom and raised her limp legs over his shoulders. She had only an instant to note the size of his erection before the crest of it disappeared into her sheath, then withdrew in a rhythm he repeated until she was ready to pull out his hair in need. *"James."*

At her voice he quickened, pumping deeper until she moved with him and broke with a force that drove the breath from her body. Her muscles closed around his shaft with an uncontrollable instinct that she guessed by his deep groan brought him the relief he needed.

It felt like he was truly hers. Her heart beat wildly as he flexed upward a final time and then fell still at her side, holding her tightly to his damp chest. Her veins throbbed in receding pleasure.

"My dress is a mess now," she whispered in resigned satisfaction.

"A little more wrinkled than before you arrived, I agree." He stroked her hair and kissed her with lingering passion. "I meant what I said. I'll give you anything you want."

She kissed him back and sat up with a sigh. "For now you can give me the apple green silk dress from the wardrobe. My sisters are going to take one look at me and know exactly what we were doing."

"Were we doing anything wrong?" he asked, smiling at her in all his alluring deviltry.

"Never mind the children, you're the one who needs discipline."

"You can't discipline a duke."

"One can try."

To her surprise he stood, refastening his trousers with some trouble, and went to the wardrobe. He handed her the green silk frock and knelt before her. "I should have said this earlier—I love you. And I trust you as I've trusted no one in my entire life."

She stared down into his face. "I love you, too, James."

He swallowed. "I think you'd better change or our absence *will* be commented on. I'm going to my room to dress for dinner. We'll try to make Lilac and Rosemary forget what happened, if only for an hour or two."

"Why would anybody attack Lilac and Quigley?" she asked, holding her dress in her hand.

He came to his feet. "I feel responsible in part. And while I'm grateful that Sir Oliver defended Lilac, I can't seem to like the man."

"Nor do I," she admitted. Although he had saved Lilac's life.

"No more grimness tonight." With that, he put on the rest of his clothes.

She nodded. Broad-shouldered, elegant, and elemental, he was quite the specimen of masculinity. He could infuriate, master her, and brighten her mood, often within the same hour.

He went to the door.

She knew she should call out after him. *James, I have something I need to tell you.*

Right after dinner.

* * *

Rosemary and Lilac had gone to visit the Duchess Suite after tea and the children had followed. Ivy did not walk into a restful scene at all, but it was a familiar one that filled her with nostalgia. Rosemary and Mary lay curled up on the bed together, oblivious to the boisterous game of checkers that Lilac and Walker were playing in front of the fire.

"You cheated, Lady Lilac!"

"How rude of you to notice, Master Walker."

"I'll chop off your head."

"Not if I chop off yours first."

Ivy cleared her throat. "The children need to have a bath and dress for dinner."

"They've already been bathed and dressed," Lilac said without looking up from the game table.

"I'd like to have a bath," Ivy announced, walking to the foot of the bed.

Rosemary dismissed her with a wave. "Don't interrupt. We're almost at the end of the chapter."

Ivy sighed. "I'll just go back to my other room and leave the lot of you alone. I thought you might want to spend some time with me."

"Why?" Lilac murmured. "You haven't spared any time for us lately."

"And now we know why," Rosemary said, lifting an eyebrow in accusation. "Whatever happened to 'All secrets shall be revealed between sisters'?"

"In due time," Lilac said, then added, "Perhaps they only realized they loved each other a day or so ago."

Mary raised her head from Rosemary's shoulder. "They met at a masquerade ball five years ago."

"They what?" Lilac and Rosemary gasped simultaneously.

Ivy stared daggers at Mary. "Traitor. Eavesdropper. I never told you that."

"Uncle James did."

Rosemary closed her book and regarded Ivy as if she were a complete stranger. "Five years ago. I attended that ball, and you never mentioned a word."

"You do remember what happened to Papa the next day."

Rosemary slid off the bed. "Have you been . . . seeing him in secret for five years?"

"Don't be stupid," Lilac said. "We wouldn't have been living like paupers if she had. Cover your ears, Walker."

Ivy shook her head in chagrin. "Don't bother, Walker. I didn't have time to tell anybody. The duke swept me off my feet."

"She's telling the truth," Walker said earnestly. "I saw him carry her to his bed when she was bleeding all over the place."

"That was not a romantic moment," Ivy said. Although when she thought back on the day of her accident, excluding the shock of what she'd undergone and Elora's arrival, it occurred to her that she had loved James for bearing her off to his room.

She sat down on the bed, Lilac and Rosemary joining her a moment later. "We knew all along," Lilac said. "I told you the night he put our dragon back on the door that he had eyes for you."

"Well, I didn't know it would go this far," Rosemary said. "If I had, I'd never have agreed to become a governess myself."

Ivy turned her head to Rosemary in disbelief. "You've done what?"

"I can't discuss it yet. It's too distressing."

Ivy frowned. "Children, go play a game by the fire—but not in the fire."

"If we'd known you'd end up marrying the duke, Rue wouldn't have taken a job and neither would Rosemary," Lilac said with a sigh. "They might have met eligible gentlemen among one of His Grace's friends."

"What about you?" Ivy asked curiously.

"I'm waiting for Terence."

"Still?" Ivy said, biting her lip in concern.

"Yes, still. And I don't want to hear another word about him after what I went through today."

"You were quite brave to throw those geraniums," Rosemary said, curling against her.

"It only made the man angrier." Lilac stared across the room. "Oliver is quite the marksman. He shot him straight in the heart. I know you didn't want to see, Rosemary. But I did. Any other man might have shot me."

"That's why I didn't want to take the chance," Rosemary said quietly. "You and that deranged creature were so close together, I knew I'd miss."

"I won!" Mary cried from the other room.

There was a knock at the outer door. Walker ran to open it, and a voice announced, "Dinner is served, and His Grace is awaiting your company."

Chapter 31

The farther that Fenwick dropped behind, the easier it became for Oliver to think clearly again. His master plan had failed. He felt a foolish affection for the manor. He had written some fine lines in that wretched gatehouse—and, what a preposterous thought, but he hoped someone remembered to feed the young dogs tonight. They had gotten loose in the melee today.

For now he had to silence that idiot Ainsley for his bumbling attack on the manor. Who had told the ass about the treasure? Joseph Treadway, obviously. Until Oliver had killed him, Joseph had been one of Oliver's casual acquaintances. Fortunately they had never been seen together except at an infrequent party or in a gambling hell. And who had told Treadway? The pawnbroker? Elora?

Oliver took no pleasure in the thought of killing another man. Perhaps he could reason with Ainsley, explain to him that the duke would not look kindly upon the accomplice in the attack upon his future sisters-in-law. He didn't think that Ainsley had recognized him. But one thing was certain—Oliver would be leaving England soon if the duke discovered the truth.

Ivy to become a duchess.

It raised the stakes. It changed the game, and Oliver didn't like his odds any longer. Whatever fortune lay hidden in Fenwick, and he now doubted its existence, it would not be found before the duke put the premises under his protection.

Oliver despised everything the bastard stood for. But at least in the Duke of Ellsworth the fair ladies of Fenwick had a genuine guardian, whereas Oliver had brought them nothing but woe.

Chapter 32

James congratulated himself on a successful dinner. He'd accomplished his goal. It had taken every drop of charm he could wring from the imaginary Book of Scoundrels to coax a laugh from Rosemary, but once she had started to entertain him with the history of Fenwick Manor, lustful ancestors and wrathful ghosts included, it seemed she wouldn't stop. While she spoke of the past, he pondered the future.

Rosemary would be the entertaining aunt his children would adore and beg to visit to escape their governess. Of course the current governess would have to give him children first. There would be the heir and the spare, then as many offspring as grace would grant. If Ivy wasn't carrying his child, it wasn't for lack of effort on his part. God knew he was more than willing to try harder. He'd been starved for her ever since she'd walked back into his life. He wanted to raise a family with her. This enormous house wasn't made for one lonely man.

Rosemary was coming to the end of her story. He glanced at Ivy, who, judging from her frown, had read his mind. Could he help it that he wanted her and couldn't hide it? He was counting the minutes until he could be alone with her again. Even if only to talk, to hold her.

He hadn't come this far to stare at her across a table.

"And then she lost her head," Rosemary said, concluding her long-winded tale.

James considered clapping, but in light of the fact that no one else at the table had raised a hand, he made do with a nod. "What a shame."

"It wasn't a shame," Rosemary said after a long amused silence. "The villainess sent twenty innocent people to the guillotine."

"Oh. *Oh.* Then she deserved what she got." He paused. "Would anyone care for dessert?"

The ladies looked at one another and laughed. At him. His fascination with Ivy hadn't escaped anyone's notice. He might have laughed at himself, too, had Carstairs not bobbed into the doorway, his silver hair disheveled, his usual aplomb replaced by an air of consternation.

"Excuse me for a moment, ladies," James said, leaving the table to lead Carstairs out into the hall.

He heard Wendover scrape back his chair and make his apologies, catching up with James in the middle of Carstairs's explanation.

"Does this have something to do with what happened today at Fenwick?" James asked in a low voice.

"God, I hope they caught the other bastard," Wendover said.

Carstairs took a breath. "I'm sorry to say that a messenger has just arrived with news of Your Grace's brother. The courier is waiting in your study."

"Thank you, Carstairs. Wendover, I'd be grateful if you

would discreetly explain to our guests why I left the table. I don't think the children need to be told anything yet."

"We don't know that it's bad news," Wendover said.

James braced himself as he strode to the study. A messenger had not arrived this time of night to announce that his brother had received a promotion. He had just sat down when Wendover reached the room. They waited for the young courier to drink a pint of ale and wipe the travel dust from his face.

"Your uncle Colonel Lord Merrit wanted me to reassure you that Curtis's life is no longer believed to be in danger. He lost one eye at Vitoria, and I offer my sorrow for that. He's expected to arrive in London the middle of this month. He's eager to come home."

James dropped his head back against the chair. "He has nothing to come home to."

"He has his children," Wendover said, beckoning the messenger to the door. "And he has you. We'll leave you alone now. Shall I tell Ivy or do you want to?"

"I'll do it. But not for a while."

"Should I ask Carstairs to make plans for you to go to London?"

James looked up. He couldn't afford to brood. "Please. Ivy's sisters have to stay here until we return, their servants, too. There isn't time to make other arrangements. I'll send some of the staff to Fenwick."

"Will you be married in London?"

His brow furrowed. In a matter of days, the household had seen an impending marriage, a death at Fenwick, now his brother's injury. "Her sisters will miss the wedding, but it will be a small affair. We could have a reception here when everything has settled down. Ivy and I will have to decide later."

"Things *will* settle down, James."

"Why do I have difficulty believing that?"

"Perhaps because our lives have undergone such drastic changes this past year. We both lost our fathers and the chance to return as heroes. At least you've found love. The rest of your life will fall into place."

James smiled. "Yes. I've found Ivy and I intend to keep her, even if it means I have to move Fenwick, brick by brick, and all those who reside within it, onto my land."

"You're marrying into quite a family."

"You don't need to convince me of that," James said with a laugh.

Chapter 33

James intended to set out for London the next morning. Not wishing to cause the duke further distress during his crisis, Rosemary and Lilac agreed to remain at Ellsworth Park during his absence, although Lilac asked whether the servants and animals at Fenwick could also be granted shelter.

"It's more than kind of His Grace to offer to house us here," Rosemary said to Ivy while they gathered outside to say their farewells on the front steps. "However . . ."

Ivy embraced her. "However, what?"

"I left everything unsettled at Fenwick. I'm not sure I can enjoy myself worrying about Quigley and the other servants."

"Of course you can," Lilac assured her. "The duke sent five or six footmen over yesterday, and a half-dozen fit young men will be more helpful in a crisis than we were."

"That's true, I suppose," Rosemary said reluctantly. "But the manor needs a mistress. Quigley won't leave his back gardens. I vow there are nights when he stays up just to catch a weed poking through his vegetable plot."

Ivy frowned, giving Rosemary another fierce squeeze. “Promise me you won’t return to Fenwick alone. As much as I’ve disapproved of him, Oliver at least defended you when you needed him.”

“It was quite dreadful to watch,” Rosemary whispered.

“We really ought to write Rue and inform her you’re to become a duchess,” Lilac said, her fair hair blowing in the breeze like thistledown.

“Have either of you heard from her?” Ivy asked, remembering her last conversation with Rue in the garden.

“Not a word,” Rosemary replied. “But then again you became engaged to a duke and didn’t bother to tell us, either. And she is traveling with the viscountess.”

“Ladies,” a male voice said behind them, and Ivy looked past Captain Wendover to James, who stood waiting in a black silk hat and greatcoat.

“You are leaving, too, Captain Wendover?” Lilac asked, her arm around Ivy’s waist.

He glanced at the duke. “I believe I should.” He bowed. “It has been my pleasure to make your acquaintance.”

“I’m sure it has,” Lilac said absently. “Oh, before I forget,” she added, “what about the dogs? Cook and Quigley never remember to feed them or let them out.”

“What about my manuscript?” Rosemary asked in panic. “What if the house should catch fire?”

“It hasn’t caught fire in three centuries,” Ivy reassured her. “It’s unlikely to happen in the next few weeks.”

“Are we ready to leave or not?” James asked bluntly, turning on his heel in his polished Hessian boots.

Ivy fell in behind him, giving her sisters a quick smile over her shoulder.

Lilac glanced back at the house. "Where are the children?"

"They're waiting in my carriage with Sally," Wendover said, walking backward to address her. "I thought to entertain them. Do take care of yourselves."

Lilac and Rosemary had disappeared into the duke's house before Ivy reached the carriage. It was a shame they wouldn't pass Fenwick Manor on their journey to London, but she wouldn't dream of asking James to let her visit the house that would forever claim part of her heart. His brother needed him. He hadn't told her everything, but she knew all the same. In fact, he had spoken but a few words to her since he received the news. It wasn't necessary. As much as she loved James, yesterday she would have grown wings and flown to Fenwick had she known of the calamity unfolding there.

"James."

He was holding his chin in his hand, so preoccupied he didn't respond. She tried again.

"James."

He turned his head.

"I'm sorry," she said, sliding closer to him. "I talked to the children this morning. They cried, but after a while they realized that their father was coming home, and he was alive. That's what matters, isn't it?"

"If he's a better man than I am."

She nestled against him. "No one's better than you."

"You didn't know me when I returned from war. I was sullen, angry at the world, disrespectful to my father, and a man you would have been well-advised to avoid."

Ivy wouldn't have avoided him even then. Nor was she about to point out that he was still, at times, sullen, angry, and disrespectful, but not nearly as often as he was sensual, tender, and protective. "He'll make it through, James. He has his family. You managed to return to yourself."

"But I have you, Ivy. Now I have a reason to stop behaving like a fool."

"The only reason you have me is because of the children."

"Yes," he said wryly. "I wanted a governess to keep them from disturbing the arrangement I thought would bring me happiness."

"And aren't we both glad that I arrived in time to rearrange the course of your life?"

"You are my life," he said, turning his face to hers.

She stared up into his eyes and felt a flame kindle inside her. "Am I?"

"Whether it is because I love you so deeply or dislike Sir Oliver as much as I do, I wonder if there isn't more to the attack on Fenwick than what it appeared to be."

She frowned. "What more could there be?"

"There are no valuables in the house?"

"No."

"No more jewelry like the pearls you tried to pawn?"

"Nothing." She felt drowsy, her eyes closing as she answered him. "Perhaps I should have traveled with the children. You and Wendover probably have a few things to talk over."

"I can talk to Wendover when we reach London. It's not often you and I are alone together."

"There was talk once that gold was hidden somewhere inside Fenwick," she murmured.

He stirred. "How long ago was this?"

"Before I was born. The family decided it wasn't true. The manor is almost bare to the bones. Wouldn't someone in the family have found it in all these years?"

"Not if it was hidden as well as you and your sisters were."

"It kept us safe for years," she said ruefully.

"Villagers were afraid to visit Fenwick," he mused. "Even my coachman warned me about the dangerous women who lived inside the manor."

"Yet his warning didn't stop you."

"An intruder being killed and hauled off by the magistrate for everyone to see might give the rumors credence."

"I wish I'd been there for them," she whispered fiercely.

"And I am grateful you were not."

"I'm tired, James."

"Rest, then."

She nodded, the rhythmic jolting of the carriage lulling her into a brief sleep. When she opened her eyes, she realized that it was twilight and her head was resting in James's lap. He smiled at her. She smiled back, drowsy and relaxed until she realized he had undone her gown and was languidly stroking his knuckles across her breasts.

"Help yourself," she said with a laugh.

"I need you, Ivy."

She sat up, one hand covering her breasts in an attempt at modesty. His wide shoulders shifted under his coat. "We'll be apart again once we reach London. There is a stool under the seat on which you may kneel."

The tone of his voice made her blood tingle. She slid

back onto the opposite seat and stared down at the floor in confusion. When she looked up again, it was to see that he held his heavy sex in one hand. His other hand reached around the nape of her neck. He kicked out the tapestried stool before she descended in a submissive position between his outspread legs.

"James—what am I to do?"

"Make love to me with your mouth."

"I've no idea where to start." This act was beyond anything Ivy had dreamt he would ask of her. Or perhaps it wasn't. One could have an intuitive understanding of certain things without having actually experienced them.

"I'll show you what to do," James said. "Do try not to bite me."

She blushed furiously as he nudged her face to his organ. She placed her hands upon his thighs for balance and parted her lips. The knob of his sex glistened with a bead of moisture. She pressed her mouth to it and then he flexed his hips, suggesting she was expected to do more.

"James, I have no practice in this art."

"Take me into your mouth. Suck me."

Her heart sped up. She grasped the silken underside of his sex and guided it to her mouth, suckling gently.

"My God." His hips bucked. She withdrew slightly, letting her tongue glide in a circle around his shaft.

"Was it that bad?" she whispered.

"No. It was that good. Sit beside me and lift your skirts. I don't want to spill my seed on your gown."

"I should hope not."

"Here." She could barely see what he was doing over the pile of skirts, petticoat, and pelisse he had lifted to give him access to her body. She noticed that he looked out the window for a long time. "You don't think anyone will see us, do you?"

"No," he said, smoothing his hands down the insides of her thighs. "I wanted to make sure we have no stops ahead for a while." He reached up and drew down the leather curtains. "Does that make you feel better?"

"Yes."

"Merciful God, Ivy, look at you. You're sweet and pink down there. Did you like what you did to me?"

"You're the one who made me stop," she whispered. "I would have done more. I would do anything for you."

He took off his coat, rolled it up under her head, all the while rubbing his shaft between her folds. She raised her hips to take him into her body. "In a carriage," she murmured, closing her eyes. "You've done this before, haven't you?"

He didn't answer, teasing her with shallow thrusts, his hands sliding under her bottom to enable a deeper penetration.

"James?" she said, shivering as if she'd never be able to stop.

"No." He shook his head. "I haven't done this particular act before in this carriage."

"What an unsatisfactory answer," she said breathlessly, opening her eyes to look at him. He stared back down at her with a dark possession that robbed her of everything but her desire to be his. "Why was the footstool there?"

"For the resting of one's feet," he said, lowering his face to hers.

His mouth captured hers at the moment he impaled her on a deep stroke. *"Oh."*

She thought she would slide off the seat. He kept her anchored with his hands and the powerful driving of his body that brought her closer and closer to release. "I love you, scoundrel," she whispered, meeting him thrust for thrust, matching his rough play with unrestrained passion. "But I want more."

"Are you certain?"

"Must I beg?"

He withdrew slightly, allowing her time to draw one breath before he grasped her buttocks and drove his cock inside her. She could not bear the tension that built until she thought she wouldn't survive another second. When at last she broke, he pumped harder into her body until he came with a shudder of relief that she felt through her own waves of pleasure.

"Comfort of all comforts," he murmured, collapsing atop her spent form.

From the window she could see that it had started raining. They had not noticed during their frantic mating. "James," she said, stroking the damp black hair upon his cheek.

"My beloved." He paused, a note of hope in his voice. "Again?"

"You're crushing the life out of me. And if I'm not mistaken, the carriage has slowed pace. We can't be discovered like this."

He exhaled and lifted himself from her tingling limbs. "Damn," he said, reaching into his vest. "I have no handkerchief."

And before Ivy could avail herself of her reticule, he unknotted his neckcloth and gently blotted the evidence of their lovemaking from between her thighs.

Ivy pulled down her skirts and sat back against the

squabs with a sigh. "Do you have another cravat somewhere in this carriage to replace that?"

"No." He appeared unconcerned. "Not unless you had the foresight to place one in our hamper."

"No," Ivy said, taking note to do so in future. "Oh, really, it's pouring, James. You won't be able to arrive in London missing your neckcloth. Wendover and Sally will perhaps for the rest of their lives wonder what—"

He was the duke. Who would question his state of dress or undress? She had no choice but to surrender to the situation. He would only respond with an answer similar to the one he had offered her about the footstool, and that response would have to be accepted.

"Ivy." She was startled when, after restoring his own appearance, he said her name and gathered her into his embrace. "Your presence is a solace to me. I admit there are times when you provoke me to extreme measures, but I have never known this peace with another person."

"May you always feel that way about me."

The thrum of rain upon the carriage roof could not compete with the primal beauty of his soul exposed to her. "Isn't that what marriage vows mean?"

Chapter 34

James always made an effort to travel in comfort, in luxury, but traveling in love was a novel experience, one that neither rain nor rutted highways could ruin. However, the weather ruled out any chance of a twilight picnic. That heavy carriage lumbered through the black deluge until even the coal braziers burning inside the vehicle could not counteract the damp.

As night approached, they stopped at a crossroads inn and took a meal in a private room with Wendover, Sally, and the children. After they'd washed and warmed themselves in front of the fire, a waiter served them roast beef, potatoes, and French beans on Wedgwood ware.

Ivy considered pinching one of the table napkins for James to use as a neckcloth. She folded it and tucked it into her throat, evaluating it as a fashion accessory. It might pass if one stood a mile away, but it definitely wouldn't deceive the experienced eye. James glanced up at her, grinned, and shook his head.

"Are we playing pantomimes?" Wendover inquired as he took a sip of wine.

"I love pantomimes," Mary said from the small corner table where she sat with Sally and Walker.

"Eat your dinner, mistress," Sally said. "We won't stop again until London."

Wendover finished his wine and glanced from Ivy to the duke. "What happened to your neckcloth?" he asked James, his tone implying he knew it was none of his business.

But now the mystery of the missing cravat was on the table, so to speak, and Ivy couldn't have come up with a plausible answer as quickly as James did.

He shrugged. "It was too tight. I took it off."

"It looked fine when you left the house," Wendover said, smiling at Ivy. "Would you like to borrow one of mine?"

"No, I would not. What's the point in dragging open all your trunks to impress the staff at Berkeley Square? Considering the reason for my return, I don't think the state of my attire will be their primary concern."

"I agree," Wendover said. "But you can't walk into the town house with a table napkin around your neck."

Ivy looked away, realizing she'd found an ally in Wendover. At least while James was engaged in a friendly disagreement about table napkins, she could repin her hair so that when she arrived at the town house, the staff would not assume her to be a slattern.

By the time they'd reached the duke's Berkeley Square town house, the rain was falling so heavily that everyone was soaked before they dashed up the front steps. No one could look presentable in this downpour.

Ivy found herself standing in an immaculate candlelit hall, dismayed at the puddles the arrival party had made on the marble floor. The staff expressed only sympathy for their bedraggled appearance, and of course for the unhappy event that had brought His Grace back to London.

"I told you," he whispered to Ivy as a maid divested her of her soggy cloak. "I could be wearing a tablecloth on my head and be forgiven for it."

It was true. By the mere act of tipping back his hat or shrugging out of his coat, he had transformed himself from a decadent scoundrel to an impeccable gentleman. Ivy decided she might as well come to terms with his abilities. She had been raised with sisters and their secret pacts could never be broken. That didn't mean she couldn't learn to penetrate the less mystifying world of the English male. She couldn't call James completely uncomplicated, however. He'd kept certain facts of his life private, and she had only begun to understand him. She looked forward to the task of taming him, even if he thought the balance of power between them should remain the way it was.

The first task James tackled early the next morning was to send for a special license to marry Ivy. She'd decided it would be in bad taste to hold a wedding in St. George's, considering his brother's condition. James agreed. He didn't want to wait a month for banns to be called and social invitations extended to people whose names he could hardly remember.

His second task was to contact his solicitors to prepare for the process of filing divorce proceedings for Curtis. His brother, of course, might argue instead for a separation. He might hope Cassandra would come home. But divorce was a drawn-out affair that required an Act of Parliament, and Carstairs had informed James that several of Curtis's servants had already sent letters offering to give signed depositions against her ladyship should they be needed in the lawsuit.

Last on his list was to visit Curtis's town house to make certain it was in suitable condition for his brother's return. Curtis would likely resent any implication that he couldn't manage on his own; James knew that from experience. But at minimum a few accommodations would have to be made, and Carstairs needed to interview a new staff.

"I'd like to accompany you," Ivy informed him as he stood in the hall waiting for his carriage. The children stood beside her. Their upturned faces reflected hope and not their usual mischief. "I explained to Mary and Walker that they had to ask your permission to come. They'd like to gather up a few of their old toys and books. Oh, and Elora is waiting outside. She wants to be of help, if you don't mind."

James shook his head in resignation. He wondered whether Ivy and Elora would eventually compare their experiences with him out of curiosity. He had no actual reason to worry. Ivy had taken possession of his heart and soul, and if she shared anything of an explicit nature, it would be with her sisters.

"A man must stand his ground in times like this." And hope that he had sons to even out the ratio of male to female in the family.

"Please, Uncle James," Walker said. "It was our home. What if our mother has come back and is waiting for us?"

"She'd have written to tell us," Mary said, playing with Ivy's parasol until James gently wrestled it from her hands.

"Mary is right." James put his arm on the boy's shoulder. His heart was breaking for his brother and the children. "She would have let us know she was back in London."

Walker shrugged off his hand. "Not if she wanted to give us a surprise."

Shock was the only word to describe Ivy's reaction to the condition of the duke's brother's town house when they visited the Mayfair residence.

She read the horror on the duke's face as she accompanied him into the entrance hall. She took a hesitant step forward and heard the crunch of broken glass under her feet. She looked back at Elora and Wendover, standing in the doorway, and whispered, "Keep the children outside."

But it was too late.

Walker had broken through the barrier of his two guardians and run into the hall, only to freeze amidst the wreckage of broken plaster, glass, and the odd piece of silverware. Family portraits appeared to have been wrenched from their mountings and shredded with a sharp instrument. Obscenities had been written on the wall in what appeared to be soot.

"What happened?" Ivy whispered, letting Mary hide her face in her skirts.

Elora put a hand to the emerald choker at her throat. "What kind of wife would do this to a man as gentle as Curtis? He gave her everything she asked for. I am sick to my stomach."

James seemed not to have heard them. "Ivy, take the children back to the carriage. We don't know who did this. The place could have been ransacked by street gangs after it was abandoned."

"Let me help," Elora said, her eyes filling with tears.

"You should stay outside with Ivy. You may help later, after Wendover and I make certain the house is unoccupied and safe to enter. And do not cry in front of the children. Hold yourself together for their sake. They've seen enough without having to remember their home as a desecrated grave."

The duke sent a crew of glaziers, carpenters, and joiners to Curtis's town house the next morning. By supper the house had been near restored to its previous condition and James agreed Ivy and Elora could unite to add whatever touches they felt would make Curtis feel more comfortable when he returned. It wouldn't be the home he remembered, but close enough.

"The children will be safe enough here with the staff," he said before he went upstairs to change.

"And where are you off to tonight?" Elora asked, arching her brow at him across the table.

"I might go gambling with Wendover. I see no reason to punish the rest of the household for my unpleasant temper. I assume you don't require my help arranging cushions or taking stock of the linens? I won't be late. In fact, I don't particularly like the idea of either of you staying there alone."

"The servants will be with us, James. Have your gentlemen's night out in London. We'll be fine," Ivy reassured him.

After informing them of his plans, he went upstairs to change into his black evening coat. No sooner had he put it on and combed his hair than Mary crept into his room. He suppressed the urge to call for Ivy, then reminded himself what the child had gone through. Or what she still might have to face when her father came home.

"Don't go out, Uncle James. I've remembered something very important."

"Mary, dear, I'm sure it can wait until morning."

She gave a violent shake of her head. "It can't."

He sighed. Poor girl. Poor, poor little wretch. "What is it?"

"Remember the man who came to the park? The gentleman who saved Lady Lilac's life?"

James stared at her. "Are you referring to Sir Oliver?"

"Yes. That's his name."

"Has he done something?"

"I think he might have."

"Tell me, then, Mary," he said, swallowing hard.

"I was eavesdropping."

"Never mind that. What did he do?"

"He hid in Lady Ivy's room and tricked her by dressing like a maid on the night the doctor came to see you. She kept begging him to leave, and I thought he was a maid, but I didn't recognize the voice until he came back to the park the day that Lady Ivy's sisters were attacked."

He managed to sound calm and unconcerned. "Why wouldn't she have told me?"

"Perhaps she was afraid of him, Uncle James."

He bent and kissed her on the forehead. "And she doesn't know that you recognized his voice?"

She shook her head. "I never said."

"She didn't make you promise to keep it a secret?"

"No. But I think she's afraid. I am, too."

"Don't be, Mary. Everything will be better soon."

"He *was* in a dark mood," Elora observed after James saw her and Ivy into his brother's house. "I don't believe he spoke a word to either of us the entire ride here."

"I noticed," Ivy said, unfastening her pelisse. "Well, I suppose he has a lot on his mind. Oh, look at this place. The workmen have performed miracles. There isn't a mark on the wall."

"Perhaps they've gone for the night," Elora murmured. "The hall is spotless. If they've worked as hard on the rest of the house, we'll have little to do. Shall I see if anyone is in the kitchen to make tea?"

"If you like."

"The drawing room is three doors down to the right. I won't be long."

Wendover shifted against the carriage squabs. "I hope your silence doesn't mean the wedding is to be canceled. I don't give a damn if you speak to me or not. But the ladies are another matter. In fact, you were rude in the extreme to Ivy and Elora when we left the house."

James watched a pedestrian dart across the street. "I'm going to kill him."

"I assume you're talking about Sir Oliver."

"Do you have any idea where he lives?"

"No. But I saw him at the club earlier. I thought you were content to let him go now that he has given up his pursuit."

A smile ghosted his face. "At our club?"

Wendover shook his head. "Can I do anything to stop this?"

"The night the physician visited me when I was bloody delirious, Oliver broke into the house, dressed as a maid, and hid in Ivy's bedroom. She persuaded him to leave. Mary apparently walked in on the end of this exchange and recognized Oliver's voice from the last day he came to the park."

"Jesus," Wendover said, covering his face. "And Ivy just told you this?"

"Ivy never told me at all. And do you know why? Not because she is a duplicitous female, but because she's afraid. Not for herself. Not for Oliver. But for me. She didn't think I could stand up to him in a duel."

Wendover lowered his hand. "Maybe you can't. Maybe it's time you accepted that. I'll kill the bastard for you."

"Spoken like a true friend who also has no faith in me," James said dryly. "Why don't we wait and see what the evening brings instead?"

Elora entered the drawing room of Lord Curtis's town house a few minutes later. Ivy admired the diamond-sapphire necklace and matching earbobs that sparkled against her sable-red hair in the light shed by a small chandelier. As lovely as she looked, Elora did not appear to have much practice carrying a tea tray. It practically crashed to the table Ivy hastily cleared for its descent.

"Good heavens, Elora," she said, laughing. "You're more dangerous than Lilac with a serving tray."

Elora grinned. "I was born to be pampered. The tea is hot, so be careful. I'll let you pour. I'm nervous tonight, if the truth be known. I have so many things on my mind."

Ivy stared at her for a moment. "I must have been retired from society for too long. I never realized that a lady was supposed to change jewels as often as she changed her clothes. Weren't you wearing emeralds when we walked into the house?" She poured from the teapot, frowning in displeasure. "This tea hasn't been steeped long enough. I need something stronger if we're going to hunt inside cupboards. I'll have to ask the maid to make another pot."

"Don't bother," Elora said. "I've sent everyone home for the night."

"And we're all alone, after what happened?"

Elora unhooked the clasp at the back of her neck and shook her head. "I wanted us to be alone. I've got my gun in case anything happens. I needed to talk to you, Ivy. I don't know that we'll have another chance."

"Do you keep a gun on you at all times?" Ivy asked as the necklace slid into the palm of Elora's hand.

"It's wise to be on guard in my profession."

"Courtesan?" Ivy asked uncertainly. "I didn't realize you considered it an avocation."

Elora smiled and removed her earbobs, dropping them into her other hand along with the necklace. In the low lights of the chandelier, the gemstones reflected a brilliance that momentarily mesmerized Ivy.

"I'd remove them, too, if I were going to plump pillows and take stock of linen wardrobes. I wouldn't even have worn them here."

"I brought the set to give to you," Elora said quietly.

Ivy looked up in astonishment. "As a wedding present? I couldn't accept anything this expensive. I appreciate the thought, Elora. I'm touched, but I don't need a costly gift like this."

Elora gave a sigh. “The set isn’t mine. I stole it from the Duchess Suite at Ellsworth. James had promised to pay me off in jewels, and I’m certain he forgot.”

“An oversight, yes,” Ivy murmured, afraid that this conversation was not going to end pleasantly over a fresh pot of tea. “Well, it was good of you to return them. If James promised you a present, he should—”

“I don’t want a gift from James.”

Ivy nodded. “That might be better, considering you hope to make a match with Curtis. I won’t say anything to James. In fact, I’ll hide these and you can put them back where you found them when we go back to Ellsworth for the wedding. I’ve a feeling that is where James would prefer to have the ceremony.”

Elora stared at the necklace in Ivy’s hand. “I won’t be able to attend the wedding.”

“Because of what you just told me?”

Elora smiled. “Because I’m about to be arrested any day for larceny. I have to leave England tonight. I’ve been warned that my last victim reported me to the police.”

“Victim?” Ivy said, taken aback. This was not the pleasant chat about making the town house comfortable for Curtis and the children that she’d envisioned. The tone of the conversation had taken a dark turn, indeed.

“I steal jewels that belong to the ladies whose lust-struck husbands I sleep with. While they’re still sleeping, of course. The gentlemen are too ashamed to admit their infidelities to their wives, and so when the theft is discovered, they invent elaborate stories about having noticed a young man or a gang lurking about the house earlier in the week.”

"You're a jewel thief?" Ivy asked Elora, swallowing over the knot in her throat.

"Yes. It seemed a harmless adventure at the beginning. Sometimes I pawn the jewels, the gentlemen buy them back, and the wife isn't the wiser. But the last gentleman I robbed decided he would be honest with his wife and bring me to justice. I'm leaving England as soon as I hear James's carriage outside the house. I want to know that you're safe before I escape. Despite everything that's happened, I've never forgotten your kindness to me the evening of the masquerade."

Ivy rose from the sofa, leaving the necklace and earbobs on the cushions, and went to the sideboard. "This calls for something stronger to drink than tea. How long have you been doing this?"

Elora smiled with a touch of pride. "From the night of my—*our* humiliation at the costume ball. My first theft was a small amethyst-studded hair comb worn by a spoiled debutante who found it great fun to gossip about my disgrace the rest of the night."

"Oh." Ivy couldn't think of how one should respond. She couldn't congratulate Elora. Nor could she find it in herself to condemn her.

"From stealing jewels," Elora continued, "I graduated to stealing other women's husbands. It gave me pleasure to sleep with the men whose wives had excluded me from society."

"And James?"

"I would have married James in a heartbeat, but he didn't love me, and I love Curtis, but he would never trust a woman like me."

Ivy shook her head. "I have to be honest, I can't imagine the duke or his brother being impressed by your résumé." She stared down at the sideboard, her nerves prickling. She wished Elora hadn't confessed any of this. It made her feel like an accomplice. "It appears that the servants have put out full decanters of brandy and whisky. Do you have a preference?"

Ivy turned slowly, sensing that Elora was not listening to her at all. Ivy glanced around the room. She saw the jewels glittering on the sofa beside Elora, the pincushion she had brought to mark repairs for the seamstress, and, standing in the doorway, a middle-aged man with a bulbous nose and ruddy cheeks.

"What," Elora called out with loathing in her voice, "are you doing here?"

Chapter 35

James received a hearty welcome back to his club. He nodded to the old friends who remarked that they had missed him. He even managed to smile at members he had never met who expressed their desire to make his acquaintance. Some thanked him for his service at Albuera. A few expressed their regret at his brother Curtis, Viscount Bramhall's, injury. He accepted their sympathy in appreciative silence.

Then he walked up to the chair in which Oliver was sitting, raised him up by his lapels, and hurled him into a table. Two glasses of claret went flying. Oliver shook his head at the assault and James punched him with all his might in the jaw.

"I'll pay for all damages," James said to no one in particular.

Oliver rubbed his chin, looking stunned. "Does that include the damage to my face?"

James pulled off his coat. A waiter took possession of it and hastily stepped behind an armchair. "Where is your mobcap, Oliver? Did you leave your apron at home? Do you mind if I dust the floor with your deceitful face?"

"An apron?" someone echoed.

"A mobcap?" said another.

The club porter arrived and summoned every waiter in the establishment to break up the fight. None of these men appeared eager to intervene. In fact, the porter decided to start taking bets on the outcome of the match. The duke had said he would pay all damages. He could afford the bill.

Society could be fickle. Society chose its darlings. A handsome poet might be popular for a season. But a duke was always in favor, especially when he had been privately wronged and took revenge in public, representing the ideals that his peers could not be bothered to uphold. This would make the papers and give the gentlemen present some good gossip for their wives.

"I have never known the duke to lose his temper," one baronet remarked as James apologized for stepping on his foot. "He must have good reason."

"It must be a woman," another said, shaking his head over his newspaper.

"His brother was wounded at Vitoria," the gentleman at his side murmured. "It's enough to make one go mad, the casualties we have suffered."

Oliver had crooked his forearm to deflect the next blow. James drew back his left fist and drove it into Oliver's belly. "Fight back, Mother Goose. Fight me, you coward."

Oliver reached inside his pocket and James took another jab, remembering how quick Oliver was with a gun. Oliver's head snapped back. This time when he recovered, his eyes blazed with anger. Defiantly he pulled out a handkerchief to dab at the blood trickling from his mouth. At last he threw a punch that glanced off James's cheekbone.

They crashed through the door and out into the hall, battling like two unchained beasts. Oliver hit the mirror hanging on the wall. It fell, showering glass on his head and shoulders. Before he shook himself off, James bore him to the staircase and down they went, heads banging, fists flying until they reached the bottom. Oliver lifted his hands in surrender to the small crowd gathered above.

"I forfeit," he said in a ragged voice. "I have wronged His Grace. I deserved the beating he gave me tonight. I have acted dishonorably toward him." Oliver leaned his head back against the balustrade. "If you challenge me to a duel, I won't fire. I am a cad," he said, speaking now in an undertone to James. "Courting Ivy was all a ploy, except that I began to care for her and her sisters. All along I sought the treasure at Fenwick."

James fought a wave of faintness. His eyes wanted to close and his head kept jerking back. "Treasure? What the hell are you talking about?"

Oliver shook him hard. "Don't fall asleep. We have to keep each other awake through the night to monitor our injuries."

James snorted. "We are not spending the night together. Explain more to me about this elusive treasure."

"The pawnbroker Ivy sold her pearls to swears there is a fortune hidden somewhere in Fenwick. I wanted to find it. I didn't realize that my conscience would interfere with my attempts."

"Forgive me if I have no tears to spare."

Oliver put his head between his knees. "I made the

mistake of mentioning my plans to Joseph Treadway one night when I was drunk. He in turn told that hulking fool Ainsley, and I assume Ainsley told Elora."

The name wrenched James out of his thoughts. "Did I hear you correctly? Elora was involved in the attack on Fenwick Manor?"

"That isn't what I said. Elora merely knew the men who attacked Lilac and Quigley. Ainsley was the one who got away. I shot Joseph, and I do not regret it. I might be a blackguard but—"

James lumbered to his feet. "Where is Ainsley?"

"Had he any brains in his bloated head, he would be en route to France. The chances are, however, that he's in a gambling hell."

"Well, I know where Elora is, and I'm not happy about it. Wendover," he called up to the slender figure descending the stairs, "I need your help. Oliver, get off your arse. If you are sincere in your regret, your atonement starts tonight."

Chapter 36

Elora stared at the scruffy gentleman in distaste. His jacket hung open. Wine stains soiled his cravat and the cuffs of his wrinkled shirt, but by far his worst offense of all was the gun wobbling in his hand. "What are you doing here?" Elora demanded. "I warned you repeatedly that you were only to speak to me in private, if then. Our association has ended."

Ainsley grunted. "We're in trouble—that's why I'm here. While you're sitting here sipping tea, Ellsworth and your poet got into a battle like a pair of lions at the duke's club. Talk of it is all over London. It's time for a holiday in Venice."

Ivy's hands tightened around the whisky decanter. "How did the duke fare?"

He squinted, evidently too inebriated to see straight. "All I know is that they almost killed each other and then, according to witnesses, took off together the best of friends." He waved his gun at Elora. "I don't suppose you managed to find out where that treasure might be hidden. That was our agreement. I keep your secret, and you keep me on the dole."

Elora's lip curled. "That was our agreement before Oliver and I realized you were willing to attack helpless women and commit murder for what could well be a fairy tale, Ainsley."

"There is no treasure," Ivy said wearily. "Don't you think we would have found it ourselves? Oh, dear heaven. Is that why Lilac was attacked? You hideous fool."

"You're up to your pretty neck in this, Elora," he said, ignoring Ivy.

"Don't believe him, Ivy," Elora said. "He's pathetic. He's no doubt lost again at the tables tonight, and I have loaned him money for the last time."

Ainsley stepped into the light. Ivy couldn't decide whether the stringy hair on his forehead was damp from rain or perspiration, but the effect was off-putting either way. "Don't you sound like a saint?" he said to Elora. "What's that beside you? Your latest contribution to charity?"

"They aren't mine," Elora said, murder in her eyes. "I'm afraid you wouldn't understand even if I explained it to you all night." She rose to face Ivy. "I'm also afraid he has a point."

Ainsley nodded toward the side door. "And I'm afraid all this chatter and stolen gems will be the end of us. Get your pretty self in the hall, governess."

"Duchess," Elora said with a rueful sigh. "She is to become a duchess in a few weeks."

"Why force me to go with you?" Ivy wondered aloud. "So far, Ainsley, all you've done is attack Quigley and behave quite stupidly. Oliver, after all, did save Lilac's life."

"Ainsley has assisted me in my career," Elora said with a sour look at the man.

"Well, who else knows that?" Ivy asked.

"Oliver and now you." Elora opened the reticule that sat on the tea table. Inside it was a pistol, which she lifted to point at Ivy. "You're to be our insurance, that's all."

"Then I suppose you'll have to kill me, because I won't go willingly."

Elora glanced at Ainsley. "I assume the coach is waiting. Why don't you go outside and make sure the street is clear? I'll take care of her."

Ainsley hesitated. "If she's anything like her sister, she'll put up a fight." He pulled off his coat, moving toward Ivy, and threw it over her head. "Move."

The smell of Ainsley's body odor on the coat alone might have incapacitated Ivy had she not immediately begun breathing through her mouth. Her muffled screams would not be heard outside the room. She needed a weapon. She turned, wondering what her sisters would do in this situation.

"I told you not to move." Ainsley made a grab for her arm. Being a drunken oaf, he miscalculated by several inches, allowing her the chance to dodge between the sideboard and the window.

She wrenched the coat from her head as he swore and staggered into the sideboard. His gun fell under the draperies. Ivy thought she detected hoofbeats on the rain-soaked cobbles. She listened until the clatter receded, taking her hopes for rescue into the night.

"Step out from behind the sideboard," Ainsley said, flexing his fingers.

"No," Ivy said.

"No?" He sounded incredulous. "Would you like your neck broken?"

Ivy looked down at the bottles and glasses arrayed on the sideboard. "Why don't we have a toast to celebrate this momentous occasion?"

"Give me the damn whisky, you impertinent witch."

"Of course." She snatched her hand away as he made another attempt to grab her, this time managing to strike her in the shoulder. Unstopping the decanter, she raised it and splashed its potent contents in his face. Allowing him no time to recover, she then brought the empty bottle down upon his dense skull.

Elora looked at Ivy in reluctant admiration. "What happened to his gun?"

"How should I know?"

"Can you find it? I never intended to hurt you, Ivy!"

She wasn't sure she believed Elora. She had a vague idea where the gun had fallen, but it didn't seem like a good moment to make a dive for it. Ainsley was weaving around the carpet like a boxer dodging the blows of an invisible opponent. Elora walked calmly around the tea table, holding her pistol high, her reticule wrapped around her wrist.

Aware that this was a temporary reprieve, Ivy began throwing glasses at her would-be captors like a barmaid in a drunken brawl.

"Ivy, stop it!" Elora cried. "Look for the gun," and then, to Ivy's amazement, Elora raised her pistol to the chandelier and shot at the links that secured it to the ceiling.

The fixture swayed back and forth in a mesmerizing arc. Ainsley looked up as the chandelier tilted, spilling burning candles and melting tallow on his recently abused head. He screamed and threw up his arm to shield his eyes. One candle remained lit in the listing chandelier. In the shadows Ivy saw Elora dart across the room and disappear through the door to the back of the house.

Ivy reached down beneath the drapes and felt for the gun in the corner. She heard footsteps in the street and a carriage door slam. Had Elora escaped and left her alone with Ainsley?

She peered through the drapes.

There was shouting in the hall. Ainsley stood up and backed into the tea table. Two men appeared in the doorway, a pair of the grimmest-looking ruffians Ivy had ever seen. She prayed it was a trick of the light and not nature that had played such unkind favor on their appearance. The tallest man stared at her with an intensity that made her feel faint.

She would rather jump out of the window and beg for the mercy of a stranger than to surrender to those fiends. Ainsley must have hired them from the roughest stews to subdue her.

"Elora?" Ainsley called again. "Where the hell are you?"

The men rushed into the room, one with a pistol in each hand, the other, as she had feared, heading straight toward her.

"Do not move!" he shouted.

Too late. She had already parted the drapes and drawn them back together. Thus hidden, she turned frantically to find the window latch.

"Did I not order you to hold still?" a deep voice rumbled, and a large familiar hand reached through the drapes to feel for her.

"James?" she whispered, hopeful but uncertain.

She gasped as a hideously bruised face poked through the drapes. It pained her to look her beloved in the eye—the one eye not swollen into a slit, that was. "What happened to you?"

"Get down on your knees."

"What?"

"On the floor. Hide behind the sideboard until Oliver or I tell you it is safe to show yourself."

She grabbed for the brandy bottle before her descent, just in case, and folded to her knees. Her position prevented her from witnessing what next occurred, but from what she could gather, Ainsley's defeat was swift and bloodless. She heard him beg, "Ellsworth, for the love of God, don't kill me. I wouldn't have harmed her. She was only to be my ticket to the coast."

"Sit down on the sofa," James said, "or I shall give you a ticket straight to hell."

"The Runners are here, Your Grace," a third male voice said, and Ivy realized that the other man at the door with James had been Oliver. Was it possible they had made amends during the evening? Was a duel no longer an inevitability?

She fervently hoped so. And she hoped that the police *had* arrived. For now, however, she wasn't sure whom to trust anymore beyond the duke. Elora had portrayed herself as a friend and had betrayed society as a whole. Oliver—she didn't know what to make of him at all. She pulled out the stopper on the brandy decanter and sniffed its contents as a restorative.

She trusted her sisters.

"Ivy?" a concerned voice said.

She trusted Quigley, Carstairs, and Captain Wendover.

"Ivy?"

Above all, she trusted James.

"Are you drinking?" he demanded.

She glanced up at the face that appeared through the drapes and recoiled. "Is it over? May I come out?"

He bent down and lifted her through the drapes to her feet. The muscular arms that offered her refuge felt like the duke's. The hard body against which she leaned comforted and radiated a male heat that her senses instantly recognized. The bliss that she knew only when he held her gradually stole over her.

But she had to steel herself to look up into his battered face without wincing. "Is Ainsley gone?"

"Wendover summoned the Runners and they've taken Ainsley away."

"And Oliver was after the treasure at Fenwick all along?"

James grimaced. Ivy suspected he might have been trying to grin, but his swollen lip contorted the gesture. "He didn't realize what the true treasure was. Or who she was, I should say."

They stepped around the sideboard into the dimly lit drawing room. Ivy sighed. "He didn't realize that there is no treasure."

"Be careful where you step," he said, holding her close to his side. "The moron broke a whisky decanter against—good God. It appears he shot at the chandelier."

"That moron who broke the decanter would be me. I was hoping to cause a distraction so that I could summon help. Elora escaped. She—"

He lowered his head to hers. "Oliver told me about Elora. I think he might have gone after her to say goodbye. Now, Ivy, please kiss me."

She hesitated. "Where? Is there a spot on your face that has not been hurt or disfigured?"

"My chin," he said wryly, pulling her down beside him on the sofa. "What a night it has been, Ivy. I apologize for being rude to you. I found out that Oliver had come to your room at Ellsworth. It did not put me in a pleasant mood."

Ivy lifted her head, relieved that at last the truth was out. "He told you?"

"No. Mary did."

"She recognized him?"

"She recognized his voice," James said grimly. "She thought you were afraid to tell me."

"I was, James. I knew you wouldn't let an insult pass unanswered." She picked up the necklace and earbobs that Elora had left on the sofa. *This* was a secret that could definitely wait another day. "You look exhausted," she said, leaning back to stroke his hair. "Why don't you fall asleep here for an hour?"

He shook his head. "We have to go back to the house. There will be questions to answer, and the children to reassure. I want to sleep beside you. I was insane on the drive here, knowing that Ainsley—"

"James?"

"I love you dearly, but whatever we do tonight, I don't think Mary and Walker should see you in your condition. We'll have to make sure they're asleep when we go back to the town house." She kissed his cheek, rising from the sofa. "Don't run away."

He caught her skirt, laughing painfully. The jewels slipped from her fingers. "Where do you think you're going—"

She left the room before he could follow her to the kitchen, meeting him in the hall minutes later with a bowl of lukewarm water and a few towels. "You were gone too long," he said.

She flinched again at the sight of his face. "James, I trust this is the last time you will scare me like this."

He preceded her into the drawing room and sat heavily on the sofa. "I scared *you*? Oliver is not the only man in London who can be accused of reckless driving on your account."

"Let me wash the blood from your face."

"If you must."

"Does your brother have a shirt somewhere in the house you might borrow?"

"I had a wardrobe sent here." He winced as she dabbed gently at the bruise coming out beneath his eye. "I love you fiercely, you know."

She smiled. "I know. Please stop fidgeting."

"Something is poking me in the posterior." He reached beneath his seat and pulled from the sofa the diamond necklace that Elora had removed from the Duchess Suite. "How the deuce did this get here? I was looking for it at Ellsworth."

She wrung out her towel. He was starting to look better. "I'll explain if you hold still a little bit longer. And by the way, I love you fiercely, too."

Chapter 37

In the end James and Ivy chose to wait to hold the wedding until Curtis had a chance to recuperate and both the bride's and groom's families could celebrate at Ellsworth Park. Sir Oliver was invited; he had asked to resume his lease on the gatehouse at Fenwick and the sisters had agreed it was a comfort to have a capable man on the premises.

Lilac and Rosemary did not lack for the attention of gentlemen at the wedding reception, which in honor of the duke and duchess was a masquerade ball. James had invited family members and friends from across England, making it a glittering affair to honor his wife. Rue had been traveling with her viscountess, and promised that although she might be late for the ceremony, she would attend the costume reception.

"That's how Ivy met your brother," Lilac confided to Curtis over a glass of apple cider. "At a masquerade."

Curtis choked down his drink. He had regained most of his strength and his spirits improved every day. He had taken the news of his wife's desertion better than anyone expected, and he wore his eye patch without complaint. "What masquerade ball was this?" he asked Lilac.

Lilac grinned at his bewildered expression. "It was a secret until recently. His Grace was going off to war and our father was—well, let's not discuss that tonight. But James gave Ivy her first kiss when they were strangers in London, and now they're married. It's quite romantic if you don't count the five years of misery that we spent before they were reunited. By the way, I very much like your costume. King Arthur, are you?"

"Yes, my lady, and you are?"

"Lilac, didn't you catch my name?"

Across the room Ivy caught sight of Lilac and then assessed the bemused expression on her brother-in-law's face. "He can take care of himself," she heard James say over her shoulder. "Besides, he needs to practice. I can think of no better way for a man to gain an understanding of women than by spending time in the company of your sisters. Meeting the four of you is the equivalent of running a gauntlet. I am rather proud to say I survived the challenge and took you as my prize."

She turned slowly. A tall handsome man in a black silk mask and Georgian courtier's long quilted coat stood before her. "I desire you," he said with a bow.

"I don't even know who you are," she whispered, toying with the feathered hat she'd removed.

"If I told you, would you allow me liberties with your person?"

She laughed. "My husband has a hot temper."

"I have a hot temperament." As he straightened, he swept his hand up her back, seeking the shape of her through her stiff skirts and drawing her into his body.

He was as hard as the columns that rose to the ballroom's ceiling.

"Sir, I must insist that you—"

"I know this won't be your first kiss, but let me try to make it exceptional all the same."

Exceptional? She tilted her face to his. As she expected, his kiss laid siege to all her senses. She had never spent an unexceptional moment in his company.

"I also realize we've only just met," he murmured, "but I have a desperate urge to bed you. Is that a possibility?"

She took a breath. The black mask highlighted the promise of dark pleasure in his eyes. "I'm not sure. This is my debut as a duchess. I ought to be mingling with my guests. It would seem highly improper to rendezvous with a stranger when I'm supposed to be an official presence at the party. My absence would be noticed, as would yours."

"There are plenty of distinguished guests who would stand in for us."

"It isn't quite the same," she murmured, already relenting.

He lifted her hand to his mouth. "Five minutes. Your room or mine?"

"Yours."

The Duke and Duchess of Ellsworth discreetly exited the ballroom, only to be arrested in the middle of the staircase by the three guests peering through the railings at the candlelit ball below.

"Mary and Walker," Ivy said, sinking down indecorously two steps below them. "I'm not at all surprised to find you here, but, Rosemary, for heaven's sake, haven't you outgrown this sort of thing?"

"Outgrown what?" Lilac asked as she slowly ascended the stairs with Curtis on her arm. "Make room for me and your father, children. We want a front-row seat."

"Oooh," Mary exclaimed, rising to her knees in excitement. "Look at the lady in the blue silk dress, Walker. She's wearing wings. She's a fairy queen."

"What lady?" he asked, attempting to squeeze his head through the railings.

"The one with the black hair walking beside the old woman holding a cane."

"God's teeth," he said. "She's the most beautiful lady in the world."

"It's Rue," the three sisters said in unison.

Curtis leaned over his son. "Walker, I don't want to hear you use that sort of language ever again. And if you get your head stuck, your rear is vulnerable to attack." Then he glanced down at the ballroom and broke into a grin. "*Who* is she again?"

A knight in light armor and a crusader approached the bottom of the stairs. Ivy glanced down at Sir Oliver and Captain Wendover, who said, "Is this a private party or is anyone invited?"

James knelt on the step beside Ivy, removing his mask to look into her eyes. "Shall I have the footmen serve us up here or are we returning to the party?"

"We can't sit on the stairs all evening," she whispered. "And there's no way to escape now without causing a stir. Besides, I should greet Rue, and her employer doesn't appear agile enough to climb the stairs unassisted."

He nodded. “I suppose I can wait a little bit longer. After all, you waited long enough for me.”

“I’ll make it worth your while.”

He offered her a scandalous smile that she trusted no one else had noticed. “And I shall hold you to your promise.”

Read on for an excerpt from Jillian Hunter's

The Countess Confessions

Available now from Signet Select

1820
England

The fortune-teller's tent was the talk of the party. It stood beyond the reach of the light shed by lanterns that twinkled in the trees. Even the footmen positioned in the garden wondered whether it had been pitched illegally or was there to entertain the guests. Judging by the chattering young ladies and gentlemen lined up on the footbridge to the dark hollow where the gypsy fortune-teller had encamped, no one cared why she'd appeared. Upon her arrival she had allegedly announced she would give readings tonight that pertained only to romance.

Few of the well-heeled guests would have found the courage to approach her if she hadn't come to the party.

"What an enchanting surprise. Lord Fletcher's wife or daughter must have talked him into hiring her. She's reading for free, I heard."

"Well, I hope she doesn't run out of inspiration before my turn."

Inspiration? It was patience the fortune-teller needed. So far Miss Emily Rowland had predicted only happy outcomes for the lovelorn, and those had exhausted her talent for deception. Each snippet of excited chatter that reached her ear only made her heart sink lower. She was doing all of this in the pursuit of love, to predict romance for one particular guest at tonight's ball, although as the evening progressed, it seemed more likely this scheme would bring about her ruination.

She sat up in her squeaky cane-backed chair, cringing as the tiny bottle that sat on the table wobbled precariously to one side. Emily had no idea what substance the green glass contained. She had borrowed it from her brother, Michael, to use for atmosphere after overhearing one of his Rom friends whisper to him over the garden wall, "Use this when all else fails."

Emily didn't believe in magic. She doubted she'd have the courage to sprinkle it on her heart's desire when he appeared. She couldn't imagine what the results would be if she dared. When the time came, she suspected she wouldn't have the nerve to use the potion, whether or not it was imbued with any power, on the gentleman she hoped would offer her a marriage proposal.

"Are you ready for me?" a man asked at the door.

"Yes. Enter." *And be quick about it,* she thought as she moved her wobbly bottle to a safer position on the table, away from the flickering oil lamp, about which her brother had said, "For the love of heaven, Emily, whatever you do, don't let the light fall to the straw."

The fifth person to seek her services happened to be a cad whom Emily disliked too much to hide it. He whipped his horse to show off, treated his servants like lumps of dirt, and was staring with vulgar fascination down Emily's bodice while she feigned interest in the palm of his hand.

"I fear, Mr. Prickett, that your palm reveals a short life line." She drew her hand away from his and slid back into her creaking chair.

"Nonsense," he said in an indolent voice. "Longevity runs in the family. Give me the name of the next lady fortunate enough to share my bed."

"Toad!"

"I beg your pardon." His face portrayed the conceit of a man who refused to believe he had been dealt an insult. "Did you say, 'Miss Todd'? I don't believe I know anyone by that name. Is she here tonight? A lady I've yet to meet?"

"How should I—"

A loud cough from behind the tent reminded Emily that a fortune-teller told her clients what they wanted to hear, not the truth. But honestly, what did she know of palm reading and French tarot cards?

She could not have been in her right mind when she had allowed her friend Lucy, Lord Fletcher's daughter, to talk her into this strategy. Once Emily had seized upon the idea, she had turned to her half brother to employ his help. She should have listened to Michael's warnings instead of letting Lucy's enthusiasm for matchmaking erode her judgment.

"You are desperate, Emily," Lucy had untactfully reminded her.

"I am desperately in love, yes."

"With a gentleman who does not realize you exist," Lucy said, her bluntness meant to motivate Emily before she became officially known in Hatherwood as an eccentric spinster.

"Perhaps it's for the best," Emily had suggested. "He notices other ladies. I've tried to make him notice me. I've done everything but turn cartwheels on the cricket field when he plays. I've dropped my reticule on his foot. I've bumped into him twice in the churchyard. And all he ever does is apologize and go on his merry way."

"You might have been too obvious."

"So in your opinion, wearing a curly black wig, tinting my skin, and telling omens are subtle ways to draw his attention?"

"You will not be yourself. You shall be a fortune-teller who slips Emily's name into his thoughts as his future beloved. As soon as you're finished, you will disappear, remove your disguise, and become Emily again. And this time when he sees you, everything will be different. He won't know why he never noticed you before. He'll wonder how he could ever have missed such a charming—"

Mr. Prickett's voice startled her back into her role. "Where am I to meet this lady?" he asked, apparently unaware that his plans for a lustful evening were of no concern to the fortune-teller.

Her brother bumped up against the tent in subtle warning. Michael was invigorated by his Romany blood, which came from the secret affair their mother had carried on a month before she married Emily's father, the man who had once believed himself to be Michael's sire as well. When the young baroness was dying, she had revealed the truth, cleansing her conscience and breaking the baron's heart by forcing him to realize he had been cuckolded, that his only son and heir was not his own.

Mr. Prickett's voice jarred her again. "What else do you see for me and this woman?"

"Separation. Woe. Perhaps even a lawsuit."

He frowned. "Why don't you give the cards a try?"

"The reading is over," she said. "I have lost contact with the other side."

"What other side?" he demanded with a doubtful look.

The other side of the tent. Or the side of me that claims some link to sanity. He can take his pick. "Go," she said, rising from the noisy chair. "Unstable elements are interfering with my ability to read or influence the future."

"But— "

"Next!"

He started to protest until a cloaked lady entered, forcing him to either make a scene or an exit. Fortunately he chose to leave. The lady who hurried into the tent perched herself on the stool in front of Emily's table. "Well?" she asked, biting her lip as she swung her cloak up from the straw. "Is our little fortune-teller ready to meet her fate?"

Emily stared across the table at Lucy's cheerful face. "Is Camden still outside?" she whispered.

"He certainly is."

"How does he look?"

"No different than usual. Well, are you going to read my cards?"

"Not again. We spent all last night reading them, and Michael has given me so many details about the deck that I'm afraid I don't remember what all the inverted positions mean."

"Make them up. None of us at the party know. There's only one person who matters. Read the future in my palm." She held out her hand. "Practice for your next customer."

"I can predict your future if, against all odds, I manage to convince Camden that he and I belong together. You will be a bridesmaid at our wedding."

"How lovely!"

"But if by any chance he recognizes me, you and I will be found out and sent to our aunts for discipline. We shall spend the next season in disgrace."

A pleasant male voice called from the line outside the tent's entrance. "Are you almost done in there? The band is tuning up in the ballroom, and champagne is being served. We don't want to miss the dance."

"That's him," Lucy said, as if Emily would not recognize the voice that haunted her dreams on a nightly basis. "The seventh in line. I'll slip out the back and listen. Or do you prefer privacy? I wouldn't want to inhibit your performance."

"Privacy? You must be joking. Michael has his ear to the tent in the event that I make an utter fool of myself and need his intervention. You might as well return to the party before your father finds out what we've done."

"Don't worry about him. He's too busy entertaining—"

A commotion of raised male voices, one of them Camden's, diverted Lucy's and Emily's attention. It sounded as if he and another man were exchanging words. But Camden never quarreled with anyone. His even temper was one of the qualities Emily adored.

"Are they arguing?" Lucy whispered, her eyes wide with disbelief.

"Hush. I think so."

"Well," Camden said, more placating than combative, "I *have* been standing in line a dashed long time, sir, but if you are in a hurry, I suppose I—"

Emily could not make out what else Camden said. A

deeper voice responded, and there followed a shuffling of feet and silence.

"I shall investigate," Lucy said before Emily, prompted by instinct, could ask her to stay.

She reached down for the handle of her basket. In it several decks of tarot cards, labeled in French and English, sat neatly tied in red silk ribbons. "Michael?" she said over her shoulder, but he gave no answer.

Had he left his post to investigate the disturbance? She turned her head to glimpse Lucy escaping the tent. No sooner had her friend disappeared than the seventh person stepped inside.

Seven. It was a mystical number from ancient times. When Michael had suggested that assigning Camden a number in line would give Emily time to prepare herself for his reading, she hadn't realized that she would become such a popular attraction at the party. She hadn't dreamed that the man she desired and one she did not know would argue over who would be the next to sit before her. No one had ever fought to be with Emily until now. If anything, she was the last girl to be invited to a party or a picnic, and often she wasn't asked at all. Now Michael was gone.

And the stranger standing before her in all his charismatic arrogance did not resemble the man she had expected, in demeanor or appearance. His hard face might not have disconcerted Emily if she had met the man before and had developed a tolerance to the impact he wielded. Under ordinary circumstances, she might not have found herself breathless from his unadulterated masculinity. High cheekbones and hollowed contours defined his face. A handsome man, to be sure. One whose vitality of presence, whose self-possession, a woman might encounter once in a lifetime. Emily realized that it was rude of her to stare. But she couldn't help herself, and he *had* made a scene to be the next man in her tent. What did he intend to conquer? Surely not a vagabond girl.

She waited for him to speak. He appeared to take her response to his magnetism for granted. Emily would have dearly loved to summon Lucy back to the tent to whisper, "Look at him. Where did he come from? Is he as attractive as I think?"

Lucy had gone, however, and some vital instinct in the back of Emily's mind set up a warning cry. *Flee. Run now or live to rue this moment.* But a dreadful suspense weighted her to the chair. His presence rendered her incapable of movement. And, really, what was there to fear? What was the worst that could happen with others outside the tent?

Seven.

Seven was a lucky number.

There were the Seven Hills of Rome. Seven Sisters of the Pleiades. Seven days in the week. Seven archangels. Seventh heaven. Shakespeare's seven ages of man.

The number did, however, possess some dark connotations. An English gentlewoman visiting London would never want to explore the stews of Seven Dials. And wasn't there a fairy-tale giant who wore seven-league boots?

Emily leaned back in her chair and stared at her seventh customer as he sat down casually on the stool. He cast an enormous shadow in the candlelit tent. She felt swallowed in darkness. He was wearing boots, too, with a long black evening jacket over a white shirt, and a pair of black pantaloons.

She had *never* seen him before. She would not have forgotten those impious blue eyes and the smile that somehow hinted he knew she was an imposter and that he fully expected to be forgiven for ruining her scheme. His impressive physique, combined with his longish dark red hair and light beard, would have made him stand out at any function Emily was likely to attend.

"Really, sir," she said breathlessly, the admonishment too restrained for a man of his presumption to respect. But who had stolen her voice?

And why had he stolen Camden's place? A true rogue rarely needed an introduction to romance, which made Emily wonder why he had ducked into the tent when she had been expecting another man.

"I hope you don't mind my switching places with the other man in line," he said, his gaze taking in her appearance as if he sensed there was something odd about it but he wasn't sure what it was. "I ran into a spot of embarrassment at the party. I noticed a person I wasn't quite ready to encounter yet. I needed shelter to hide out and collect my thoughts. I'm sure someone with your experience will understand. You must be used to keeping secrets."

Experience? Secrets? Never in her twenty-five years had Emily been confronted with the type of man the vicar had always warned the ladies in his congregation to avoid. Hatherwood produced one or two scoundrels a century, if that.

She was instantly drawn to the playfulness in his eyes, delighted and appalled by his unabashed male authority. So, a stranger had thrown her off course. She would simply have to recover and resume her role before the gentleman he had usurped, Camden, was sitting before her.

"What happened to the man who was next in line?" Emily asked, refusing to acknowledge his aplomb. The nerve of him. Supplanting Camden for his convenience.

"Who?" She realized then that he spoke with a deep Scottish brogue. "Oh, *him.* He was kind enough to give me his place."

"But . . . did he leave? Voluntarily, that is?"

"I've no idea. Does it matter?"

Obviously it didn't matter to this interloper. Poor, polite Camden must have been too intimidated to object. After all, what kind of person pushed ahead of guests he didn't even know at a party? Who did he think he was?

Perhaps she didn't want to know.

She realized then that there were seven deadly sins, and that the man who stared back at her with false guile looked prepared to commit at least one of them before the night came to an end.